where he would be
screened from view
by the trees,
but he wasn't quick enough.
A rider
came out of a narrow,
treeless slash
in the prairie,
two hundred yards ahead.
Behind him
rode four others,
their hands on their weapons.

Breck thought
he'd seen the leader before.
The man shouted in warning
and jerked his rifle from its boot,
firing across the saddle horn.
A bullet
screamed past Breck's ear
as he threw himself from his horse.
His own gun was in his hand
as he hit the ground,
and he fired twice
in rapid succession . . . .

SHOOT-OUT AT BUFFALO GULCH

BERNARD PALMER

LIVING BOOKS
Tyndale House Publishers, Inc.
Wheaton, Illinois

First printing, Living Books edition, September 1985

Library of Congress Catalog Card Number 85-50731
ISBN 0-8423-5849-8

1

Late evening darkness swallowed the desolate, sun-scorched Kansas prairies, hiding the thistles and soap weed and scattered cactus on either side of the tracks. The headlight on the proud new Baldwin ten-wheeler struggled valiantly to search the area ahead of the cow-catcher, but with scant success. It stabbed a faint yellow hole in the night, scarcely stretching farther than the ribbons of steel to the outer edges of the grade. It dimly revealed a small wedge of tie ends, cinders, and buffalo grass that appeared to be scurrying forward, continually beyond the reach of the laboring engine.

The locomotive clattered noisily over the iron rails, dragging a baggage car, four passenger coaches, a private car—seldom seen in that part of the country—and a caboose. The engine was supposed to hold back the sparks by pulverizing them in the stack, but that feature was not as effective as its designer claimed. Glowing coals and bits of fire spewed out at intervals, along with acrid black smoke that filtered through the open windows, clogging the nostrils and staining the faces and hands of the passengers. The long-distance travelers were easily distinguished from the locals. Their clothes were grimy and their eyes reddened by the sting of the smoke and cinders, and by lack of sleep.

John Breck lowered himself into the cramped quarters of the coach seat. His spurs rattled against the wooden floor as he straightened his long legs. The toes of his boots kicked the seat in front. His companion on the narrow bench seat opened a calm hazel eye and surveyed him critically.

Breck's hunched figure and haggard features, now hidden by grizzled, week-old stubble, made him appear little different than the others who wearily rode the train west. To the casual observer he was just another restless cowhand, drifting from one ranch or cowherd to another. But those who noticed those piercing gray eyes, the tied-down holster and slender fingers that never seemed to be far from the handle of his Colt Peacemaker, shuddered and turned away.

Breck was one of a vanishing breed—men who stalked silently through the wilderness of the West. Some traveled the outlaw trail, moving restlessly up and down the lonely trails and hills of the back country. The settlements they preferred were on the fringes of the frontier, ruled only by the law of the six-gun. They were a tense lot, those lean, hard-eyed drifters. Always alert. Always suspicious of every stranger, of every approaching rider or opening door. They confided in no one and trusted no one.

Others of their crowd were intrigued by the challenge of law enforcement. They pinned on a badge and prided themselves in how tightly they could keep the lid on *their* towns. But there was a sameness about such men, whether they wore a star or kept to the dark side of the law. They lived by the gun, and most would die by the gun.

There had been a time in the now-distant past when life promised to change for Breck. That was when Helen had fallen in love with him; when he had put up his six-gun and together they had traveled to a new, untrammeled territory where his reputation had not preceded him. He would have made it too, but for a ruthless man's lust for land and gold that had robbed him of Helen and the gentling force she had been to him. He still bore the marks of her tenderness and loving Christian spirit like a brand on a wild-eyed maverick.

The kids were growing up under the watchful eye of his sister, who was so much like his wife that it bothered him. He thought about the ranch on the eastern slope of the Rockies, the place he called home. He harbored a yearning to go back and live as other men, but few saw that side of him. He was a silent, brooding individual who kept his emotions locked deeply within, far from the view of others.

It had been five years since Helen had been killed; yet the ache in his heart was undiminished. And for some reason not even known to himself, an uneasy restlessness kept him moving.

Breck had only met Asa Hunter recently. They were strangers when they changed trains in Kansas City and found themselves sharing the same seat on the Colorado-bound train. Before they had traveled fifty miles they were friends, as close as he had ever been to another man since he bought the Triangle B and got acquainted with Chris Duncan.

Hunter, like Chris, was younger than Breck by several years. The two travelers were as different as the well-dressed Easterner's sophisticated New York City was from the coarse, home-

spun prairie towns of Texas, which John Breckenridge had just left.

Asa Hunter was handsome, proper, dapper;
a slight, well-knit individual whose bearing matched
the refinement of both his clothes and his speech.
Yet the Easterner's lean, weathered features—
features that appeared to be out of place on one
so genteel—had a hardness about them. There
was a firm set to his jaw, and determination flecked
his usually mild eyes. To all outward appearances
he was not armed, but Breck noted the small,
telltale bulges under his coat. He was carrying
weapons. Probably a pair of Spies .38's or similar
small guns in suspender holsters.

That added an intriguing dimension to the
New Yorker. Hunter could be a gambler headed
for the gold-rush towns where a good hand with
cards could make a stake or mend his fortunes in
a hurry. He could be a fugitive running to the
territories beyond the reach of the law. He might
even be a tenderfoot on his way west, afraid to
be unarmed in such a wild, untamed area. But
none of those descriptions fit the young man beside Breck. He lacked the deceit and shifty eyes
of a gambler. He was cautious and alert, but not
uneasy. Instinctively Breck knew he could not be
an outlaw. And he certainly was not a tenderfoot.
He had the calm assurance of one who knew exactly what he was about and how to take care of
himself.

The guns set Breck to wondering, and for a
time he let his thoughts roam to the man hunched
in the seat beside him, trying to sleep. Not that
he really cared. In this part of the country a man
was accepted as he was—no questions asked.

Still, there were times when it helped to know

the sort of man who was next to him. Not his name or his position or the money he had. He had been told that such things were valuable as gold back east. But here they were chaff, as useless as the tumbleweeds that bounced across the hills in early fall. What counted was the worth of a man's word, his skill with a gun, and the strength and stability he showed in a crisis.

With Hunter, however, even those things didn't matter much. Tomorrow they would reach Buffalo Gulch in Colorado Territory. John would buy a couple of horses and the supplies he would need and head for the hills around Leadville in an effort to find paying color. Hunter would go about whatever business had brought him to the area, and they would probably never see one another again unless his close-mouthed companion was also planning to work the hills for gold. But that seemed unlikely. Breck had given him opportunity to say so, and he failed to respond. If he did intend to prospect, his plan was to go alone.

Not that Breck held that against him. He had been alone since Lee Corbitt had picked him up as a kid.* There were advantages to being alone.

Dismissing his traveling companion from his mind, Breck scooted low in the seat and pulled his hat over his eyes, trying ineffectively to close his ears against the rhythmic clanking of the iron rails and the constant murmuring of the passengers. There was an uneasiness in the coach, and the hours dragged by.

A little after 2:30 he stirred and sat upright, envying Hunter's ability to sleep. For a time he listened to the clanking of the wheels on the rails

---

*Kid Breckenridge

and the heavy breathing of those fortunate enough to be asleep. Finally he got up and moved down the aisle where he paused beside two other passengers who were having the same difficulty he was.

"Every time I ride this confounded train," a portly drummer grumbled, "I swear I'll never do it again."

"Beats walking," his companion reminded him.

"Not by much, it don't."

Even as he spoke there was a shrill squeal of brakes and the train lurched to a halt, almost throwing the trio to their knees. The men caught themselves by grasping the backs of the seats nearest them and bracing their feet.

A moment later they were erect, eyeing each other with growing uneasiness.

"We ain't near any town," the salesman said irritably. "What are we stopping for?"

"Probably another hotbox or a pulled drawbar."

He shook his head. "Not this time! I *know* what they're like. We hit something."

Breck wasn't experienced enough in riding the rails to know what was taking place, but the sudden halt so far from a town grabbed at him convulsively. His pulse quickened and new sweat moistened his forehead beneath his broad, brimmed hat. There were other reasons a train might be stopped on that desolate stretch of track. Ominous reasons.

"We'd just as well sit down and try to get some shut-eye," the disgruntled drummer mumbled. "We'll be here a couple of hours."

Breck left them and moved to the front of the car. He paused in the narrow space between doors, his ears straining for some foreign sound that would indicate the reason for the sudden stop.

The searing wind had died with the disappearance of the sun and a breathless, super-heated hush settled over the prairie. Sweat soaked his shirt as he moved down the steps and leaned forward to see what was going on at the front of the train.

It was a moment or two before his eyes grew accustomed to the darkness. When he could pierce the gloom of the cloudy, starless night, he was able to make out the shadowy figures of several men on horseback, clustered at the rear of the engine. They were about to be robbed!

His gray eyes hardened, and his hand moved to the butt of his gun. His first reaction was to move forward to do what he could alone. But if he had learned anything from Lee Corbitt it was to think before making a move. It would be stupid to blunder ahead on his own, especially when he didn't have to. There were those on the train who would be eager to help.

He went back aboard and walked briskly through the train, choosing his men hurriedly. When he saw an armed passenger, he motioned him toward the front. The grizzled, hard-bitten men didn't know for sure what was happening, but they knew they were needed. They got up and pushed between the seats to the forward door.

Breck tried not to alarm the few women and children, but fear leaped to their eyes as they saw grim-faced cowhands, prospectors, and gamblers pulling their six-guns and crowding forward.

He stopped briefly at the seat of his companion, Asa Hunter, and shook him awake.

A woman in front turned imperiously, her fat jowls quivering. "What is it?" she demanded loudly. "We're paying passengers. We have a right to know!"

Ignoring her, Breck motioned Hunter to the rear of the car.

"I'll need more guns than I've got," the Easterner said under his breath when he saw that the others were heavily armed. Breck held out a Henry rifle. Expertly his companion checked to be sure that it was loaded, and they stepped out into the warm night air.

In grim whispers Breck placed half the force in the hands of a hard-faced old rancher with a livid scar that angled from his cheek bone to his chin, parting his gray whiskers. They were to approach the front of the train from the other side. Breck would take the rest and attack from their side of the tracks.

He moved stealthily forward, his Colt Peacemaker in his big fist. Asa, beside him, had the battle-scarred Henry ready. Their companions were clustered close behind, ready to dive to one side and fire at any instant. It would only be a matter of moments until they would be discovered, but they used that time to close the gap between themselves and the bandits. It was the only chance they had for a swift and sure victory.

2

At that instant one of the gang saw Breck and his men. "Watch it!" he shouted. The bark of his big gun drowned the last of his words.

A barrage opened on both sides. A horse screamed in pain and terror as a bullet missed the outlaw it was intended for and caught the animal high in the shoulder. He reared, and his rider crashed to the sod.

Another gunman leaped from his mount and flung himself to the hard turf in an effort to make a smaller target. But he was not in time. Hunter caught him with a bullet before his body came to a stop. He jerked convulsively as the big slug slammed into his shoulder, shattering the bone and effectively taking him out of the battle.

A bit to the left of the injured man, Breck saw the flame at the end of a barrel, and hot lead slashed through the flesh of his upper arm. But there was little pain, and he was scarcely aware that he had been shot. His own weapon bellowed and another outlaw jerked upright, staggered forward, and sprawled lifeless on the prairie.

The men behind Breck and Hunter scrambled farther to one side for the cover of darkness behind clumps of prickly, spearlike soap weed. The blackness behind each little clump of vegetation was small, but by this time the clouds had parted just enough to let the slivered crescent moon shine through. The shadow made by the yucca might serve to partially hide a man. At least it was enough to give a measure of comfort, whether it actually helped or not.

The passengers threw a thunderous barrage of lead at the bandits. The outlaws, returning fire, added to the din. The battle was as fierce as any of the participants had ever seen.

Asa selected a target, raised to one knee, aimed, and squeezed the trigger. The bandit's weapon hand jerked upward, and the slug from his gun went harmlessly overhead.

For an instant the outlaw remained erect, frozen motionless by the impact. Only an unnatural slouch to his torso indicated that anything was wrong. Then his knees buckled and he swayed, struggling to level his heavy gun and continue firing. But before he could do so he collapsed slowly, the strength going out of him. The weapon wavered and slipped from his fingers, falling to the ties. His left hand reached for it, clawing desperately, but it was too far away. He struggled to pull himself forward, but the effort was too much and he slumped to the ground.

The men still on the train were aware of what was going on. They extinguished the kerosene lamps and those who could scrounge guns began to shoot from open windows. Others herded the few women and children into corners away from the line of fire.

Outside, a bullet slammed into one of Breck's men. He turned in time to see the youthful cowhand drop his rifle and clasp his hand over the reddening stain on his chest. So much blood could only mean a severed vein or artery, probably near the heart. He reached over impulsively and touched the young passenger's hand. Anger at his own helplessness leaped within him. There was nothing he or anyone else could do.

His gaze met those calm brown eyes, and a faint smile lifted one corner of the dying man's lips. He spoke, and the words were so low Breck had to bend close to hear them.

"Go on," the boy whispered. "Take care of 'em. There's nothing you can do for me."

At that instant a rifle shot sounded from the back of the train. John Breck jerked his lean frame erect. The passengers! The outlaws weren't wasting any time.

"Hunter!" He shouted, grasping his companion's arm. "Come on!"

Together they dashed to the rear.

They could see no one at the back of the train. That meant the bandits had approached from the opposite side. But where were the men he'd sent over there? What were they doing that they didn't realize what was going on behind them? Or—

Breck hadn't moved three steps when half a dozen guns fired, almost in unison. He flung himself under the train, scrambled to the other side and ripped off a shot that caught one of the outlaws in the hip. The renegade went down in a heap. Hunter was at Breck's side a moment later, the old Henry barking.

The sudden hail of bullets from a new quarter panicked the outlaws who were planning to board the train. They quickly mounted their horses and started across the prairie, shooting wildly as they fled.

One of the gang, evidently the leader, screamed at the deserters, and two reined in, turning uncertainly and waiting, as though trying to make up their mind whether to fight or run. Hunter ended their indecision and the battle. He was aiming at the one who gave orders, but the outlaw's horse lunged forward, taking the slug in his hip. Shrieking in pain, the big stallion reared, front hooves clawing the air. The injured animal stretched upward and froze, motionless as a granite boulder for one breathless instant. Then he lost his balance and fell backwards so suddenly the rider could not scramble out of the way. The fall drove the saddle horn into the pit of the man's stomach, ruptured his abdomen, and knocked the wind out of the powerful buckskin. The big stallion lay still momentarily, fighting for breath. Then he struggled to his feet and moved shakily away, leaving the train robber motionless as death.

Breck and his companion eyed the outlaw intently, but there was no movement, no sign that he was alive. The fighting at the front of the train broke off, as abruptly as it began. An unnatural silence settled over the battleground. The strange hush lacked reality. Breck felt separated from the events of the last few moments, as though he hadn't been involved. It was a bad dream that had happened to others or would go away when he was finally awake.

But it was real. He knew the body of the youthful passenger was still lying facedown on the other side of the train. The bandit leader was dead, killed by the sledgehammer blow of the saddle horn when his horse fell on him. One member of the outlaw gang was injured, but still breathing. He moaned plaintively for someone to help him. Others had been wounded, but apparently had managed to escape.

The conductor, white-faced and trembling, stepped down from a coach and approached the silent knot of passengers who had been fighting for the safety of the train and its occupants. They were looking down at the dead man and his injured companion.

"I—I'll get somebody to take this body up to the express car," he said to no one in particular. "We'll have to take him to Buffalo Gulch for burial."

"Don't forget me," the wounded man pleaded.

"The fireman knows a bit about patching people up," the conductor told him, his voice icy. "Don't know if he'll work on you, but he might."

The injured man tried to struggle to his feet, but could not make it. Breck went over, grabbed him by the shoulders, and lifted him erect.

"You can lean on me," he said quietly.

"They made me go with them," the outlaw said, pleading to be believed. "I was down on my luck and they offered me a job. I thought it was bustin' broncs or herdin' cattle till I saw the rails. By then they wouldn't let me go."

Four passengers who hadn't taken part in the fight carried the bodies of the two train robbers to the front to lay them with those who had been killed in the assault at the engine.

Breck helped the wounded outlaw across the cinder-strewn ties to the front of the train. The only sound was the crunch of boots against the cinders and the heavy breathing of men still struck silent by the fierce battle. Nobody in the tense little group had anything to say. They stopped and watched as Breck got the fireman to examine the outlaw.

One of the onlookers swore darkly. "If it was me, I'd let him die. Wouldn't waste any time on the likes of him!"

Breck whirled on him. "You don't know what you're saying! After all, he's a man!"

"Not in my book he ain't!"

He could see what the man meant. A fine, clean, upright lad had died back there. A boy who hadn't lived long enough to really know what life was. And for what? To keep the likes of the wounded outlaw and his companions from robbing the train and probably raping the women. Because of him and the rest of the gang, they had *all* faced death. Still, to speak so callously of letting someone die without trying to help him was more than Breck could understand.

The fireman was aware of the callous, angry attitude of the passenger, and of the others who agreed with him. But he ignored them as he went about cleaning the outlaw's wound and bandaging it.

"You're just savin' him for a hanging," someone said.

"I hope so." His gaze came up. "I surely do."

While that was taking place, the engineer examined the bodies of those who had been killed, going through their pockets in a search for clues to their identity.

"Recognize them?" Hunter asked.

"Never saw those two before, and they ain't carrying anything to tell us who they are," the trainman replied. "But there's a poster on this other guy in the marshall's office in Buffalo Gulch. Saw it myself when I was in there the other day."

Breck stared at the bodies. He had seen all three at one time or another. The black man was

Jericho Turner, a gunman from up Nebraska way whose six-gun was known to be for sale to the highest bidder. He had killed three men in a hassle over a faro game in Abilene a few years back. Rumor had it that all three were unarmed, but nobody knew for certain. And those killings weren't the only ones credited to Turner. He was supposed to have killed nine others, not counting Indians or Mexicans.

The one lying next to Turner Breck knew only as Baldy. He had seen him once when he came blustering through Texas cutting a wide swath with that mouth of his. Breck remembered him as talking a good fight. He had set up shop at a front table in the town's biggest saloon, boasting of his skill with a hog leg, regaling his audiences with lurid accounts of the men he had faced down and the gun slingers he had buried. He sounded like a real bad man, but nobody knew for sure how much of it was true.

A couple of weeks after he hit town, an argument had developed when a drunken cowhand called him a liar. Baldy hadn't acted all that much like a gunfighter then. He kept his hand away from his gun and backed off. Not long after that he moved on, leaving town in the middle of the night.

Breck didn't doubt that he had killed. There was a cold, ruthless gleam in his eyes and a desperate cut to his features. He was the sort a man didn't turn his back on if he wanted to see the sun come up the next morning.

Breck wasn't surprised that Baldy and Turner were involved in a train robbery. They would have done most anything to earn a few dollars. But the third man—the leader who was killed at the rear of the train—had been different.

Gordon Ludwig was a gunman. Breck had seen him several times and had heard about him far more often. He was lightning with a six-gun, men said of him. Those who had seen him in action spoke of his cool, unruffled manner and his awesome speed. Few lawmen dared to face him, but he gave them no reason for fear. Modest and soft-spoken, he didn't cause trouble when he hit town. His killings were neat and done in out-of-the-way places. There was nothing messy about him.

It was said that Ludwig had killed twenty-six men before he was twenty-six years old, but nobody could prove it. Others maintained the number was twenty-nine, while still others claimed he had lost count at thirty-three. He traveled alone, kept his own counsel, and drew only when he had to. He lived, and lived well, by his gun. The fee for his services was high.

"Friend?" Hunter asked quietly.

Breck started at the sound of his companion's voice.

"Friend?" he echoed. "He wasn't my friend. Can't say I ever talked to him, but I've seen him."

"Gunman." It was not a question but a statement of fact.

"Gunman. He came through Dodge City once when I was there." Thoughtfully, he looked up. "He was a bad one. Killed a lot of men in his time. But there's something I can't figure out. He was a loner. I've never heard of him teaming up with anybody. And especially robbing trains. It doesn't fit."

"Maybe he decided it was time to branch out."

"Maybe," Breck said doubtfully. "I suppose most anything's possible with a guy like that. But it doesn't add up!"

3

The men were still gathered around the bodies when Cornelius Devin, who had dressed hurriedly at the first sound of shooting, rushed up from the private car. He was spare and skinny as a Kansas jackrabbit, a weasel-eyed little man in his early fifties, whose gaunt features gave no sign that he had ever smiled. His forehead, pale as a dead fish, stretched up from his eyebrows to a thin, irregular line just forward of his ears. The little hair he had was sparse and scraggly as a nester's cornfield in the dog days of August, and his mustache was gray—almost white.

Although it was still the middle of the night, he was properly dressed for tea or for a meeting of the bank's board of directors back in New York City. His gray trousers and black coat and waistcoat were clean and unwrinkled. His celluloid collar was neatly buttoned in place, fastened with a narrow string tie. He looked every inch the esteemed railroad executive.

Except for the fact that his head was bare and there was a wild gleam in his eyes, there was no indication that anything out of the ordinary had happened to disturb him. When he spoke his voice was calm, and carried the tone of authority.

"What's going on?" he demanded.

"We've had a bit of a problem, sir," the conductor informed him apologetically. "But everything is under control now."

Mr. Devin surveyed the situation with the attitude of one used to taking charge. "Don't just stand there," he ordered. "Get those bodies in the express car, and let's be on our way. We're running a railroad, and we have a schedule to keep!"

The conductor cleared his throat, and his cheeks colored slightly. "Begging your pardon, Mr. Devin, but we can't be moving quite as quickly as either you or I would like. In order to stop the train, the outlaws piled ties on the tracks. Some are jammed between the cow-catcher and the rails. We were fortunate not to have been derailed."

"But we weren't," Devin retorted coldly, as though the conductor's explanation of the reason for the continued delay was completely unacceptable. "That is the important thing. And the bandits have been fought off. Now, we must be on our way. So move those ties, my good man. *Move them!*"

"Yes, sir!" The scarlet in the conductor's cheeks spread as he quickly enlisted the aid of the passengers. They pried loose the timbers that were jammed under the front of the engine, and the engineer attempted to back up in an effort to get free. The ties stubbornly resisted their efforts, but there was plenty of help and everyone on board was anxious to get moving as quickly as possible. The sweat coursed down their dirt-streaked cheeks and soaked their shirts as they struggled with the ties, but finally they succeeded. The last timber was removed and they were able to go on.

While this was taking place, Cornelius Devin stood to one side barking orders like a drill sergeant with a batch of new recruits. At that moment he looked at the work force, not as paying customers, but as gandy dancers; workers who were there to accomplish the task at hand.

The job was almost finished when the railroad executive first saw the blood on Breck's shirt sleeve. Immediately his expression changed.

"This man's been wounded!" he exclaimed, motioning to the conductor, who came hurrying up, anxious to do his employer's bidding. "See if there's a doctor on the train," Devin continued.

"Yes, sir!" The conductor turned quickly and ran toward the first coach. "Right away, sir!"

Moments later a gnarled, waspish individual slouched off the train and approached the knot of men who had gathered around Breck. He was carrying a small black doctor's bag.

"Where's the one who got in the way of the slug?"

A burly, rough-hewn cowhand stepped aside and gestured in Breck's direction.

At first the excitement and tension of the shoot-out made Breck oblivious to pain. Now, however, a dull throbbing seized his muscular upper arm and radiated outward from the injury into his shoulder and neck and down toward his wrist. Blood had soaked the sleeve of his shirt and then dried, leaving it stiff and grimy with dust. Apparently the bleeding had stopped, but the pulsating ache continued to build.

"You're in luck, cowboy," the doctor said, cutting away the sleeve and examining the wound. "It went on through. We aren't going to have to dig it out."

"Could have told you that," Breck commented quietly.

The doctor swabbed the bullet hole with a wad of cotton soaked in the new carbolic acid he had received in his last shipment of drugs. It stung fiercely, but Breck gave no sign of pain.

"Hurt?" the doctor asked.

He nodded. "It's tolerable."

"Can't do any good if it don't hurt some."

When he finished, Devin pushed forward. "Here's my card," he said. "Send me a bill for your services."

"There ain't goin' to be any bill," the doctor retorted, brushing the card aside. "I'm indebted to this cowboy, same as everyone else."

Devin fastened the lower button on his waistcoat and drew himself up to his full height, eyes narrowing.

"Suit yourself," he said coldly.

"I'll do that, friend. You can count on it."

The railroad executive frowned after him. Who did that so-called frontier doctor, who probably had never seen a medical school and had picked up his dubious skills from who knew where, think he was?

Devin wasn't used to being treated with such lack of respect. Back in New York he was recognized for who he was and accorded the esteem of his position.

For a moment he wished the doctor was on his payroll, so he could fire him. Devin's nervous fingers went down to the lower points of his waistcoat and tugged at them.

The wind had died suddenly, as though hushed by the ferocity of the battle and overwhelmed by the silence that enveloped the tense, hard-bitten men. Breck adjusted the bandage on his arm and walked about, trying to ignore the throbbing pain.

The conductor took a step or two toward him, stopped, and pulled out his heavy gold watch, staring intently at it. Breck didn't think he could see either the hands or the numbers, but that didn't seem to matter.

"We're late, gentlemen," he announced loudly, glancing quickly at Devin to be certain he heard the decisive tone in his voice. "We've got to hurry. Everybody back on the train! Step lively!"

Breck fell in beside him, with Asa at his other elbow. "Just who is that bird Devin?"

In spite of the fact that he was determined to get the train moving promptly, the conductor stopped and faced his companions. "Bird?" he echoed, his scowl cold and disapproving. "I don't believe I follow you. What do you mean, 'bird?' "

"Devin," Breck repeated. "Who is he? And how come he thinks he's so all fired important? He acted as though he owned the whole shooting match!"

The conductor was disturbed that anyone would have to ask the identity of the most important personage on the train. "He almost does," he said crisply. "*Mister* Cornelius Devin just happens to be president of this railroad."

Breck turned and started toward the coaches once more. "Glad I ain't workin' for him."

The railway employee stood tall and straight. "And I," he blurted indignantly, "am proud to."

Breck and Hunter climbed aboard and made their way to their seats. Before they reached them, the train began to move forward. It crawled slowly at first, belching smoke at every turn of the wheels, then gathered speed. The laboring of the engine and the rattle of iron against iron disturbed the hush of the prairies as they lumbered through the night.

Breck leaned back and closed his eyes, trying to ignore the throbbing ache in his arm so he could get to sleep. But every joint in the rails jarred him, driving pain into his shoulder and down to his fingertips. In silence he fought against it, but it would not leave. Now and then nausea over-whelmed him, and he was sure he was going to be sick. After a time the queasiness in his stomach eased slightly. He even dozed occasionally.

Morning came and shortly before 6:30, when the sun was just beginning to gather strength for another blistering day and the wind was picking up, they stopped for water.

"If you leave the train," the conductor announced, "be sure to be back in thirty minutes. We have some time to make up."

Hunter and Breck stood, stretched some of the weariness from their bodies, and made their way to the end of the car where they descended to the parched, sun-packed ground.

"Murphy's, Colorado," Breck read aloud. "I've never been here before."

The town, if it could be called a town, was a scattered handful of shacks and widely scattered buildings bordering the right of way. The depot stood a little to one side, a sorry wooden structure already showing neglect and decay, though it was the newest building in the scruffy community. It was narrower and shorter than most buildings, with an upstairs where the agent lived and an office and waiting room on the first floor. There was a window on either side of the open door and a sign above that proudly proclaimed the name of the place to the passengers who were supposed to come flocking in, but never did.

Hunter pushed his bowler hat back on his head and wiped his forehead with his hand. It was hot and getting hotter. Riding the train that afternoon would be miserable.

"Suppose we can find a cafe to have breakfast?" Breck asked.

Hunter didn't answer immediately. He was staring down the wide street that led out into the desolate, treeless prairie. It was not easy to understand why anyone would settle in such a place. As far as the eye could see, the land was an arid, browning desert, dotted with yucca, cactus, and sage. Grass grew there, of course, but it was sparse and dry, lifeless as tinder.

A lone rider was making his way out of the miserable little town, puffs of dust coming up around his horse's hooves with every step. Breck and Hunter watched him in silence. They didn't see or hear the station agent approach until he spoke.

"I hear tell you had some excitement last night," he said.

They nodded, curiosity gleaming in their eyes.

"How would *you* know anything about that?"

He chuckled good naturedly. "Mr. Devin—he's the president of this railroad—the whole shebang—he sent the conductor in with some messages to telegraph to Buffalo Gulch. He told about it." The depot agent paused, surveying Breck critically. "You must be the one who got shot up."

"I was clumsy. Didn't stay out of the way."

"You stopped 'em. That's all that matters." He spat a stream of tobacco juice on the nearest railroad tie. "It's like I was tellin' the missus just last night. Things are really gettin' bad with these train robberies and all. It's almost so a body don't dare go anywhere!"

They asked him about a cafe, and he volunteered to have his wife fix something. "You don't want to eat over at the hotel if you can help it." He wrinkled his face distastefully. "My missus is the best cook in town, if I do say so myself."

They followed him up the narrow stairs at the back of the depot to the living quarters. The station agent's wife had the same bleak, weary appearance as the depot and the town behind it. She was spindly and bony, built like one of the occasional cottonwoods that struggled for survival against the heat and wind and sudden temperature changes. A severe, sharp featured individual, her beady eyes were set close together beneath straight, pencil-line eyebrows. Her hair was pulled tightly about her head and caught up in a knot at the back of her neck.

The woman accepted Hunter quickly enough. "It was easy to see that he was of good English stock and character," she was to boast to her friends at Literary that night. "But the other one!" She rolled her eyes upward and shuddered. "It's the likes of him as is making this country unfit for decent folks."

Nevertheless, she hurried to fix breakfast for them, and by the time the engineer sounded his whistle to call the passengers back to the train they had finished eating and were on their second cup of coffee.

They left Murphy's exactly thirty minutes after they arrived, making it midafternoon when the train finally rumbled to a halt at the Buffalo

Gulch station. Word of the attempted robbery had been telegraphed ahead, and half the town was at the station, crowding around the passengers as they got off. They wanted to learn, firsthand, everything that had taken place.

"Here," Hunter said when he and Breck were finally on the platform alone, "I'll carry your bag."

"I can manage," Breck retorted sternly.

"You'd do the same for me." With that his younger companion picked up both carpetbags, and they made their way to the town's only hotel. By the time they checked in, the engineer had switched the president's car to a little-used siding and the trainmen had made their report of the attempted holdup to the local marshall.

Breck and Hunter got clean clothes from their bags and went down to the first floor to take their baths. The proprietor's wife had already filled the tub with warm water and laid out a bar of strong homemade soap and clean towels. They flipped a coin to see who would be first, and John won. He settled into the tub while his companion lounged in the lobby, waiting his turn.

Breck relaxed somewhat as he scrubbed the grime of the long trip away, and the pain in his arm even eased a bit. The weariness of the long ride fled as he dressed and strapped on his gun. Funny how much better a man can feel after getting rid of the dirt and putting on clean clothes, he thought.

Hunter lingered in the tub longer than Breck. It was after five when he finally came out, wearing a new tailor-made black suit with a high-cut vest, white shirt, and narrow tie like Devin had worn the night before. He put on his hat, hiding a sheaf of brown hair, and approached his companion. Few would have recognized him for the begrimed young man who had gone in to have a bath.

"It's been a long time since we had those eggs and bacon at Murphy's this morning," he remarked. "Let's find that cafe you've been telling me about."

Breck surveyed him critically. "I would never have believed it. A regular dude! A silk-sock Sam!"

"Watch it, John." Hunter grinned. "You're apt to get me riled."

"You and Devin would make a good pair."

"We both know how to enjoy the better things, if that's what you mean."

They took a couple of steps toward the door.

"You've got me plumb outclassed," Breck continued. "Maybe you'd rather go over to the Bon Ton by yourself."

"It'll be hard," Hunter retorted, smiling slightly. "But I guess I can put up with you a day or two longer. Just don't act like we're too close friends, will you?"

Breck paused. "I ought to go over to the stable and buy a horse."

Before Hunter could reply, the door creaked open and a tall, angular stranger entered the hotel lobby, bringing a blast of warm air with him. He stepped inside and looked about, as though searching for someone in particular. His hard eyes slitted, and his fingers hovered over the bone handle of his six-gun. Breck saw that the bottom of his holster was tied in place with a rawhide string and the trigger thong was hanging free. But he didn't need those clues to let him know that the stranger was a gunman. He could read it in the other's weathered features.

Their eyes met and held briefly.

"Howdy," Breck said, his voice mild. "Looking for someone?"

"That depends. Is your name John Breck?"

Breck nodded.

"Mr. Devin wants to see you right away. You're to come with me."

"Sorry, but I'm busy right now. Tell him to come to the hotel in a couple of hours if he still wants to talk to me. We ought to be back by that time."

"You don't seem to understand, mister," the stranger said, a threat in his hushed voice. "Mr. Devin wants to see you *now*. He ain't used to waitin' on people he wants to see. And he sure as shootin' don't plan on comin' over to the hotel to talk to you. He sent me to get you, and that's exactly what I'm fixin' to do—one way or another. Understand?"

Breck's manner did not change. Except for a slight tightening of the muscles around his eyes, there was no indication that he caught the threat in the stranger's manner.

"I appreciate your position," he said, his voice still cool and mild, "but that doesn't change things. Devin knows where we'll be. If he wants to see us, he can come over."

The stranger's hand moved closer to his weapon. "Know something, Breck? *Mr.* Devin's not going to like that. And I don't think you and me ought to have trouble over a little thing like who goes to see who. Just come along and he won't need to know a thing about it."

"I don't care whether he knows about it or not," Breck shot back. "And I don't like being ordered around like one of his railroad flunkies.

I don't work for him, and I'm not about to start. You can tell him that for me."

He eyed the gunman coldly, his own hand close to his weapon. It was one of those tense, unpredictable moments when anything could happen. A false move or a wrong word and trouble could explode—the kind of trouble Breck was determined to avoid if possible.

"Come on, Asa," he said quietly. "We've got things to do." They started past the gunman, who held up his left hand in warning. His right was on the butt of his six-gun.

"Nobody walks out on Joe Curry!" he snarled.

The lean, hard-eyed cowhand smiled bleakly. "If you're Curry," he said, his voice firm, "I just did."

Curry hesitated, and for an instant his hand quivered slightly, as though uncertain whether or not to draw. He would have pulled on an ordinary man. But Breck was no ordinary cow-puncher. Of that he was certain. The calm way he carried himself, the look in his eyes, the way the gun was a part of him—all of that added up to the fact that John Breck was not one to be taken lightly. So Curry hesitated, and the advantage of surprise that he might have had was lost.

Reluctantly he inched to one side. His lips quivered, and the color fled from his leathered cheeks. Breck and Hunter went by him and without looking back made their way out the door and started for the livery barn.

"Do you always treat strangers that way?" Hunter asked, giving Breck a sidelong glance.

"When that stranger happens to be a hired gun, I do."

"He could have shot you."

"He was thinking about having a go at it," Breck admitted.

"And it didn't scare you?"

"Not when he backed down."

"You didn't act very scared to me."

Breck did not reply. Helen had always told him there was nothing wrong with backing down, nothing wrong with letting the other man think you were a coward if it saved the life of one or the other. But she hadn't understood. To back down, to appear to waver, was the surest way he knew of having to use his gun. She had never been able to grasp that, and now she was the one who was gone—killed by a coward—a man who beat up women and used his weapon only when he was sure he had an unbeatable advantage.

Letting others think you were afraid didn't buy peace, Breck knew. It only made gunplay much more certain. He wished he had been able to get her to see that, to have made her understand before her death that he hated to draw the Colt strapped to his side, that he used it only when there was no other way.

They walked up the boardwalk, crossed the street, and passed the saloon on the way to the livery barn. The sun was low over the hills to the west, but neither the wind nor the heat had abated. Two barefooted boys of ten or twelve were playing tag in the street, completely oblivious to the scorching weather. A dog of uncertain ancestry that evidently belonged to one of the boys was sprawled in the shade, lying on his side, eyes closed, panting heavily.

Beyond the harness shop and the blacksmith stood the livery stable. It was a big building, with double doors in the front and a haymow in the loft above. Breck approached a slovenly, pot-bellied individual with soup stains on the front of his shirt and a pack of chewing tobacco in his pocket. He sat in an old captain's chair, leaning against the building in the only shade on the lot. His eyes were closed, and he was breathing heavily.

"I'm looking for the boss."

One eye opened as the man surveyed the tall cowboy quizzically. "You're talkin' to him. Name's Wagner."

"I'd like to buy a horse."

The man brought the front legs of the chair forward, thumping against the hard ground. "Just exactly what kind of horse are you wanting? We got horses, and then again, we got *horses!* Depends on what you're lookin' for."

"I'd like something big," Breck said. "Seventeen, maybe eighteen hands. An animal with a good head and a broad chest. One who could carry me all day with no trouble."

The other man got to his feet, noting Breck's tied-down gun and the cold, even stare of his eyes.

"I reckon you do, at that." He waddled into the barn, motioning for Breck and Hunter to follow. "I think I've got just what you want. A dun built just the way you described him. He's the kind of a horse a man like you ought to have."

The dun was in a back stall. He was everything Wagner said he was—a big horse built for a big man. He had an intelligent head and eyes that showed he didn't miss a thing. His chest was broad and powerful and his legs sturdy. He wasn't one of those spindling racehorse types that could go like the wind for a mile maybe without folding. The dun was a working horse with lasting qualities as well as speed. A man's horse. The instant Breck saw the animal he knew he had to have him.

"How much?" he asked skeptically.

Wagner bit off a chunk of tobbaco and wiped the dribble off his chin with the back of a grimy hand.

"Seein' it's you and you appreciate a good horse when you see one, I'll make him $100."

"For one horse? I don't want your herd! Just the dun."

"I know, but you get yourself in a tight spot and you'd give a sight more than that to have him under you."

That was true, but Breck couldn't let the owner of the animal know that.

"I can buy a horse for a sawbuck."

"Ain't it the truth! You want a ten-dollar horse, I've got a ten-dollar horse. A whole passel of 'em. I've even got one I'll let you have for eight. Course he ain't much to look at, and he ain't much for ridin', either, but he's cheap. That's one thing you've got to say for him. He won't cost you much."

Breck dickered for a time, making Wagner an offer and waiting for him to refuse and make a counteroffer. The haggling went on for half an hour. Finally they settled on a price of sixty dollars, and Breck counted out three twenty-dollar gold coins. The price for the dun was too high. Breck was aware of that, but nobody else around Buffalo Gulch had a horse that was half what the dun was, and Wagner was sure Breck would relent and buy him, even at an inflated price.

Once that was settled, Breck bought a Texas saddle that had been left by some drifter who couldn't pay his feed bill and a rangy, long-legged pack mule with the disposition of a mountain lion and the stamina of an old longhorn bull.

Asa didn't want to buy an animal, but the livery barn had few good saddle horses to rent. He finally decided on a horse and buggy. That wasn't the fastest way to travel, but it was better to have a good animal in harness than a wind-broke nag under a saddle.

"We'll pick them up tomorrow," Breck explained. "OK?"

"Suit yourself," the livery barn owner said. "Of course, you're payin' for the feed from now on. Those animals are yours."

Breck and Hunter were on their way back to the hotel when they saw Devin and his man Curry at the far end of the street. The two men were leaving the railroad right of way and heading uptown.

"Oh, oh," Hunter murmured. "Here comes trouble."

Breck slipped the thong from his heavy Colt Peacemaker and approached warily, his gaze fastened on the gunman at Devin's side. The sun was beginning to hide its blazing face behind the western hills, and the wind swept down the granite-hard dirt street. The two boys, who had been playing tag a few minutes before, were still on the street, running after a rolling hoop with a stick.

Breck didn't like the idea of having kids around at a time like this. If there was trouble, they were apt to be hit. Mentally he noted where they were and moved over a few feet so the boys would be out of the line of fire. The distance between the four narrowed in the tense moments that followed.

"Good afternoon, gentlemen," Devin began when they were less than a dozen paces apart. He pulled a thick gold watch from his pocket and noted the time. "You informed Mr. Curry that you would be returning to the hotel in two hours, but I see you are ahead of schedule. I like that. It tells me you're the sort of men I want to do business with. Reliable. Punctual. Admirable qualities!"

Breck ignored the conciliatory remark. "You wanted to talk to us?"

"That's right. When you refused to come see me, I decided to come to you. I hope you understand that I don't usually do that."

Breck waited in silence for him to continue.

"I like what I know about you both, Breck."

"How did you know my name?" he demanded.

The railroad president's lips lifted into a brief, mirthless smile. "I make an effort to find out about the men I am going to hire."

Breck's sturdy frame stiffened. "*We* may have something to say about that."

"I know, I know," Devin repeated hastily. "But don't turn me down before you hear my proposition. I think you'll find it very interesting."

"Go on."

"This is no place to discuss such matters. I want you to come and see me in my railway car where we can speak in private. We can't talk in your hotel or out here. Too many people."

Breck glanced at his companion, a question in his eyes. He was ready to turn Devin down, but wanted his friend to have a voice in what they did.

"It won't hurt to listen," Hunter said.

"Fine. You sound like an astute young man." Devin studied his watch once more. It seemed to Breck that he must live by that watch, as often as he consulted it. "Come over at 7:00. The others will be out to eat by then, and we can be alone." With that, Devin turned and walked away, Curry following him in silence.

Breck and Hunter went to the Bon Ton across from the town's biggest saloon, had supper, and walked briskly back to the private car, parked on a siding just beyond the depot. Rounding the newly painted station, they became aware of the guards at the coach. Curry and another lean, hard-featured gunman were at the front, studying every move for some sign of trouble. At the far end, two more rifle-carrying men were scarcely visible in the shadows.

Hunter stopped. "What do you make of that?" he asked softly. Breck studied the situation a moment longer, then looked at his friend.

"I'd make," he said quietly, "that Mr. Devin is a scared man."

4

As they approached the car, Curry stepped to one side, his rifle cradled in his arms, and motioned them up the steps. "Mr. Devin's expectin' you."

Breck paused and knocked lightly. The railroad president must have heard them approach, for he opened the door immediately.

"My friends are just leaving for supper at the Bon Ton," he said, a thin smile parting his lips. "The girls want to have a look at the untamed West."

"They won't find it there."

"That's what I tried to tell them."

Breck stepped into the private coach and looked around. At first glance, he noted two women and a young man, evidently Devin's traveling companions. An older man sat erect in a chair off to one side. The car was the same height and length as the one he and Hunter had been in, but the similarity ended there. The windows were twice as wide and almost as high, with heavy drapes to keep out the sun or prying eyes of ordinary people.

The carpet was finer than anything Breck had seen on his trip to St. Louis. The pile was soft and deep as a thick stand of well-watered buffalo grass. It was richly colored in blues and reds laid out in an intricate design, and it reached from side to side and end to end of the special car's forward section. The ceiling and walls were of polished wood, and there were reflectors behind the kerosene lamps that lighted the interior, mirroring the elegance of the furnishings.

The front half was a sitting room with ornate overstuffed divans and chairs, and a special desk for Mr. Devin when he was of a mind to work. What lay behind the wood partition Breck did not know. He supposed it was the sleeping quarters for those traveling in the coach. And there was probably a small galley.

When he was in St. Louis, he had heard about fancy first-class coaches and a dining car on some of the eastern trains. But as far as he knew, such luxury hadn't yet reached west of the Mississippi.

The young man who was lounging in the coach was dressed very much like Hunter, in a fine tailored suit and patent leather shoes and spats. He had a certain refinement about him, a dapper gentility that was strangely out of place in the rough, uncultured West.

The young women who were staring openly at Breck and Hunter were as foreign to the rugged, forbidding plains as their male companions. They probably wouldn't know what it was to wash a dish or churn butter or make a bed. They would never have milked a cow or helped with the wash or picked up buffalo chips. Helen had been just as beautiful. More so, now that Breck thought about it. But she was as firm and capable as they were soft and helpless.

He noticed the dresses they were wearing— made in the latest styles in crisp, shiny material more suited for a fancy dinner or going to church back in New York City. Apparently they didn't know that they were in a part of the country where people didn't go for frills. Clothes in the West were mostly handmade, of cloth chosen for its low price and long durability.

He didn't suppose they would stay in Buffalo Gulch long enough to learn much about the country or the people. But if they did, they would soon change their ideas about clothes and a lot of other things.

At first Breck only noticed the two young ladies, who were carbon copies of each other. They had to be sisters. Then he became aware of a third young woman, who was sitting off to one side as though she wanted to make it evident she did not belong with the others.

She was a sharp-eyed redhead, about nineteen years old. Freckles splattered across the bridge of her nose and onto her cheeks, and an impish grin lighted her features. She was dressed more simply than the others, more like the Sunday-go-to-meeting clothes of the local belles. She had a calm self-assurance that was not apparent in her companions. Her firm hands were browned by the sun. It was obvious that she had learned to work and knew how to take care of herself. As his gaze met hers, a friendly smile flecked her lips.

He was still motionless when the stately, white-haired individual about Devin's age and with the stature and bearing of a military man came from a chair in the far corner and extended a hand.

"Name's Claude Nester," he said in a deep, rich voice.

"A business associate of mine," Devin said

lamely, as though embarrassed that he hadn't introduced Nester to his guests. "And I want you to meet Claude's daughters, Libby and Abigail, and their gentleman 'friend, Charles Snyder. Charles graduated from Harvard this spring. He's having a bit of a holiday before he gets down to the boring chore of earning a living."

"The girls are being married in the fall," Nester informed the visitors bluntly.

"Papa!" Libby protested, blushing.

"It's the truth. And the truth never hurt anyone."

"You didn't have to say it *that* way. You make it sound as though you're warning them to stay away from Abigail and me." Although she included Breck in her remark, it was obvious that she was referring to Hunter.

Charles Snyder spoke up quickly, breaking the clumsy, unnatural silence. "Maybe you two are the ones to help me. I bought a new rifle before we came west. Figured I could get in some buffalo hunting." He glanced from Breck to Hunter. "Either of you ever hunted buffalo?"

"I reckon most everybody out here's hunted buffalo at one time or another," Breck told him.

"That's good news. You'll guide for me, won't you?"

"Sorry. I can't take the time."

"I'll pay you well."

"I have other things to do," he said. "But you won't have any trouble finding a guide. There's always someone in a place like this who'll accommodate you."

Devin cleared his throat as though to inform the others that it was past time for them to leave. Nester moved toward the door. "I don't know

44

about the rest of you," he said, "but I'm getting hungry. Coming Melinda?" He looked at the red-head, and she got to her feet and joined them.

Only then did Devin acknowledge her presence. "I'm sorry," he said in a tone that denied the truth of his words. "I'm forgetting my manners. Gentlemen, this is Melinda Grainger. Her father is our chief surveyor and a member of our board of directors."

She smiled and offered her hand before following the others out into the stifling night.

When they were gone, Devin motioned for Breck and Hunter to be seated. The porter came in with coffee, serving them in silence. Although he was Devin's personal servant, the railroad official did not speak until he finished his duties and left the room. Devin spooned sugar into his coffee and thinned it with a generous helping of cream.

"You saw the guards outside." His words were more a statement than a question.

"We could hardly miss them," Breck said.

"The idea of having bodyguards is repulsive to me. It's so melodramatic—like a play one of those traveling companies would put on. Besides, I'm used to taking care of myself."

Breck saw the set to his jaw and realized that that small frame hid a fighter. Devin was a fancy talker and dressed like a picture in one of those eastern magazines, but Breck would have bet that he could take care of himself.

"My board was afraid to have me come out here without someone to guarantee my protection," he continued. "I finally told them I'd get guards if anything happened."

Breck thought about that. "Why would they

be afraid something would happen to you?" he asked. "You don't look like you'd have a lot of enemies."

Devin's eyes narrowed, and his voice hardened. "Everybody's got enemies."

"Even you?"

"Even me." He paused, staring into his coffee.

"And who would these enemies be? If you don't mind telling us," Hunter said. Devin looked at him and his expression was grim.

"The people who are trying to take over the railroad and get rid of me and my associates," he said, watching the two men. "They tried twice to do me in while I was back home. Last night they tried again with that fake train robbery."

"Fake train robbery?" Breck echoed. "You could've fooled me."

"It looked real enough to me too," Hunter added.

"Don't let that deceive you," Devin remarked. "That was the way they intended it to look. They didn't stop the train to rob it. They were after me."

Breck remained silent while the railroad president selected a cigar from the humidor on the desk beside him, bit off the end, and moistened the cigar with the tip of his tongue.

"I suppose you have a good reason for believing that," Hunter said, settling back in his seat.

"Indeed I do. It seemed strange to me at the time. Mighty strange. But it was not until after I got back to bed that I sorted things out." He hesitated, and they waited for him to continue. "Did you notice the sequence of events? They piled ties on the tracks to stop us and launched the first attack at the front of the train."

Breck nodded. "That's the logical place to start."

"I agree. But the Wells Fargo car was right there, behind the coal car. That's the place most train robbers hit. The express coach. But not these robbers. Nobody made a move for it. And that's not all! I found out later that the real gun fighters were at the back of the train. And they were after *my* car."

Breck hadn't really considered that. There had been no reason for him and Hunter to think it was anything other than a normal robbery—at least until now.

"As nearly as I've been able to put things together," the railroad president went on, "the leader of the outfit was a man by the name of Ludwig. Gordon Ludwig. I did some fast checking on the bandits whose names we had. There was a message about them waiting for me when we got here.

"Pinkerton's in Denver said they were sure Ludwig was the leader of the gang, in spite of the fact that he had never been involved in a robbery of any kind that they knew of."

"You sure of that?" Hunter questioned.

"Pinkerton's were sure. They said Turner, the black, would have been smart enough to lead the raid, but both Baldy Edwards and Ludwig were from the South, and outlaws from the South usually ride together."

"Could be," Breck said. "I suppose Pinkerton's figured southerners wouldn't take orders from a black."

"Exactly. They'd ride with him because he was lightning with a gun, but wouldn't let him tell them what to do."

47

Breck had known southern outlaws like Lee Corbitt. What Devin said would have been true of him and his men. "But what about the others?" he asked. "One of *them* could have been bossing the gang."

"Maybe, but Pinkerton's figured the others were scum picked up to help with the job. Small-time thieves or drifters who were down on their luck."

"There was the outlaw who was wounded. What does he say?"

"Nothing so far. He's scared and is willing to talk, but he claims he doesn't know anything." Devin dragged deeply on his cigar and sent a stream of blue smoke upward as he expelled the air from his lungs. "Gave his name to the marshall as Edward Jacob O'Holloran. Says Ludwig and Baldy picked him up in a saloon in Denver. They bought him a horse and sent him out here with two other bar flies. There were eight altogether."

"You could be right about Ludwig," Hunter said, sipping his coffee. "He was a gunman, that's for sure."

"I'm fully convinced of it. And they're out to get me!" He tapped his armpit significantly. "I've taken to wearing guns again."

Breck glanced out the window at the armed guards. "Looks to me like you've got all the protection you need."

"I've got *more* protection than I need. I have only gone into this matter to acquaint you with the entire picture. I want you to know exactly what you are going in to."

"We haven't said we would go into anything," Breck corrected him.

A brief anger flecked Devin's eyes. "You will! I'm going to make you an offer you can't refuse." Before either Breck or Hunter could reply, he continued, "This takeover attempt has been in the making for a year or more. I won't bore you with the details of the manipulation that has been tried, or of the extraordinary measures I have been forced to go to in order to withstand their efforts.

"But they haven't given up. It's coming to a head at our next board meeting, I have been reliably informed. One of our directors, Edwin Knox— we were in the war together—came under personal attack some months ago and ran from New York to this area. Word is that he's hiding out until the board meeting."

Breck's cold gray eyes searched Devin's face. "I take it that you want us to find him."

"Not at all! Please wait until I've finished. His niece started worrying about him and finally came out west on her own to look for him. Nobody has seen her since. I want you to find *her!*"

Breck uncrossed his legs, spurs jangling. "What makes you think she hasn't holed up with her uncle to wait until the board meeting?"

"If that's what's happened, I want to know it. If she's being held somewhere against her will, I want to know that too."

"You think that's possible?" he asked.

"With the men involved in this mess, anything is possible."

"Sounds like it's a tough job you're askin' us to take on," Breck said quietly.

"It is a tough job. A mighty tough job." He formed a tepee with his hands. "I would probably have sent to Denver for someone to take care of things for me, but when I saw the way you two handled yourselves in that train robbery I decided you were the ones I needed. It's worth a thousand dollars apiece if you find her."

The muscles in John's jaw tightened. "She must mean a lot to you."

The railroad president tugged at one corner of his mustache. "Edwin Knox is the one who means a lot to me. He saved my life at Bull Run."

"And you need his vote at the board meeting," Hunter added.

"I *have* to have his vote," Devin retorted coldly. "If you want the truth of it, I'm finished without Knox. But I want to find the girl too. And I must admit that I'm not the only one who's interested in locating her. The other side would give a great deal to get to her first."

"I see," Breck said. "That's why you need someone who can handle a gun."

"Precisely."

"Then you don't want us," Hunter countered. "You can hire gunmen."

"I want men I can trust," Devin shot back. "I'm hoping gunplay won't be necessary. I had enough of that in the war to last the rest of my life and then some. But I won't lie to you. There is a possibility that there will be shooting. A definite possibility."

For an instant all was silent in the railway president's coach, save for his hard breathing. "How about it?" he finally asked. "Do I count you in?"

John glanced at Hunter and shook his head almost imperceptibly.

"Afraid not," he said.

"Same here," the young easterner replied.

Devin was annoyed. "What's the matter?" he demanded. "Isn't the ante high enough?"

"I don't know about Hunter," Breck said. "We haven't talked it over. I just don't care for traipsing around these parts looking for some girl, especially when there's apt to be shooting."

"I'm not asking you to break the law."

"We're still not interested," Hunter put in.

"I could raise the fee a bit. Say an extra $500 if you find her alive and bring her back to me."

"Nope."

"You're making a big mistake."

"Maybe. Maybe not."

"It could be the easiest money you've ever earned. I don't care if it takes three hours or a week. The pay's the same."

Breck rose to leave. "Was that all you wanted to talk to us about?"

"Sleep on it," Devin urged. "We can talk again in the morning."

"There's no need of that," Hunter told him. "It won't change anything."

The gray-haired railroad president glared at them as they left his car and stepped down to the cinders. He wasn't done with those two yet, not by a long shot!

5

The sun was gone, and oranges, scarlet, and gold faintly streaked the western horizon, a final rearguard action before giving way to the inevitable darkness that relentlessly stalked the land. Though color still lined the resting place of the sun, night was upon the prairie. It hid the ugliness of the shabby little settlement, wrapping stark, ungainly buildings in one great opaque curtain. Here and there yellowing fingers of light wavered feebly in an occasional window along the boardwalk, revealing the fact that there were those who were still at work.

Breck and Hunter scrunched noisily over the cinders on their way to the depot and their hotel. The heat of late afternoon had lessened slightly with the coming of nightfall, and the wind had died to a whisper. Somewhere to their right a coyote cried out his loneliness and another, as sad and mournful as the first, gave answer, howling his dejection to the razor-thin crescent of moon.

"What do you make of Devin and his proposition?" Hunter asked.

Breck shrugged. "I couldn't figure it out. He's a hard man, and I don't reckon he does much for anybody unless it helps him too. Why would he be so anxious to find that girl?"

"It's not because he feels sorry for her."

"That's the truth." They made their way to the crossing at the opposite end of the depot and turned, passing in front of the small, darkened building. "Makes you wonder what kind of a mess a girl like he described has gotten herself into."

"But it's no concern of ours."

Breck glanced quizzically at his companion. "You're right, Asa," he said. "It's no concern of ours."

Her parents, or whoever looked after her, ought to have known better than to let her come out to a place like this alone, even to look for someone who meant a lot to her. Anything could have happened. She might never have reached Buffalo Gulch. And if she had, Devin's enemies could have gotten to her first. From the way he talked, the fact that she was a girl wouldn't have stopped them.

Still, it was not the sort of thing Breck wanted to get involved in. Come morning, he would tell his friend good-bye, pick up his horse and pack mule, and start into the hills. Stories of Leadville had been abundant ever since the gold strike there. He was going to see if all they said about color lying around for the taking was true.

The saloon across the wide street from the hotel had been busy when Hunter and Breck went to see Devin, but now that darkness had settled in, it was really coming to life. Already the hitching rail in front was lined with saddle horses.

The player piano inside was jangling noisily in the precise rhythm that marked its tunes. But the saloon had another attraction. An off-key soprano was belting out the words to a lonely, sentimental ballad in an impromptu solo. She could not quite keep up with her mechanical accompaniment, but that didn't bother either her or her audience. No other sounds came from the saloon, and when she finished there was a wave of clapping and cheering.

"Sounds like a busy night," Hunter said. He was about to say more, but at that instant a shot rang out. John saw the brief burst of flame from the narrow space between two store buildings on the opposite side of the street. Effortlessly he palmed his gun and fired, but in the darkness there was no way of knowing whether his bullet had found its target.

The din from the saloon was so loud, few even knew that a rifle had been fired. Breck crouched momentarily, trying to peer through the opaque gloom to catch the telltale sign of movement.

In that tense moment Hunter coughed weakly and clutched Breck's good arm, the one that still held his weapon. "I—I—" he managed weakly. But the effort was too much. The words choked off, his knees buckled, and he collapsed on the walk.

"Hunter!" John cried, dropping to one knee and grasping his friend's shoulders. The easterner opened his pain-dimmed eyes, gasping violently for breath.

". . . Papers," he whispered between bloodstained lips. "Pocket . . ." His hand moved uncertainly toward the inside breast pocket of his coat, but he couldn't quite make it. His lips parted once more, but he could not speak. Only a thin, gurgling sound came out. Then his hand fell lifeless to his side.

Two men in front of the saloon saw what

happened and moved forward slowly, glancing in every direction as though trying to determine the location of the gunman who had fired the shot. Breck heard them coming, but did not look up. He reached quickly into Hunter's coat pocket, removed the papers, and shoved them inside his shirt. His shoulders screened the act from the men who were heading toward him.

"What's this all about?" the stubby, sandy-haired stranger demanded, an ominous tone creeping into his voice.

"Yeah," the tall one snarled, "what's goin' on?" His hand hovered over the six-gun on his hip.

Breck caught the hushed challenge in their tone. It was obvious that they thought he had killed Hunter in order to rob him. They were going to take over—killing him and stealing what he had too. Slowly he got to his feet and pointed to the spot where the shot had come from.

"Someone shot him from over there," he said. "But I don't know if the guy was after Hunter or me."

The strangers moved apart, pale hard eyes fastened coldly on him.

"Why did you do it?" the beefy spokesman demanded.

"Me?" Deliberately and with great calm he returned their stare. He was in a precarious position. There were two of them, separated just far enough so he could not take one without the other getting him. "You know better than that," he replied evenly.

"You callin' us liars?" Sudden anger tinged the gunfighter's words. It was a challenge, bait he was certain Breck could not refuse.

John's lithe frame stiffened and his eyes met

theirs, glancing quickly from one to the other. There was no fear in his manner, and they found that disconcerting. Only a fool, or someone uncommonly fast with his gun, would stand up to two of them. And Breck didn't appear to be a fool.

"Take it any way you want."

"You killed him!" the spokesman repeated. "We'll swear to it."

Before Breck could reply, another stranger came out of the saloon and rushed across the dusty street. The gunmen saw him coming and backed hurriedly into the darkness. Breck was left alone with the body of his friend.

"What's goin' on?"

John saw the star on the newcomer's chest. "I'm right glad to see you, marshall. Somebody bushwacked my friend just now as we walked up the street. Don't know if they were after him or me."

Marshall Hank Corrigan knelt beside the dead man and touched the still face with the back of his hand. "He's dead, all right."

Breck nodded.

By this time, men from the saloon and the hotel lobby, seeing the commotion on the street, had rushed to the scene. They looked to see if they knew the dead man, watched the marshall and Breck momentarily, and listened to learn more of what happened before moving on.

"Help me get him over in the light so I can have a look," the marshall said.

Together they carried Hunter's inert form to a place under the big window of the hotel where half a dozen kerosene lamps in the lobby spilled light out on the walk, the hitching rail, and a narrow strip of dirt street. As they lowered the body to the walk, Breck could feel Corrigan's searching gaze upon him. He surveyed Breck's cold, expressionless features and the tied-down holster on his hip.

"Ain't see you around these parts before. Been here long?"

"Name's John Breck. Hunter and I just came in on the train this afternoon," Breck replied, nodding towards his friend's still form. He didn't know whether the answer satisfied the marshall, but it was several minutes before Corrigan said anything more. He bent over the easterner's body again, examining it carefully.

"There's no powder burns on the wound," he said at last. "You didn't do it."

Breck looked at him evenly. "Could have told you that."

Corrigan ignored the irritation in the tall man's voice. "Any ideas who might have had it in for this chap?"

"I only met him on the train out from Kansas City. I don't know much about him, except that he was mighty good with a gun when the going got tough in that train robbery."

"I see." His eyes were piercing. "I wondered if you weren't on that train." He paused and straightened. "Could that slug have been meant for you?"

Breck paused. There were at least half a dozen men who would give anything to get him in their sights. He shrugged slightly. "Who doesn't have enemies?"

"Enemies who hate him bad enough to kill him?"

"I reckon there's some of them too."

The corners of the marshall's mouth tightened.

"I'm sure there are."

Breck did not reply, and Corrigan did not press for more information. Instead he bent over the body and went through the pockets carefully. While he did so, Breck stared into the darkness, searching the street for some sign of the killer. Whether the rifleman had intended the shot for Hunter or was aiming at John, he still didn't know.

"This may explain something," Corrigan said, drawing something out of one of Hunter's pockets. "He was a Pinkerton agent."

"No!" Breck exclaimed, the word exploding from his lips. "That can't be!"

"Here are his credentials. There's no mistaking it. He worked for Pinkerton, all right."

John was totally surprised. Hunter had seemed so refined—so eastern. Yet, in the gunfight at the train he had handled himself with a coolness and skill that had been impressive. The pieces to the puzzle now fell into place.

Corrigan continued his search, finding $129 in Hunter's pockets, a letter from a sister in Boston, and a return ticket to St. Louis.

"Whatever brought him out here," the marshall said, "he didn't plan on staying long."

The marshall finished searching Hunter's body and sent for the undertaker. He waited with Breck until the hearse pulled up.

"You be careful now, Breck," he said softly as Hunter's body was picked up and loaded inside. "I don't want to have to get Joe to put you in the ground too. We try to discourage that around here."

"I can take care of myself."

"I've heard men say that before. Just remember—that bullet might have been intended for you!"

John went to the undertaker's and made arrangements for a service the next morning. He hadn't known Asa Hunter long, but he didn't want him taken out to the cemetery and buried without a regular funeral, as though nobody cared about him.

"Kin?" the undertaker asked.

Breck shook his head.

"We can't have no regular funeral. The only preacher we've got is in Denver for a spell."

"I'll find somebody to take care of it."

The undertaker squinted skeptically, but he said no more about the matter. There was old Effie Malone. She was known as a praying woman. He might be able to get her, but the undertaker doubted it. The last he had heard, her rheumatism was acting up again. A time for the service was agreed on, and Breck went back to the hotel.

It was a two-story clapboard building with the paint peeling from the false front and an aging sign that beckoned to the few travelers who found their way to Buffalo Gulch. Breck acted unconcerned about the possibility that the gunman had actually been after him, but he moved cautiously. His eyes searched the street ahead, prying into the passageways between the buildings and the deep shadows of an occasional recessed doorway. He moved his booted feet as quietly as possible, his hand not far from his gun. Yet there was no hesitation in his walk, no fear in his manner.

It had been an hour since Hunter was killed, and the sidewalk on either side of the wide thoroughfare was almost deserted. The small groups of men that gathered in the doorways and along the boardwalk, talking in hushed tones about the shooting, had gradually dispersed. Some went back to their homes, some to the steps of the general store, and others to the hotel lobby or the saloons along the street.

They wondered about the identity of the man who had been killed and the reason. It wasn't often these days that there was a shooting on Main Street in Buffalo Gulch. There had been a day, the old-timers remembered, when the killing of a man wouldn't have caused more concern than the stealing of somebody's horse. Probably not as much. But now it was different. So the shooting was a thing to cause excitement.

John paused some distance from the hotel, searching the area carefully. All was quiet. While he watched, one of the group on the steps of the store got up and detached himself from the others, walking to the corner and heading toward one of the houses on a side street. A block ahead a drunk staggered out of a saloon and wobbled uncertainly to the livery barn, passing the darkened land-office building and the barber shop on the way.

Still Breck did not relax. There was no one suspicious in sight, but that didn't mean the killer was not hiding somewhere, studying his every move and waiting for the right moment to strike. To be careless now might be to invite a bullet.

He paused outside the hotel, feeling the warm breath of a fitful wind on his face. With one final look around he went inside.

"You John Breck?" the night clerk asked, stopping him as he started up the steps.

Instantly alert, John turned quickly.

"Yes."

"You had a visitor a little while ago."

Breck frowned. "That couldn't be. I don't know anybody here."

The night clerk shrugged indifferently. "She said she'd heard about that guy getting shot a little while ago and wanted to find out about the funeral. She was fixin' to go to it. That's all I know."

Breck mumbled that he didn't know anybody in Buffalo Gulch except the marshall, and he'd just met him.

"She must think I'm somebody else."

"You couldn't prove it by me."

The clerk went back to the dime novel he was reading and Breck made his way upstairs and down the hall to his room. Having anyone ask for him was disturbing, especially a girl. Like he said, he didn't know anybody in town except the marshall and he certainly didn't know any women. There had to be some mistake.

Of course, there was a possibility that it was someone Asa Hunter had met on a previous visit. Though Hunter was from the East, he had been as close-mouthed as anyone Breck had ever met. His job with Pinkerton's could have taken him to the grubby little Colorado town a dozen times. He might even have had a family there, for all anybody knew.

Now that Breck thought about it, the marshall acted as though he had never seen Hunter before. That would indicate his youthful friend had never been there. Most town marshalls made a practice of meeting as many newcomers as they could. And when they did, they seldom forgot them.

He lit the kerosene lamp on the rickety table in the corner, locked the door, and sat down to read the papers his friend had wanted him to have. The marshall had been right about Asa's association with the Pinkerton Agency. He was an investigator working out of the St. Louis office and had been assigned to locate eighteen-year-old Cassie Knox, who had left New York for Buffalo Gulch in an effort to find her uncle.

Breck's eyes widened, and he read the letter again. Cassie Knox! Hunter had been sent to look for the same girl Devin was so anxious to find!

6

Breck stared at the report in his hand. It couldn't be true, yet there it was. All in carefully formed letters and words written by a Pinkerton secretary. Hunter had come west to find an eighteen-year-old girl. Devin hadn't mentioned her first name, but how many girls by the name of Knox could be in Colorado looking for their Uncle Edwin?

He put the detailed account down briefly, then picked it up again. Starting once more at the beginning, he read the report slowly, a word at a time. No wonder his friend turned down the railway president. He wasn't working for Devin, that was sure. That probably meant he had been hired by the railway president's enemies.

Breck pulled in a long, deep breath. He had always heard that Pinkerton's would take either side of any case, as long as they were paid for it, but he had never quite believed that. Now he wasn't sure about the detective agency. He wasn't sure about anything. It was all very confusing.

There was a description of the girl in the report, along with a faded tintype to show Hunter what she looked like. Dark, wavy hair framed the soft oval of her face, almost reaching her shoulders, and a tantalizing smile lifted one corner of her mouth. Even the poor quality of the picture could not hide the flawless texture of her skin. She was 5' 2", the report said, and weighed approximately 110 pounds.

Suddenly Breck heard muffled footsteps on the rough, board floor, coming down the hall in the direction of his room. Quickly he got to his feet, inched to the door, and listened, his gun in his hand and his lithe body taut as a steel spring. Whoever it was paused outside the door for an agonizing moment, then moved on at a brisk pace. Breck heard a key rattle in a lock. The door to a room down the hall swung open and closed noisily. It seemed obvious that whoever it was had gone inside. Breck waited for a moment, then returned to the chair and the long, detailed report. He found his place again and read on.

The girl's ma had died when she was ten. She had been raised by her pa, a poor, itinerant preacher who roamed the outer reaches of the western frontier. Cassie had gone along, passing out hymnbooks, playing the piano, and singing for him, in addition to keeping their clothes clean and doing the cooking.

Her Uncle Edwin had been a Union general, fighting on half a dozen fronts. When the war was over, he married an actress by the name of Fannie Martin. She didn't stay with him long, but ran off to live with a wealthier man without benefit of either divorce or remarriage. Her husband became rich railroading, and she did everything she could to get him to take her back, but he refused.

When Cassie's dad died, she went to live with his brother and became a daughter to him. For four years all went well. Then there was trouble. Cassie saw that her Uncle Edwin was increasingly disturbed about the developing opposition to the way the railroad was being run; so she was not surprised when he told her he had to go west on business.

Shortly after he arrived in Buffalo Gulch, he wrote saying things were worse than he expected and he might be delayed getting back. When she didn't hear from him again after several months, she went west to see if she could find him. That was the last anyone had heard of her.

"Our client indicates there may be trouble," the report said. "So proceed with caution."

Breck leaned back in the chair and closed his eyes, trying to sort things out. It was all too bewildering. It didn't make sense. He went over the papers again, noting the details. Then he stood, folded the report once more, and slipped it into the bottom of his carpetbag. Once that was done, he went to the window and stared out into the darkness.

Devin was mixed up in this. He *had* to be. Yet, there was no way of knowing whether he and Edwin Knox were on the same side or if they were enemies. Devin had said they were partners, and the report seemed to verify it, but the railway president had to be ruled out as a reliable source of information. He was vitally involved himself and could have a good motive for straying from the truth.

Breck unbuttoned his shirt and turned back to a rickety chair where he sat down and pulled off his boots. It had been a long, hard day and he was suddenly exhausted. The full effect of all that had happened since the attempted train robbery wracked his sturdy frame. The strength seemed to flee from his legs, and his injured arm was aching again. Placing his gun on the chair within easy reach of his right hand, he blew out the light and went to bed.

Come to think of it, Devin wasn't the only one who was suspect. The background information Pinkerton's gave Hunter came from an unnamed source. The informant might have been as reliable as the detective agency thought, or he could have been lying through his teeth.

Breck closed his eyes, and a moment later he was asleep. The sun was streaming in his open window, and the heat of another day was beginning to build when he stirred restlessly and opened his eyes. Instantly he was awake, sitting up and swinging his feet over the side of the bed.

Breck dressed and went down to the Bon Ton for breakfast. It was only seven o'clock, but Buffalo Gulch was wide awake. The drummer who came in on the train with him was at the desk checking out, and a spring wagon lumbered up the street to stop for supplies at the general store. The barber shop was open, and the smithy next door was noisily hammering on a horseshoe. Only the saloons were quiet.

Breck found an empty table in the corner near the kitchen and sat down with his back to the wall. When he finished breakfast, he made his way along the rough boardwalk to the depot. The slight, coarse-featured agent studied Breck's lean face momentarily before getting a pad of paper from one of the pigeonholes behind him.

"Write it down here," he said. "The message you want to send."

Breck took the stubby pencil, moistened the lead with the tip of his tongue, and copied the Pinkerton Agency's St. Louis address. "OPERATOR ASA HUNTER SHOT AND KILLED YES-

TERDAY," he wrote, hesitating just long enough to read it over again before signing his name.

The agent wasn't satisfied with that and read it aloud to himself for verification and turned back to the desk in his office. "I'll get this sent in a few minutes."

Breck left the dusty little building and made his way to the livery barn for his horse. Had he lurked around the corner of the depot for a moment, he would have seen the depot agent whisk off his sunshade, take a wide-brimmed hat from the nail just inside the door, and leave. He hurried in the direction of Devin's private car, a copy of the telegram in his hand.

Breck knew nothing of that. His mind was on the funeral that would be held at 10:00 that morning. It was 8:00 already, and he still didn't have anyone to speak over Asa's grave. He asked the hotel clerk about it and the proprietor of the general store, but neither could help.

"I think my wife could do it," the store owner told him. "She's the religious one in our family. But she didn't even know the man. Besides, it wouldn't be a proper thing for a woman, him being murdered and all."

Breck couldn't see what that had to do with it, but he didn't say anything. The man was entitled to his own opinion. He stopped at the barber's and checked with the marshall, but could find no one. Finally he went back to the undertaker's.

"Get anyone to speak?" the man asked, glancing at his watch as though to remind him that the hour for the burial was fast approaching.

Breck shook his head. "We'd just as well get started."

They were ready to leave for the cemetery when the door opened and the freckle-faced young lady Breck and Hunter had met in Devin's private car came in. She glanced about quickly, disappointment marring the attractive lines of her face.

"Isn't the preacher here?"

"There's not going to be any preacher," the undertaker answered. "The only one we've got is in Denver. There ain't no one else around to take care of it."

She turned to Breck. "But you *can't* bury him without a preacher!"

"We have no choice as I see it," he told her. "I've been all over town. There ain't no one else to do it."

"There *has* to be some Bible reading! You can read, can't you?"

"I reckon so," he answered reluctantly, "but not at a funeral."

She ignored his protest. "And you," she continued, whirling on her heel to face the undertaker, "you have a Bible, don't you?"

He thought for a moment, tugging at a wayward strand of greasy black hair. "There's probably one around here someplace." He started for the stairs that led up to his living quarters. "I'll see if I can find it."

"If it was a fitting thing for a lady to do, I would," she said. "But folks might get the wrong idea about me and Mr. Hunter. They might think we were something to each other that we weren't." She paused and her voice grew stronger. "So you're going to do it."

Breck fell silent. He didn't know why she had to be so blamed stubborn, but then, come to think of it, there was no reason why he shouldn't do the reading.

The undertaker was back in a moment or two, dusting the cover of the Bible with his hand. "It was in the bottom of the trunk we brought west," he explained.

Melinda opened the Bible to the fourteenth chapter of John. "This is the place," she said, "starting with the first verse."

The reverent way she took the Bible and turned to the part she wanted Breck to read reminded him of his wife. Come to think of it, that determination in Melinda's eyes was just like Helen's. When she made up her mind a thing was right, there was no use in trying to stand against her. She wouldn't be backing off.

They left the undertaker's and walked behind the hearse. Breck held the reins of the line-back dun in one hand and carried the big Bible in the other. Melinda Grainger was beside him, her eyes filled with tears. He tied his horse at the cemetery gate and reluctantly took the place of the preacher, standing at the head of the casket. The girl and the undertaker stood five or six feet to one side.

Breck opened the Bible to the place Melinda had marked and found the first verse of John 14.

"Let not your heart be troubled; ye believe in God, believe also in me," he read aloud. "In my Father's house are many mansions: if it were not so, I would have told you. I go to prepare a place for you. And if I go and prepare a place for you, I will come again, and receive you unto myself; that where I am, there ye may be also. And whither I go, ye know, and the way ye know.

"Thomas saith unto him. Lord, we know not whither thou goest; and how can we know the way? Jesus saith unto him, I am the way, the truth and the life; no man cometh unto the Father, but by me. If ye had known me, ye should have known my Father also; and from henceforth ye know him, and have seen him."

When he finished reading, he paused. He knew from the funerals he had attended that there should be a prayer, but he had never prayed in public in his life. Desperately he eyed Melinda. She seemed to understand what was troubling him and bowed her head.

"Our Father and our God," she prayed aloud, "I didn't know Mr. Hunter, so I don't know if he was a Christian or not. But I ask that you comfort his family if he had any. Amen."

When she finished praying, she raised her head and the funeral was over. Breck was surprised to see that she was dabbing her eyes with the corner of a lace handkerchief.

"By your prayer I take it that you didn't know Hunter," he said.

"I didn't," she explained, "but *I* was responsible for his death."

The corners of his mouth twitched. "Now wait a minute. I can't believe that!"

"It's the truth! I caused his death as—as surely as though I aimed the gun and pulled the trigger."

Breck eyed her intently. Could that mean what he thought it did? It wasn't possible that she was the one who hired Pinkerton's to locate Cassie Knox! She wouldn't be mixed up in a mess like that. What would she have to do with railroads and power struggles? There had to be a mistake. Or did there?

"*That,*" he said pointedly, "takes some explaining."

"I—I suppose it does." She stopped suddenly, glancing fearfully about. "I—I want to talk to you anyway, Mr. Breck," she murmured.

"Go ahead. I'm listening."

"Not here. I'm going to the livery barn to buy a horse. Meet me there, and we can go for a ride." Before he had opportunity to protest, she walked away.

"Pretty little vixen, ain't she?" the undertaker said when Melinda was out of hearing. "I don't know about you, but I figure she didn't quite tell the truth in that prayer of hers. She *had* to know the guy. There ain't no other reason for her comin' to the funeral like she did."

Breck shrugged. "It doesn't much matter, does it?"

"I reckon not. But I wouldn't mind havin' a pretty little gal like that cryin' over me."

Without answering, Breck mounted his bronc and rode off. He was glad the undertaker hadn't heard what the girl said to him about being responsible for Hunter's death. He was one of those men whose tongue was loose on both ends and hinged in the middle, a talker who couldn't be trusted to keep anything to himself. The story about her being at Hunter's funeral, mourning over him, would be all over town by dark. And there wasn't anything Breck could do to stop it.

He was on his way up Main Street in the direction of the livery stable when Corrigan came out of the jailhouse and stopped him.

"Got somethin' you might be interested in," the marshall said. "Get down and come in."

Breck swung off the big stallion, tied him at the hitching rail with a slip knot that could be released in an instant if necessary, and followed the marshall inside.

"I did some lookin' around this mornin'," Corrigan began. "There's blood on the ground between the store and the saddle shop. You're a better shot than I thought you were."

"It doesn't sound all that good to me. I didn't stop him."

"You hit him hard enough so he couldn't carry his rifle away. Had to stash it in a pile of old boards where I found it. He must have been in an all-fired rush to get away from there. The gun wasn't hid too good."

Breck sat down and crossed his legs, waiting silently for the marshall to continue. Instead of speaking, however, Corrigan went behind his desk and picked up a heavy rifle of strange design—a new turnbolt weapon with a tubular magazine beneath the barrel. A quick glance told Breck it was an outstanding firearm.

He examined it carefully. "What kind of a gun is it?"

"I've never seen one before, but it's got the name Vetterli engraved on the barrel. I read about it one time. It's a new gun—a Swiss army rifle."

Breck's features clouded as he considered that piece of information. "How could a gun like that get way out here?"

"That's what I've been askin' myself since I found it."

Breck pulled himself erect. There was only one place such a weapon could have come from that he knew of: Devin's private car. But why?

7

The hostler had saddled a horse for Melinda, and she was waiting impatiently in the shade at the livery barn. The toes of her riding boots were gray with dust from her restless pacing in front of the barn, and she waved her quirt subconsciously. The man at the stable had brought a chair out of the office so she could sit down, but she only used it for a moment. Then she was up and moving about once more. When Breck finally rode up, her finely chiseled features brightened and her voice came alive. A stranger would have thought him to be a close and trusted friend she hadn't seen for years.

"I'm so glad we're going for a ride," she told him, moving toward the wiry little sorrel. There were still traces of hurt and panic in her manner left over from her reaction at the funeral, but she was fighting to overcome it. "It's such a lovely day."

He wiped the sweat from his forehead and wondered what she could possibly find enjoyable in such heat, but he said nothing. Some folks liked pickled pigs' feet too.

"Don't you think it's gorgeous, John?" she asked, pausing shyly as the words came out. "I mean Mr. Breck."

"John's fine with me," he said. "And I reckon it's the kind of a day you say it is. At least you seem to like it."

He dismounted and held the high-spirited gelding while she swung easily into the sidesaddle and took the reins from him. It was quite obvious that she knew what she was about.

"I take it you've done that a few times," he told her approvingly.

Her smile winked. "A few times. We *do* have horses back east, you know."

He stepped into the saddle and headed the dun toward the western outskirts of Buffalo Gulch. Touching the big stallion's flanks with the spurs, he caught up with Melinda in a few long strides.

"They gave you a lot of horse there," he told her.

She snorted her indignation. "You should've seen what they tried to push off on me!" The lines around her nose and mouth deepened indignantly.

He scarcely heard what she was saying. The sun had washed the haze away from the towering crags in the distance and was sweeping the rugged slopes with a fiery white light. The shadows grew shorter, giving warning that noon was almost upon them. The heat of summer continued to increase sharply as the day grew older, hour after blistering hour.

Sweat wilted the collar of Breck's shirt and moistened his cheeks and the back of his neck. He could feel the perspiration under his coat and wished he had taken the time to leave it at the hotel before making the ride. He glanced Melinda's way. She had acted as though she had to talk to him immediately, but she remained silent so long he wondered if she might have had some other motive for getting him out of town.

"You said you wanted to talk to me?" he asked at last.

She pulled in a long, deep breath and slowly expelled the air. Again pain flecked her eyes. "I've *got* to talk to you! You're the only one I can trust!"

He smiled gently. "How do you know you can trust me?" he asked.

"I have to trust somebody," she replied, as though that explained everything.

He reined in and waited patiently for her to continue.

"When I told you I was responsible for your friend's death," she went on, "I meant it."

He was resting his hands lightly on the saddlehorn. "You said you didn't even know him. How could you be responsible for his death?"

"I know it sounds strange." Hurt marred her soft, brown eyes. "But it's true. You see, he was working for me. I hired Pinkerton's to find Cassie Knox, and he was assigned to the case."

His gaze hardened. So she had hired Pinkerton's. That meant she was undoubtedly the one who had furnished information for the report in Hunter's pocket.

"Don't tell me you're mixed into that mess, too!"

Her temper flashed. "Just what do you mean by that?" she demanded coldly.

He shrugged. "Forget it."

But she was not one to put such an accusation aside so easily. "I don't know what you're talking about. I'm not mixed up in *any* mess! And that's the truth. It so happens that Cassie Knox is the very best friend I ever had. She came west four months ago, and I haven't heard from her since! And neither has anybody else that I know of!"

Tears filled her eyes and she tried to blink them away, but without success. "I'm afraid something terrible has happened to her."

He hesitated momentarily, not understanding everything that Melinda said, but knowing she wasn't guilty of Asa's murder. "What makes you think you're responsible for Hunter getting killed?" he demanded roughly. "He was in a dirty business, a business that makes a lot of enemies. He probably had a dozen men who were anxious to see him dead."

"That's what I've been trying to tell myself since—since I heard that he had been shot. But it's no use. I know he would still be alive if it weren't for me."

"Tell me something," he persisted quietly. "Why would anybody kill a man for trying to locate this friend of yours?"

She shook her head. "It doesn't make sense. I know that. But neither does the note I found when I got up today. It was on the floor of my compartment this morning, and it wasn't there when I went to bed last night."

She took the folded piece of paper from the cuff of her sleeve and handed it to him. He spread out the sheet carefully and read it. The letters had been formed with bold strokes that made them shout at him.

"YOU HAVE BEEN WARNED! FORGET ABOUT CASSIE KNOX AND GO BACK EAST BEFORE IT'S TOO LATE!"

Breck's lips tightened angrily. She was right— the note didn't make sense. Anyone who knew her could see that she was harmless enough. Why would anyone want to threaten her? Or was it this Cassie Knox they were afraid of? But if that were true, why? What possible reason could there be for anyone not to want a young girl to be found?

"Why *don't* they want Cassie found?" he asked curiously. "Any reason that you can think of?"

She shook her head. "But I do know this. Cassie has to be in terrible danger. They'd do *anything* to keep me from finding her."

"Then you're in danger too."

Her eyes flashed. "I can take care of myself. But I've got to find her and warn her."

Instinctively Breck glanced about to see if anyone was watching them. The prairie stretched endlessly from horizon to horizon. There were hills to the west, climbing out of the flat land in the direction of the Rockies. The land to the north and to the south rolled in a series of ragged canyons and steep hills and sharp, twisting ravines, dotted here and there with scattered cottonwoods and aspens among the sage and soap weed. To the east, in the direction of Buffalo Gulch, the prairie leveled out, a vast parched grassland with fewer trees and more yucca and cactus and sage.

Breck surveyed it all with a practiced eye, but he saw no movement, no telltale flash of light from a rifle barrel, no sign that anyone knew where they were, or cared. But that didn't mean they should relax. The only safe way to travel, Corbitt had told him, was to react as though someone was noting every move and would strike out at you if he could.

"We'd better ride," he said softly, "in case we're being watched. The wrong people might be able to figure out what this conversation is about."

Although he spoke calmly, Melinda jerked herself erect and turned in the saddle to stare across the dismal barrens in the direction of the town. She was breathing heavily.

"Don't do that!" he exclaimed in a sharp undertone. "If anyone is watching us, you'll give it away that we're on to him. And he'll be that much more careful."

"What should I do?" she whispered in subdued tones.

"We came out for a ride." He gathered up his reins and clucked to his horse. "Let's go for a ride. OK?"

He started forward at a leisurely walk, and Melinda clucked to her gelding and joined him. They moved slowly over the narrow, sun-baked trail. The smell of sage was in the air, and scattered clumps of yucca broke the tinder-dry of the buffalo grass with spots of faded green. For several minutes they rode on in silence.

"Do—do you think anybody is watching us?" she stammered uncertainly.

"Not that I could see, but we don't dare take a chance."

He remained silent, waiting for her to continue, but it seemed as though she had finished talking. If she wasn't going to talk, he was.

"Suppose you tell me what's going on?" he asked.

"What do you mean?"

"I'd like to know exactly what's going on," he said firmly.

She nodded. "I owe you that much," she said, more to herself than to him. "I—I'm not sure what you want to know or where to start."

"I want to know everything, and a good place to start is at the beginning. How did you and this Cassie Knox get to be such good friends?"

She breathed deeply, and a tiny smile lifted one corner of her mouth. "This isn't the first time

I have been in this part of the country," she began. "Our family came out here four or five years ago when Papa was surveying the route for the railroad.

"Cassie was here with her pa at the time. He was trying to get a church started, and she was helping him. I started going to the services, and Cassie and I were together every chance we had." She paused for a time. "It wasn't only that we were two lonely girls the same age in a strange western town. We hit it off from the first time we met. I'm sure we would have been best friends no matter where we lived."

He knew something about that type of friendship himself. He and Chris Duncan had had it. He and Hunter would have had it too, if the younger man had lived and they had been able to spend more time together.

"Papa was about to finish his work, and we were going home when a couple of drunken cowboys tried to break up the meetings. Cassie's pa went out to stop them. Papa always said he was a brave man in spite of the fact that he was a preacher. Anyway, Reverend Knox was accidentally shot and killed."

The trail dipped into a shallow valley and crossed a narrow, twisting tree-lined creek that had shrunk to a trickle in the summer heat and would be but a memory by the end of the month. They stopped and allowed their mounts to drink while Melinda went on with her story.

"Did I tell you that Cassie's mother had died?"

He shook his head. He knew that, but Melinda hadn't told him.

"Well, she was dead, so Cassie didn't have anyone to look after her except her Uncle Edwin in New York City. Papa got in touch with him, and it was decided that we would take her back east with us.

"That was the way Papa and Edwin Knox got together," she continued. "The next thing we knew, Mr. Knox had put some money into the railroad and after a while was elected to the board of directors. So it worked out fine for everybody."

She paused so long, Breck thought she figured she had told him everything.

"But how did your friend's uncle come to leave New York for Colorado Territory? And why was Cassie so concerned she felt she had to come out to find him?"

"I'm coming to that." She smiled again. "When Edwin Knox came home from the war, he courted and married an actress. Cassie said Fannie had never loved him, but married him because he was the best catch in sight."

Breck did not think it necessary to tell her that he knew that part of the Knox story as well. It would be interesting to see if her account matched the one in Hunter's report.

"They had only been married a few years when somebody else came along. She ran off with him. That was before Mr. Knox got involved in the railroad and made himself rich. When she learned how wealthy he had become, she came and wanted to move into his house again, but he wouldn't allow it. He said he didn't trust her.

"Anyway, Cassie and her uncle got along very well together, and it looked as though she would live with him until she got married and had a home of her own. Then something happened. It had to do with the railroad. I really didn't understand it then, and I still don't now. But Papa was worried about it too. I think there were some men who were trying to get the railroad away from Papa and his friends. Finally, a year ago, Cassie's uncle said he had to come out here. She didn't know why. And if Papa knew, he wouldn't tell me.

"Mr. Knox made the trip, and at first he wrote to Cassie regularly. Then the mail stopped coming from him, and her letters were sent back. She got so worried that she decided to come out to see if he was all right."

"I see." Breck reined in and stood in the stirrups, surveying the long, rolling hills that continually reached higher until they led to the towering Rockies in the distance. "And when did you start to worry about your friend?"

"Almost the same thing happened with her as with her uncle. She wrote me often at first. Then her letters stopped coming, and I was so concerned Papa suggested I hire the Pinkerton Agency to find her. He always said we were together so much we were more like sisters than friends."

He swung in the saddle to face her. "So that's why you feel you're responsible for what happened to Hunter?"

She nodded. "Only there's more to the story. I went to Pinkerton's New York office and they sent a man out from Kansas City." She paused, and he saw her shudder. "About a month later that detective was found with a bullet in his back."

"And you know that to be the truth?"

"That's what they wrote me. They also said that a new man by the name of Hunter was being assigned to the case from St. Louis. That was when I decided to come out to find Cassie myself.

But I didn't have any idea I was on the same train with the Pinkerton man until the two of you came back to the Devin private car and I was introduced to you."

"Does anyone else know about this?"

"All of the people with Mr. Devin," she told him. "When word came that Mr. Hunter was murdered, I was so upset I told them everything."

Dismay showed in his eyes.

"You don't think anyone in that railway car could have been responsible for what happened, do you?" she asked doubtfully.

"Let's face it. The railroad's mixed up in this whole affair, and everyone in that car's got something to do with the railroad. I'd say it easily could be someone who traveled west with you."

"But they're my *friends!*"

He shook his head. "In something like this, you can't trust anyone."

Her eyes widened. "Not even you?"

He turned quickly away. He liked to think he could be trusted in any situation, but what *would* he do if the chance for great wealth presented itself? It was enough to make a man stop and look at himself.

"Why're you telling me all of this, Melinda?" he demanded, changing the subject abruptly.

The light died in her eyes. "I—I don't know. I thought—"

"That I would help you?" he asked, finishing the sentence for her.

"You were a friend of Mr. Hunter's. I—I thought you might—" The words choked off as she read his refusal in his eyes.

"I'd like to," he said, "but I'm leavin' for the hills, soon as I can get my gear together. I've got some business to attend to."

She smiled bravely. "I'm sorry to have bothered you. Thank you for listening to me." With that, she turned her horse and headed back to town.

Breck glowered. That was just like a woman! Trying to make him feel so guilty he would put his own plans aside and get embroiled in a nasty knockdown, drag-out fight that could only mean trouble for himself and everybody else. Well, she wasn't going to get away with it. He could tell her that much.

They left their horses with the hostler at the livery barn and walked up the street in the direction of the hotel.

"I'm going to the Bon Ton," he told her grudgingly. "Would you like to have dinner with me?"

She shook her head. "Mr. Devin is expecting me, thank you." With that she was gone, the faint scent of her perfume lingering in his nostrils.

As he watched her walk slowly up the street, he noticed a corpulent, expensively dressed woman of forty or so had stopped her rig in front of the cafe. She got out, and was about to tie the horse to the hitching rail when he went over to her.

"Could I help?"

Her smile was warm, but held just the right reserve so he would not think her forward.

"I've always heard about the gallantry of western men," she said, "but I must confess this is the first evidence I've seen of it. Thank you."

He took the reins from her plump hand and tied them to the hitching rail.

"Haven't I seen you somewhere before?" she asked curiously.

"I doubt it. I only got in yesterday."

Her features brightened.

"I know now! I was on the train when you and your friend organized the men and drove those thieves away." She extended her hand to him. "I want to thank you on behalf of myself and the other passengers."

He felt the color tinge his cheeks.

She smiled again, swept into the cafe regally, and took a chair at a table near the window. He followed her, but seated himself some distance away with his back to the wall where he could easily watch everyone in the room.

"Never let nobody sit behind you," Corbitt had told him when they rode together in the early days.

Breck had just been a kid, but that was something his outlaw companion had hammered into him.

"If you don't let nobody sit behind you, you ain't so apt to get shot in the back."

8

Breck ordered a steak and leaned back in the chair to wait for it. He looked around the room with growing uneasiness. Why had Melinda Grainger come to him? She said it was because he was with Hunter, but that was no reason. Why should that make him want to help find her friend? If he had been inclined to get involved, he would have taken Devin up on his offer. That way, at least, he would have made some money on it. Helping Melinda would get him nothing more than trouble.

The waiter brought him a large T-bone smothered in potatoes and was pouring the coffee when the door opened. A tall, well-dressed stranger came in. His dark suit was tailored to fit his hulking, muscular frame; he was wearing a white shirt with a narrow black tie. John had never seen him before, but it was obvious that he was an important personage in Buffalo Gulch.

The waiter looked up as he entered. "Good afternoon, Mr. Richards."

"Good afternoon, Adolph." A row of white teeth showed as he spoke. "How's the Missus?"

The waiter flushed. "Mr. Richards," he protested, "you know I ain't married."

"You should be, Adolph," Richards told him, chuckling. "You should be."

With that, he made his way over to the woman who had talked with Breck outside the cafe a few minutes earlier.

He flashed his toothy smile. "You must be Mrs. Knox."

"Yes," she acknowledged proudly, her voice loud enough for everyone in the room to hear. "I'm Mrs. Edwin Knox."

"I'm Sam Richards."

Her face shone. "I'm delighted to meet you. I've been looking forward to it."

"And I have been anxious to meet you. I'm sorry I wasn't at the train when you came in." He sat down opposite her, and she laid her plump fingers on his arm.

"You're forgiven."

They talked casually about the weather and the attempted train robbery. Mrs. Knox mentioned Breck's part in breaking up the robbery with a broad, patronizing smile in Breck's direction. He looked down quickly and attacked his meat as though he hadn't eaten in days. The couple stopped talking just long enough to order, but when Adolph went back to the kitchen, they leaned forward until their heads were almost touching. Their voices were so low even those at the nearest table could not hear what they were saying.

Casually Breck studied the wife of the missing Edwin Knox. She had been a beautiful woman at one time. Even now, she was strikingly attractive in spite of her sagging jowls and the dark circles beneath her puffy eyes. She had the quiet self-assurance of one born to the stage.

It was easy to understand why Edwin Knox had been attracted to her. Yet, there was a hardness in her features that she could not quite conceal. Breck read her as a cold, calculating woman who usually got what she wanted. It lurked in her eyes and in the strong-willed set to her mouth. She would be a formidable adversary.

The waiter returned with more coffee, and Breck took the opportunity to question him casually about the man conferring with Mrs. Knox.

"He must be a mighty important man in these parts," he said.

"That he is," Adolph replied, keeping his voice as soft as Breck's. "He's just about the richest man around. He's the only lawyer we've got, and he owns half the bank and all of the Eagle's Nest—that's a saloon up the street." The waiter drew himself even straighter, and pride put a smile on his lips.

"He always comes in here to eat. Says he likes the way *I* take care of him." Adolph finished pouring the coffee, but did not leave immediately. "But don't you pay no 'tention to that talk about me havin' a missus. I ain't never sparked a gal in my whole life."

Breck finished eating presently and left the cafe, stepping out into the boiling sun. There had to be a reason for Knox's wife to come all the way to Buffalo Gulch from New York City. A mighty good reason. A woman like her was more suited to the opera house and the genteel drawing rooms and restaurants of the eastern seaboard than the stark furnishings of a frontier hotel.

He walked briskly to the hotel. Stopping in front momentarily, he pushed his hat back on his head. She had come west for much the same reason as Devin and his companions—that was evident. The railroad was the only common denominator in the arrival of so many easterners in such a brief period of time. Fannie Knox had come looking for her husband—John would have bet on it. Why else would she appear at the last place he had been seen?

A lone rider was approaching from the west, making his way slowly up the wide, dusty street. He had been riding long and hard. Sweat had dried on his mount's withers, and the strength seemed to have gone out of that proud body. The horse plodded wearily in the direction of the livery stable, his head down and his ears back slightly. John watched until the stranger dismounted and led his horse into the barn; then he turned and went into the hotel. He was halfway across the lobby when the clerk at the desk recognized him.

"Breck," he said loudly, "the kid who hangs out over at the depot's been tryin' to find you. Says the agent's got a telegram for you and wants you to come over."

He shook his head. "Nobody would be sendin' me a telegram."

The man at the desk shrugged indifferently. "I said I'd tell you and I did. You can go over there or not. It don't make no difference to me."

Breck was about to go upstairs when he remembered the message he had sent to the Pinkerton office in St. Louis. He turned back and made his way out the door to the depot for the second time that day. He was some distance from it when he saw that the door was closed. That had to mean it was locked. *Nobody* in Buffalo Gulch would be inside with the doors closed on such a day. He was about to turn back when the slight, broad-featured agent came scurrying across the tracks.

"Just a minute!" he called out, his voice bellowing. "I'm coming! I'm coming!" He recognized Breck. "Oh," he said, "it's you."

By the time he got the door unlocked, Breck was beside him.

"I've got a message for you," he said importantly. Scooting nimbly behind the counter he fished a sheet of paper from the pile on his desk. "It's from Pinkerton's."

John read it at a glance. "ARRIVING ON FRIDAY TRAIN. IMPERATIVE I SEE YOU." It was signed P. J. Jacobs.

"Sounds like you're goin' to have company," the agent ventured, a question in his voice.

John folded the paper and stuffed it into his pocket. "It does for a fact."

"Them Pinkerton men sure do get around. Comin' in here all the time, dressed fit to kill and money janglin' in their pockets."

He surveyed Breck quizzically. "You workin' for 'em, too?"

"Me?" Breck laughed without answering. Let him ponder over that for awhile. Might keep him busy so he wouldn't be running over to Devin with every little thing that happened.

Outside the depot John paused. A fancy rig was pulling away from the private railway coach. Claude Nester was in the front seat; his daughters were in the back. A small spring wagon pulled by a team of mustangs was following with their luggage.

They recognized Breck and waved to him. He returned the wave. The buggy, with the wagon trailing it, rumbled past the general store and the jail at the far end of town. Wherever they were going, they were fixing to stay. And it looked as though everything they had ever owned was making the trip with them.

He scratched his forehead thoughtfully. There was something strange about their leaving the private coach and the minimal comforts of the little frontier town—as strange as their making the trip west in the first place, or as Mrs. Knox leaving New York City. It was surprising enough that they would leave the east for Buffalo Gulch. Now they were going on, beyond the few comforts of the rowdy railroad community, away from the hotel, such as it was, and the Bon Ton, which, by western standards, was a very good cafe. Going off into the hills they would find neither.

His first thought was that they might be going camping, to do some hunting on their own. But he didn't quite see them as the type, even with a wagonload of gear.

No, they had to have a specific destination, within a half a day's journey. If it was farther, they would have left home earlier in the day. Whatever their destination, it had to be a nice house, like the living quarters on a large and prosperous ranch.

He first thought that everyone in the car except Devin and Melinda were leaving by buggy. But that wasn't true. Charles Snyder was missing. This struck Breck as strange, especially since Snyder was engaged to one of the Nester girls.

There could have been an argument and she had left him sulking in Devin's private car, but that didn't seem likely. He was Claude Nester's guest, and Nester was one of those who was protective of his daughters. Snyder would have to make a favorable impression if he wanted the gray-haired railroad executive's blessing on their marriage.

There might be another reason why Snyder wasn't with the rest of the party. The man who killed Hunter took a bullet doing it. If Snyder was the murderer, he would have a slug in him somewhere, and that would cause people to wonder. It wouldn't be long until somebody would be adding things up and find out that they didn't come out right. He would have to be hidden until he healed. That would explain why he wasn't with the others when they left town just now.

Nester's future son-in-law scarcely seemed the sort to be a party to a killing, though. He was more suited for the waltz or an afternoon tea party or a concert. Yet, Snyder was one of the few in the entire area who could have had access to a Swiss Vetterli army rifle. He was from a wealthy family, and he traveled with a wealthy crowd. It wouldn't have been difficult for him to have someone bring the rifle over from Europe. It was also possible that he had been abroad and had brought it to America himself. He was still a suspect in spite of his refinement and gentility. Breck had knocked around enough to realize that the most innocent appearing tenderfoot could actually be a ruthless killer. Snyder must not be ruled out.

John made up his mind suddenly. He went to Devin's special railroad coach, climbing the steps to knock on the door. He didn't know how he would get Melinda alone, but he had to talk to her. Somebody had to hammer some sense into her. He knocked a second time, and she opened it.

"Mr. Breck," she said. "Won't you come in?"

He did not move. "Could I talk to you? Outside?"

"There's no need for that. The others have

moved out, and Mr. Devin's in his compartment in the far end of the car. He fell and broke his arm last night."

John scowled. Devin, too, could have been Hunter's killer. It could be that Devin hadn't broken his arm at all. He could have caught the slug from Breck's six-gun after killing Asa Hunter. If his arm was splinted and bandaged, no one except the doctor and Devin himself would know the truth. And he could have easily acquired a Swiss army rifle. He didn't seem as much of a possibility as Snyder, though. Breck's scowl deepened—there were many things about this affair that he did not understand.

"I feel foolish standing out here," Melinda said once more. "Can't we go inside?"

Still, Breck hesitated, shifting uncomfortably from one foot to the other. "You're sure nobody's goin' to hear us?"

"Would you like to check for yourself?" she asked icily.

"You can't be too careful about a thing like that," he blurted.

She stepped to one side, allowing him to enter the plush living quarters. He made his way to a large overstuffed chair and sat down, squirming uncomfortably.

"There are things I need to know," he began roughly.

A mirthless smile lifted one corner of her mouth. "I thought you couldn't get involved—that you're going to the hills."

He ignored her remark. "I saw Nester's party pull away just now, but Snyder wasn't with them. You wouldn't happen to know where he is, would you?"

"How would *I* know? He's engaged to Abigail."

"You know whether he's around or not," he retorted irritably.

"They told me he had gone to Leadville on an errand for Claude—I mean Mr. Nester. He took the early-morning stage."

John hitched himself closer to her. "Did you see him last night?"

"He wasn't around then either. They all went out for supper together, but Charles didn't come back." She realized, then, the reason for the questioning. "You don't think *he* had anything to do with Mr. Hunter's murder, do you?"

"I don't know what to think." He pulled in a long breath. "But I can tell you one thing. I'd feel a lot better if you weren't stayin' here. It's no place for you."

"Like I told you, I can take care of myself."

"I just don't want to see you hurt, that's all."

Her features softened. "I appreciate that, Mr. Breck. Honestly I do. But you don't have to be concerned about my living here. Mr. Devin's having the car pulled to Denver by tonight's train. I have to move out. I was packing when you came."

The muscles in his face tightened. "And just where do you think you're goin'?" he bristled.

"To the hotel, of course."

"That's even worse! What you ought to do is get yourself on the next train and go back to New York where you belong."

"And not find Cassie?" she echoed indignantly. "You sound just like Papa. I'm *not* going home until the two of us can go back together."

"If that's the way you feel about it, OK!" he exploded. "But if you get yourself in trouble, don't come runnin' to me for help."

"You have already informed me that you are not going to get involved," she retorted. "And that's fine. I don't need you or anyone else. I'll find her myself."

He stared at her quizzically. "I don't know why I bother with you!" he exclaimed, his voice crescendoing. "I've never seen such a cantankerous female. Can't you *understand?* I'm just tryin' to keep you out of trouble."

At that moment a thin voice called imperiously from the far end of the coach, "Melinda! Is that you? Are you all right?"

"I'm fine, Mr. Devin," she exclaimed loudly enough for him to hear.

"Who's there?"

"Someone to see me, but he's just leaving."

Breck stood abruptly. "Here," he said, thrusting the telegram into her hands. "This is what I came over to show you."

She read it slowly, the color fleeing her cheeks. "Oh, no!" she whispered tensely. "Not another one!"

"Pinkerton's doesn't give up easy," he said, "especially when one of their own's been killed."

"I don't want him to come! Is—is there any way we can stop him?"

John shook his head. "Not that I know of. He wouldn't turn back now, even if you did catch him. They aren't going to quit 'til they find out who's been responsible for the deaths of those two agents."

She looked up, her lips trembling. "Will you see him?" she asked. "Just to talk to him, I mean."

"That's the least I can do."

She was relieved at that. "I want you to discharge him for me. Make him understand that I want them to quit work immediately. I don't want them on the case anymore."

"I'll tell him, but don't get your hopes up. Like I said, two of their men have been killed. They aren't going to slack off until they find whoever was responsible."

"But I—I won't pay them."

"I don't think that's goin' to make any difference."

She held out her firm young hand. "Thank you."

He was about to leave when the inside door opened and Mr. Devin came in. His features were ashen, and his left arm was in a sling. The other hand held a derringer.

"Oh, it's *you!*" he muttered. "I thought we had another robbery on our hands."

"I was just leaving."

"Next time do your arguing somewhere else. How do you expect a body to sleep with that going on?"

Breck ignored Devin. "I'll be back later and help you move," he told the girl.

"That won't be necessary," the railroad president broke in. "I've already made arrangements for my porter to get her things to the hotel." He glanced at Melinda and back at the visitor. "I've tried every way I know to get her to accompany me to Denver, but she won't hear of it." He paused dramatically. "Maybe you can talk some sense into her."

"I've already tried."

Devin laughed drily. "So that's what all the shouting was about. If I'd known that, I'd have stayed in bed."

He staggered uncertainly into the back half of the private car, leaving the door open.

"How about havin' supper with me tonight?" John asked when the railroad president was gone.

"I wouldn't want to get you involved."

"There's something I have to show you."

"And having supper with me is the only way you can do it?" she said icily.

"It's the easiest way to make you believe it."

Exasperation clouded her eyes. "You make me so angry!"

He smiled pleasantly. "I'll see you at six. OK?"

"If I'm not in the lobby by six," she said, "don't wait."

9

Melinda Grainger moved to the hotel later that afternoon. Breck was in the lobby when she swept in, the porter and one of the railroad men bringing her bags. She spoke to him, stopped at the desk long enough to register, and followed her luggage up to a room on the second floor.

John considered going up to tell her that Fannie Knox was in Buffalo Gulch, that he had seen and talked to the buxom, strong-minded matron. In some ways it would have been simpler than taking her to supper. But Melinda was the sort who would have to see for herself. The instant she heard about it, she would have insisted on going to the cafe. So in the end it was better to get her to the Bon Ton and show her the plump Mrs. Knox.

After a time he went up to his room, cleaned his boots, and shaved. A few minutes before six he went down to the lobby and found a chair in an obscure corner. Although it was out of the way, it was situated so he could command a view of both the front door and the stairs while he waited.

He expected her to appear promptly. In fact he thought at first that she might be there before he was, but there was no sign of her. He got up, paced to the front door, and stared into the shimmering late afternoon heat.

The clock on the wall struck the hour, and there was still no sign of Melinda. He waited another fifteen minutes before concluding that she wasn't going to show up.

Fannie Knox was already in the cafe when John Breck appeared and took a table some distance from her. She saw him come in and lifted her pudgy hand in greeting. He didn't know whether that was an invitation to join her or not, but he decided to ignore it if it was. Adolph came to his table almost immediately and took his order.

"She's here again," he said softly. "That fine-feathered friend of Mr. Richards. Just look at her, would you? She must have *piles* of money and she's awful pretty."

Mrs. Knox was watching, and Breck wondered if she suspected they were talking about her. It would probably have pleased her to know they were. She was the sort who enjoyed being noticed. But it bothered John.

"I'll have another steak, Adolph," he said loudly, "and a *big* cup of coffee."

"Yes, sir. Coming right up!"

He hadn't reached the kitchen when Melinda came into the cafe. Breathless, she stopped in the doorway and looked around, finding John almost immediately. For an instant she hesitated, her cheeks flushing darkly, before she started for a table of her own. Breck got to his feet and started for her, but he hadn't moved more than a step or two when she saw Fannie Knox. She froze where she was, her gaze riveted on the older woman.

Mrs. Knox glared irritably at her. "Do I *know* you?" she demanded.

John had planned only on showing the girl that Mrs. Knox was in town. He hadn't counted on a confrontation. As wrought up as Melinda was, anything could happen. He hurried over to them.

"Miss Grainger," he said, "this is Mrs. Edwin Knox."

"I believe we've met," Melinda replied coldly.

Fannie managed a tight little smile. "I'm sure there's some mistake. I—I don't remember you."

"But I remember you!" Her voice rose. "I'm Cassie's friend."

The color seeped from the older woman's cheeks, leaving them a pasty gray. "Oh yes . . . Cassie. Edwin's ungrateful niece. I remember you now."

Anger flashed in Melinda's eyes, and John took her firmly by the arm. "I'm sure you ladies will want to get together to talk over old times, but that will have to wait until another day. Good-bye, Mrs. Knox."

She nodded curtly at the girl by his side, and Melinda mumbled something unintelligible as he led her away.

They sat down at the table.

"Is this your idea of a joke?" she snapped irritably.

"If you'd come over here with me at six o'clock, like I asked, this wouldn't have happened."

"I was writing a letter and time got away from me," she said angrily. "I'm sorry about that. But it's no excuse for what you did. Getting me over here face to face with *that* woman!"

"I had nothing to do with what happened just now. You ought to know that. I figured you and

I would walk over here from the hotel, find a table, and have a nice quiet meal. When the time was right, I was going to point her out to you. I didn't know you were goin' to charge right up to her like a riled up she-bear."

She started to reply hotly, but checked herself. "That wasn't being fair," she admitted.

"The fact is," he added, grinning, "I had to come over and rescue her."

"Exactly what do you mean by that?"

"I was expecting a hair-pullin' contest and I figured, mad as you are, that she was a sure loser. I could see the two of you rollin' around on the floor, clawing an' screaming."

Melinda giggled in spite of herself.

After she gave Adolph her order and he went back to the kitchen, she leaned forward until her lips were almost in John Breck's ear. "Why do you suppose *she's* here?"

"Probably for the same reason you are."

Her eyes widened. "To find Cassie? You heard what she said. She hates her."

"To find her husband then. I have a feeling that when one is located, we'll find the other."

John Breck went to the depot to meet the Friday night train from the East. He didn't know who he was looking for, but figured he should be able to recognize a Pinkerton agent. He had seen a few over the years.

Four men got off at Buffalo Gulch that night. Two were cowhands who obviously were traveling together, seedy individuals down on their luck and looking to strike it big in the hills around Leadville. The third was a drummer selling hardware, and the fourth was a portly, balding fellow with a carpetbag and a boisterous manner.

None of them looked like a detective, but the fat one was the most likely, if the real Pinkerton man hadn't missed the train. He was older than John expected anyone working for the detective agency to be, and his flushed face and bulbous nose spoke of too much whiskey. His clothes were grimy and slept in, and his shoes were scuffed and unpolished. He was hardly the type to represent the largest and most formidable detective agency in America.

Breck approached him slowly.

"Are you P. J. Jacobs?" he asked.

"The one and only," the agent blustered. "You must be Breck. Did you say you wanted to carry my bag? As I remember, it's a 'fur' piece over to the hotel from here."

He handed the carpetbag to John, who took it with his good arm and started off. His companion hurried to catch up. "Gets mighty awful uncomfortable toting that thing around. How're you doin, cowboy?" he asked. "Enjoyin' yourself?" He acted as though Breck was on vacation.

"Tol'able," he answered. "Tol'able."

They went to the hotel, where Jacobs checked in and climbed the creaking stairs to the second floor where most of the guests were lodged. For his size and weight he was surprisingly agile. He kept pace with John going up and was a step ahead when they reached the room to which he had been assigned.

"It's time to eat," he said, patting his stomach. "Past time. I always think better on a full stomach." He paused. "As I recollect, there's a pretty good eatin' establishment here. Let's see if I can still remember the name." His pudgy features crinkled thoughtfully. "The—the—I've got it now—the Bon Ton! Never forget a good cafe. What say we saunter down there and see if they've got a couple of nice, juicy steaks just for us."

"Go ahead," Breck said. "I'll be along."

"Suit yourself. But don't waste too much time. I'm buying."

As soon as the hall was empty, John went down to Melinda's room and knocked lightly. At first all was silent, and he knocked again. He heard footsteps crossing the rough board floor, and a moment later the key turned in the lock. The door opened an inch or so, revealing a narrow crack of light.

"You all right?" he asked.

"Why wouldn't I be?"

"Just checking."

"Like I told you, I can take care of myself."

"Not until this mess is cleaned up," he continued softly. "You don't know what you're up against."

She stared haughtily at him. "When I want your advice, I'll ask for it!" The door slammed noisily.

He turned on his heel and stormed down the hall. He should have known better than to try talking to her about anything. She had a mind of her own, that one. Nobody could do anything with her. His spurs rattled noisily on the boardwalk as he hurried after Jacobs. He reached the cafe just as the detective was placing his order.

"Thinking about that steak must have got to you," he said. "Sure didn't take long for that errand of yours." He paused. "I ain't had a decent meal since I left St. Louis." Jacobs hailed the waiter and added, "Bring us two of those steaks and a couple of the coffee cups that never get empty."

"Yes, sir." Adolph's smile lighted his features, and he scurried away.

Breck glowered across the table, still annoyed at Melinda for her stubborn attitude. If she fooled around and got herself in trouble, she'd wish she had paid more attention to him.

"I'm goin' to let you in on a little secret about yourself," Jacobs said, biting off the tip of his cigar and fumbling for a match. "You've either got a man-sized bellyache or you've had a whale of a fight with your best girl."

"She's *not* my girl!" he exploded, "but she's the most obstinate, stubborn, mule-headed woman that ever wore skirts!"

"Want to talk about it?"

"No!"

"Suits me. I've never been much on helpin' out with woman trouble."

John knew there was something more he should say—that he should explain to the Pinkerton man, but he couldn't. He didn't even know where to start.

Adolph brought their meals, Jacobs crushed the fire from his half-smoked cigar and placed the stub carefully on the saucer that served as an ashtray. When they finished eating and Jacobs had smoked the rest of the cigar, they went back to the hotel together.

Before going into his room, the agent checked the door and those on either side.

"They're empty," he said. "But you can't be too careful."

"How do you know those rooms are empty?" Breck asked.

"See those matches?" the Pinkerton man said quietly, pointing to the match sticks on the floor leaning against the doors. "As long as they haven't been moved, you know the room's empty."

He motioned Breck to sit down and went over to his carpetbag at the end of the bed, extracting a thick sheaf of papers. "I brought the Knox file along."

"If it's the same stuff Hunter had, I've already read it," John explained. "When he was dying he had me get it from his pocket."

"He only had the preliminary information. You'll find this to be in much greater detail. You can take a look at what I've got if you want to."

"Why should I?" he asked. "It don't mean nothin' to me one way or the other."

The detective was unperturbed. "Suit yourself."

Breck's eyes narrowed. Somehow he hadn't expected a remark like that from a Pinkerton man. In fact, this fella wasn't *anything* like Breck expected a Pinkerton man to be, and he wasn't too sure he trusted him.

10

"Don't get your back up," Jacobs remarked jovially. "I just want to lay it all out to you so you'll know what's goin' on."

Breck crossed his legs, bumping a spur noisily on the floor. "Shoot. I'm listening."

"I'm not goin' to repeat what you already know, except to say there's a big fight shapin' up over control of the Great Western Railroad which Devin, Knox, and this Melinda Grainger's pa are involved in."

Breck nodded silently.

"But there's more to it than that. A lot more. There's only one route to Leadville and that's through the Grand Canyon of the Arkansas River. The Great Western is layin' track in that direction fast as they can."

"I was over that way once a spell back," John told him. "It's just a notch in the canyon walls about 3,000 feet deep. Didn't look wide enough for a pack mule, let alone a train."

"It's narrow, and that's a fact. There's just barely room enough for a train to get through, accordin' to the surveyor."

"That shouldn't be a problem then."

"It wouldn't be, 'cept that Leadville's booming now that they've found silver up there and opened the mines. There's 100,000 pounds of ore a day bein' dug out and waiting to be hauled by the first railroad to get there."

Breck was surprised at that. He knew Leadville was booming, but not that it was such a bonanza. He had been discounting the stories he had heard.

"But that's not all. The Missouri Pacific is just as determined to get there first. They're headin' toward the pass too. They've got the state militia, as many sheriffs and marshalls along their route as they can buy, and a passel of local gunslingers to enforce their right to go through the canyon."

John could still see the hard eyes of the railway president immediately after the attempted train robbery and could hear the steel in his voice as he barked orders to the passengers struggling to get the ties off the track. He was a rich man, and he hadn't made his money by letting others shoulder him aside.

"I don't reckon Devin's taking that sittin' down," he observed.

"You bet he ain't. You can bet your bottom dollar on that. Rumor has it that he's bringin' in Bat Masterson and some of his old cronies to protect the gandy dancers and stir up a bit of trouble for the other outfit."

John thought back to something the railroad president had said about the men who held up the train. Devin had been certain the outlaws weren't real thieves, but were after him. This would explain why. But there were still some things he didn't quite understand.

"Why would this fight for control come now, when they've got troubles from the outside?" he asked. "Most outfits stick together when the going's hard."

Jacobs shrugged. "Who knows? Maybe some of the Board of Directors have sold out to the other side. Maybe they've been afraid Devin would lose out and decided to go along with the opposition. Or maybe they saw what was waitin' for 'em at Leadville if they could be in charge of the railroad when it got there first, and they got greedy."

Breck got to his feet and paced to the window where he turned and faced the Pinkerton man. "I still don't see why this man Knox is so all-fired important. Why's everybody so concerned about him?"

"I don't know any particular person's reasoning, but I can tell you what I know. He owns a sizeable bloc of shares. Maybe enough to be a decidin' factor in the battle that's goin' on now. As near as I can make out, that's why everybody wants him. He's the key."

John returned and sat on the edge of the chair.

"And what about this niece of his? How does she figure into it?"

"She doesn't."

"Now wait a minute!" John broke in. "Devin tried to hire Hunter and me to locate her, and two of your men have been killed tryin' to find her for Melinda Grainger. Don't tell me she ain't important. I know better!"

"I didn't say she wasn't important," Jacobs continued. "I said she doesn't figure in this railroad fight, and she doesn't. The Grainger kid is the only one who gives a hoot about her. Devin and the others are anxious to locate Knox. They figger Cassie's with her uncle and lookin' for her will lead 'em to him. That's all that means anything to them."

John pulled in a deep breath. The moment had come for him to keep his promise to Melinda. "The Grainger gal asked me to talk to you."

Jacob's thin lips tightened. "Well, go ahead. If you've got to talk, talk!"

"She's plumb daft, I know, but she's decided to look for Cassie herself. She wants you off the case."

The detective straightened. "How come she made up her mind to that all of a sudden?"

"She says it's her fault that Hunter and the other detective were killed. She doesn't want that to happen to anyone else, so she's goin' to look for her friend on her own."

"That's the stupidest thing I ever heard!"

"I agree with you on that." Breck's lower jaw stiffened. "But did you ever try to argue with a woman—especially that one?"

The big man got ponderously to his feet and stared around the room. Then he made his way to the window and looked down on the darkened street, now almost devoid of people.

"If she wants to get us off the case, there's nothin' we can do about that. But I can tell you this much. We ain't quitting, with or without her as a client. If we start lettin' our people get killed, *none* of our men'll be safe. No, cowboy, we're stayin' on this case as long as it takes to find the rascals who hired the guns that killed Hunter and Copes. You tell her that for me, will you?"

"I'll tell her, but she ain't goin' to like it."

Jacobs took out another cigar and bit off the end, but he clamped it between his teeth without lighting it.

"Now that we've got that settled, let's go on. Ain't you goin' to ask me that question again?"

"What question?"

"The one you threw at me when we first met. You wanted to know how you figured in all of this."

John tugged at the lobe of his ear. "I'll have to admit the thought's been on my mind."

The agent removed the cigar from his mouth. "How'd you like to be on our payroll?"

"Me?" John's eyes widened. "I don't know nothin' 'bout bein' a detective."

"You're a smart character and you can handle that iron on your hip. Don't try to tell me different. I can tell by lookin' and talkin' to you. Besides, I've checked you out. You're just the man we need to find the girl and wrap this case up."

"Not me!" John Breck spoke quickly. "I've already turned down two people who asked me to do the same thing. I'm goin' to tell you what I told them. I'm headin' for the hills to do some prospectin' for a spell. I ain't hirin' my gun out to nobody."

Jacobs eyed him slyly. "You'd be sure that little gal you're so worried about was taken care of proper-like."

"I've already done everything I can for her. It wouldn't do any good for me to try. She won't pay no attention to me or to anything I say."

The Pinkerton supervisor reached for his cigar again. This time he lighted it, cupping his hands about the end as though he was out in the wind. "How about seein' me after breakfast and givin' me your answer?"

"I can take care of that right now."

"I'll be eating about 7:30." Jacobs took out his watch once more and held it in his fat hand. "Come to my room at 9:00, OK?"

Breck didn't know why he agreed to see the Pinkerton detective again. He wasn't going to change his mind. Come Monday morning he would be on his way into the hills, searching for the vein that would make him rich. He had a feeling that Melinda still harbored hopes of getting him to help her, but he could do nothing about that. He couldn't let her turn his life upside-down trying to keep her out of trouble—especially when she wouldn't listen to anything he told her.

"I'll see you tomorrow," Jacobs said as John started for the door. "I'm goin' to meet with that little firebrand who hired us and try to get her to head back to New York on the next train."

"Good luck."

Jacobs nodded. "I figure I'll need it."

The Pinkerton agent went down to the lobby, found a chair near the door, and picked up the dog-eared, week-old paper. He had read most of the news before leaving St. Louis, but he went over it again slowly, absorbing the words. With the thoroughness of one who had spent many days and weeks alone in places where there was little to read, he devoured everything in the old newspaper—the news stories, ads, everything, page by page. He was turning to the back of the paper when the door opened and Melinda Grainger entered. She took two or three steps into the big room and paused, looking about uncertainly as though unsure what she should do next.

He would have recognized her anywhere. Her slim figure, the firm set to her delicate features, and the determination gleaming in her eyes gave away her identity. He could have picked her out of a crowd as the sort who would travel more than halfway across the country to locate a friend who had disappeared. He got to his feet, approached her quickly and introduced himself.

"You have credentials, of course?" she asked.

"Certainly."

As he reached for them, two slender, cold-eyed men with heavy weapons slung low on their hips came in. Jacobs and Melinda moved to one side to allow them to pass. He took his Pinkerton credentials from an inner coat pocket and showed them to her.

"I also have a copy of the letter you wrote our New York office asking us to take the case."

Once she had satisfied herself that he was who he said he was, she allowed him to lead her to a far corner of the almost empty lobby.

"The clerk gave you my note?" he asked.

She nodded. "But somehow I expected someone more—more—"

"Dashing?" he asked helpfully. "Dignified?"

"I don't know how to say what I—I expected, but you certainly don't look the way I thought a Pinkerton man would look."

"This is one of my many disguises," he told her. "Actually I'm a thin, handsome young buck with all my hair, a new broadcloth suit, and elegant manners. But right now I'm on a case, so I'm made up like this."

She laughed and relaxed a little.

"I tried to convince John Breck that he ought to be working with us too."

Her eyes flashed. "Didn't he tell you that I don't want you to work for me anymore?"

"He told me," Jacobs replied cryptically. "But I'm afraid it isn't going to do any good. My orders were to pursue the case to a successful conclusion."

"I also wrote to your St. Louis office telling them I'm dropping the case. They can send a bill to my father in New York."

He laughed drily. "I *am* the St. Louis office," he informed her. "And unfortunately I'm here in Buffalo Gulch, so I can't get any mail. Won't be able to until I get back home, and I ain't goin' there until this matter is taken care of."

"I've tried to explain," she said, her lips trembling. "I don't want anyone else killed on my account."

"Sorry, young lady, but we ain't stoppin' now. Them's my orders."

"I thought—"

"It's like I told Breck. If we don't find the killers in this affair, none of our people would be safe. So we'll be staying until we get them and see them swinging at the end of a rope. Every outlaw in the West has to learn that shooting one of our agents is a sure ticket to bein' hung."

She picked up her purse and was about to leave when he stopped her. "One moment, Miss Grainger. Now that we're on the case and plan to stay on it until your friend is found, I must ask you to go back to New York."

"You sound just like John Breck. Did he put you up to this?"

"We make our own decisions," he informed her coldly.

"Well, I don't care what you say. I'm not going."

"We're only thinking about your best interests," he reminded her. "You'll be much safer there."

"I've always been told that even the worst of men out here won't allow anyone to hurt a girl of good reputation."

"Unfortunately not every man out here is like that. There are plenty of outlaws in and around every town—even Buffalo Gulch—who would put a bullet in you for the price of a few drinks."

Her cheeks blanched and it was a moment before she could speak, but she was still adamant. "In the unlikely event that I meet up with one of the more unsavory characters," she said, "I have this." She opened her purse and showed him a small Remington Over and Under .41 caliber derringer.

"Have you ever *fired* it?" he asked skeptically.

"Do you want a demonstration?"

When it was obvious that he was not going to talk her out of her resolve to stay in the area until her friend was found, he ended the conversation. They were both going upstairs, so he walked with her to her room. At the doorway she paused and held out her hand.

"Thank you, Mr. Jacobs."

"It's been my pleasure."

He was about to leave when his narrowed eyes noted that her door was slightly ajar. Certain that she would have locked it before going out for the evening, he pointed to it silently and motioned her to one side as he spoke again.

"Good night, Miss Grainger. I'll see you in the morning for breakfast."

"But—"

"I'll be in the lobby at 7:30."

With that he jerked a Smith and Wesson .32 from a shoulder holster and kicked open the door. The instant it moved a shot rang out.

Jacobs fired twice through the wall.

There was the sound of running feet and the clatter of spurs on the windowsill. The Pinkerton agent fired again, dashing into the room. The light from the hall was feeble, but he could see that no one was inside. Whoever had been there had left through the open window.

He leaped forward, staring into the darkness outside.

11

For an instant Melinda remained motionless, staring around the darkened room, though she could see nothing save the dark form of the bed and the dresser and the open window that looked out onto a side street. Her breathing was quick and shallow.

"He shot at me," she murmured in tones so soft Jacobs could only guess at what she was saying. "He shot at me."

"He's gone now," he told her crisply. "Where's the lamp?"

"I'll get it." She made her way to the dresser, but was trembling so violently she could not strike the match.

"Here, let me do that."

By the time Jacobs had the yellow flame burning, John Breck and several others, hearing the shots, had rushed to the room and were pushing their way inside, demanding to know what had taken place.

"The lady had a visitor who wasn't very polite," the Pinkerton agent replied.

John saw the open window and realized what had happened. Palming his Colt Peacemaker, he climbed out onto the ledge and made his way to the back of the building, where he jumped lightly to the shed and then onto the ground.

John made out the hoofprints of a horse tied to the rickety board fence. There was a small pile of fresh manure in the alley and the boot prints of a heavy man jumping from the shed roof. The one who made them must have been in a big hurry. When Jacobs started shooting, he had decided to get out of there. Unfortunately he had reached the ground in the alley where there were a dozen places to hide.

Cautiously Breck moved forward in the darkness, a step at a time. His big frame tensed, and his senses were keenly alert to every sound. He could hear the hotel patrons in Melinda's room, their muffled voices high-strung and excited. He couldn't make out what they were saying, but wouldn't have listened if he could. His attention was on other things.

A deadly calm took hold of him and every sound, every movement, however slight, was intensified. Nothing in that narrow alley escaped his attention. A cat hopped up on the fence at his shoulder and leaped to the ground, scurrying away. He jerked his weapon to the ready, but did not squeeze the trigger.

Breck searched up and down the long alley, but there were no other signs of the would-be assailant. Satisfying himself that the gunman was no longer nearby, he went back to the hotel and up to Melinda's room. By the time he got there, Jacobs had managed to get the curious hotel guests back to their rooms, and he and Melinda were alone. John burst in without knocking, concern narrowing his pale gray eyes and deepening the lines in his weathered cheeks.

"See anything?" Jacobs asked.

"Not a thing." He holstered his gun and faced

Melinda. "That settles it! You've got to get out of here pronto! Go back east before those guys get to you, Melinda. You could be hurt bad. Killed maybe."

Her face was ashen, but defiance marred the gentleness of her eyes. "I don't take orders from you," she informed him coldly.

"It'd be a sight better if you did." He paced to the window and searched the area with a practiced gaze. "Don't you see?" he continued, turning back. "This is just the beginning. They're out to get you, and they'll stay with it until they do."

"But why? I haven't done anything to hurt anybody."

"Maybe you haven't and maybe you have. You're out here trying to find your friend. That might be enough to make them want to stop you."

"I'm *not* leaving," she snapped. "You'd just as well quit hounding me about it."

Breck glanced at Jacobs. "I never *saw* anyone so stubborn."

"No one's going to blame you for anything that happens to me," Melinda snapped.

"I agree with you, John," Jacobs said. "She can't stay in the hotel anymore. Any ideas?"

"We could take her over to the marshall's. I've never met his wife, but he's an all-right fella. They'll put her up for awhile, I'm sure."

"Now wait a minute!" she exploded. "Don't *I* have anything to say about this?"

Jacobs faced her sternly. "Whoever got in this room once, Melinda, could do it again—any time he has a mind to. We can't leave you here and let you risk gettin' shot."

She still hesitated. "I—I could ask for another room."

"That wouldn't make any difference," Breck said. "The other rooms aren't any more secure than this one. You can't stay here. You've got to go to the marshall's."

Jacobs nodded grimly.

"All right," she agreed at last, "but I still think it's foolishness."

"Think what you like."

She got her things together, and they went downstairs. Jacobs made arrangements to leave most of her luggage at the hotel with the night clerk until they could send someone for it.

They left through a side door, stepping out into the still night air. John set the small suitcase on the ground and looked about, his hand close to the butt of his six-gun. As his eyes grew accustomed to the darkness, he was able to make out a team and wagon standing near the corner and two saddle horses at the hitching rail across the side street. But the residents of Buffalo Gulch were inside somewhere. There was no one in view.

"Everything OK?" Jacobs asked softly.

"So far." Breck picked up the suitcase and they started forward, turning at the corner and walking warily up the boardwalk.

The town's business district was as dark as the side street, save for the Eagle's Nest, its four competitors—scattered along the thoroughfare at irregular intervals—and the Wells Fargo office. There the lamp shining through the window indicated that the manager was working late.

Marshall Corrigan and his wife Dora welcomed Melinda to their home. Dora was a plump, bustling woman with gray streaking her once-blonde hair and a trace of Swedish tinging her voice.

"I am so glad to have you here, my dear," she said. "It's been lonely for me rattlin' around in this big house since our daughter got married and moved to Denver." She glanced at her husband. "Now I have someone to talk to at breakfast."

Hank led John Breck and the Pinkerton supervisor into the parlor and closed the door. "I'm right glad to meet you, Jacobs," he said. "Heard you were comin' and figgered on seein' you tomorrow. Frankly, I don't like what's goin' on."

The detective's eyes slitted. "Meanin' what?"

"No offense, mind you. I know you've got a job to do, but so do I, and I'm just tryin' to get a handle on things." He pulled up a chair and sat across from his guests. "We've always got a few guys who are quick with a gun floatin' in and out, and we have our share of killings. But there are altogether too many gunslingers comin' to Buffalo Gulch these days. Seems to me that we've got trouble brewing."

Jacobs took out another cigar. "You want to talk now or in the morning?"

Corrigan looked up at the clock, which had just struck 10:00. "Tomorrow's fine if it suits you."

"Come down to the Bon Ton and we'll have breakfast," the Pinkerton agent said. "We can talk there."

The marshall paused. "If it's all the same to you, I'd rather meet in my office. Too many itchin' ears in the Bon Ton." Though he spoke mildly enough, it was obvious that this was not a request but an order.

Once the place and time of the appointment was settled, the marshall turned to Breck. "I've been meanin' to look you up and tell you about the man you thought you shot right after Hunter was killed."

John waited for him to go on.

"You didn't hit the killer. There was this big, ugly dog that's been 'round town the last few months. Come in with a wagon train, I reckon. Friendliest mutt you ever did see. Thought be belonged to everybody in Buffalo Gulch.

"Anyway, I found 'im dead yesterday afternoon fifty yards or so from the place where the Vetterli had been hidden. He was shot in the heart. I figure he come up alongside the gunman about the time the guy fired and the dog caught the slug you intended for the man."

"Are you sure about that?" Jacobs put in quickly.

"I found a bloody footprint of a dog on the pile of lumber where the gun had been hid. Should have seen it the first time, but I didn't."

With that, the subject changed. Corrigan and Jacobs began to talk about some of the cases the Pinkerton man had been on, but Breck was not listening. He was thinking about Devin with his heavily wrapped shoulder that could have been a bullet wound. The way he remembered, the flash of the rifle had been shoulder high. If so, Devin couldn't have been the one who murdered Hunter. Of course he could have gone down on one knee to shoot. That would have put him low enough so the slug could have killed the dog and still wound the murderer.

Then there was young Snyder who had been unaccounted for since the morning after Hunter was killed. He still might have been the killer. Finding the dog didn't clear him completely. True, he might have made a trip for Devin or his prospective father-in-law. But he could also have been nicked by Breck's bullet. If he had, he still would have hidden out, so no one would know about the wound.

The fact that Breck had killed the dog did not completely prove that Devin and Snyder were innocent. Yet, he now had no more reason to suspect them than anyone else. It was more mystifying than ever.

On the way back to the hotel an hour later, Breck said, "At least we know Melinda's well taken care of for a while."

"Unless she does somethin' foolish."

"Like what?"

"Like goin' out to look for that friend of hers. She's only safe as long as she stays at the marshall's."

John fell silent. He didn't speak again until they approached the hotel.

"You still lookin' for someone to work on the Cassie Knox case?"

Jacobs nodded. "And the killin' of our two agents," he added.

"I've been thinkin' on it. Somebody's got to take care of that girl, or she's goin' to fool around and get herself killed."

A grin lifted one corner of the fat man's mouth. "Are you meanin' what I *think* you do?"

"I'll probably kick myself in the morning."

"I don't know about that, but I for one will sleep a sight better knowin' we've got you and that gun of yours on our side."

The Pinkerton agent stopped abruptly and faced him.

"Tell me something. You sweet on her?"

"Me?" Breck straightened suddenly.

"Stranger things than that have happened."

"Not so's you could notice."

"You don't need to get so riled up about it. I was just asking."

They were at the head of the stairs when Breck spoke again.

"If you must know," he said, keeping his voice down, "I keep thinkin' about the row that gal's tryin' to hoe by herself. I reckon if anybody needs help, she does."

After Jacobs talked to the marshall the following morning, he took John to his room, provided him with the notes, interviews, and background material on the Cassie Knox case, and gave him several last-minute instructions.

"I think you know enough," he concluded, "to keep your eyes open. Don't trust anybody."

That would be easy for Breck. He was not a trusting man.

He spent the morning reading the material. It was quite likely that Edwin Knox was somewhere in the area—if he was still alive. Several witnesses had seen him in Buffalo Gulch and gave detailed descriptions of him. One, Sam Richards, the town's only attorney, knew him by name. Knox had come in to get some papers filled out. Richards claimed he couldn't specify what they were because it would be a breach of ethics. But Breck wasn't sure he had any. He seemed to be the kind whose talents were available to the highest bidder.

There really wasn't too much to the interview with Richards. He had seen Knox around town on several occasions. Knox had seemed to be preoccupied, as though he was afraid of someone or something. The attorney couldn't figure it out, but something had obviously disturbed the railroader. Knox approached Richards on the street and made an appointment to meet with him in his hotel room at 10:30 that night. He had kept the appointment, but complained of being sick and said he hadn't eaten for three days.

The papers were prepared by Richards's secretary the next morning. Knox had been most emphatic that they had to be ready by the next afternoon.

That much of the report was routine enough. Edwin Knox was known to be something of an eccentric, given to exaggerated methods of secrecy. Asking Richards to come to the hotel at 10:30 at night was completely in character. So was his insistence that the papers be ready the following day.

It was the final chapter of the tale that confused Breck.

According to Richards, Knox had the papers made out, but didn't come in to sign them and pick them up. He was seen once late that afternoon, when he went to the livery barn where he bought a horse and rode out of town. That was the last anybody in Buffalo Gulch had seen of him.

The following week someone broke into the lawyer's office and stole the Knox papers. They were all that was taken.

Breck talked with Jacobs about it.

"Did you ask Corrigan if Richards reported the theft?"

He shook his head. "I figured you would do that."

Jacobs headed for the marshall's, but stopped abruptly and came back. "There's somethin' else

I've got to tell you that I didn't feel free to say before."

John scowled suspiciously. "Go on."

"I'm still on the case."

"I figured that."

"But not the way you think. You see, I'm also workin' for Cornelius Devin to find out who's behind this takeover business and who hired those gunmen who tried to rob the train."

Breck stood quickly, towering over the pudgy Pinkerton agent.

"That might change things."

"What do you mean by that?"

"Devin just might be the man we're after. If he is and you're workin' for him, what do we do then?"

Jacobs's beady eyes narrowed, and he took the cigar from his mouth. "We grab him, John. We grab him."

Breck stepped forward and thrust out his hand impulsively.

"I think you and me are going to be able to get along."

"Sounds like it, for a fact." Jacobs stuffed the cigar back between his teeth, turned, and waddled out the door.

12

Melinda Grainger and Dora Corrigan got on well together. They fixed breakfast for themselves and the marshall—a big meal with eggs and potatoes and two kinds of meat. When Hank went to the jailhouse before going on his rounds, they made up the beds, baked bread for the week, and did the ironing. They were finished before noon.

"This is just like when Emma was home," the older woman said happily. "Many hands make light work."

"That's what my mother used to say."

"It's true, too." Dora set out a plate for herself and one for her guest. "Hank won't be home today. Said he would get something at the cafe." The smile left her face. "He's worried, Melinda. There are strange men coming to town. Bad men."

"I know."

They ate in silence and washed the dishes, drawing water from the reservoir on the stove. When that was done, Melinda changed to a clean dress, combed her hair, and put on a hat, fixing it in place with a long, ornate pin. Dora watched her uneasily.

"Do you think you should be going out?" she asked.

"I don't know why not."

"That nice Mr. Breck was very concerned about you. He doesn't think it's safe. I know he won't approve if you go traipsing off by yourself."

"Oh, bother that nice Mr. Breck!" Melinda exploded. "I asked him one little favor and he tries to run my life!"

"Hank seemed to agree with him, and so did that cigar-smoking Mr. Jacobs."

"But, Dora," Melinda protested, "I'm only going to run a few errands, and this is the middle of the day." She laid a hand on the older woman's arm. "I don't want to do anything dangerous either, but staying here all the time doesn't make any sense." Noting the concern in Mrs. Corrigan's eyes, her manner changed. "I'll be back in an hour."

Reluctantly the marshall's wife watched her go.

Melinda crossed the vacant lot in front of the Corrigan house and started up the dusty side street in the direction of the sprawling business district. There were no clouds in the sky, and the heat of the summer sun hammered down relentlessly. She was glad she had put on a hat. The sun and heat reddened her cheeks and brought out those terrible freckles. She didn't know why she had to be plagued with them. They were one of the curses that went with red hair.

She was in front of the Bon Ton Cafe when the door opened and John Breck came out. He saw her immediately.

"I thought you were told to stay with Mrs. Corrigan!" he blurted out.

"You ought to know by this time that I do my own thinking," she informed him.

"You don't *think*—you just *do!*"

"Thank you!" she retorted. "Now if you'll excuse me, I have some things uptown to attend to."

"I was going to come out and see you, Melinda," he told her, trying to keep his irritation from showing. "Why don't I walk back to the Corrigans' with you? We can talk on the way."

"That would be nice, but I'm not going to the Corrigans' right now. I have other things to take care of."

"But you shouldn't be out here alone. It isn't safe."

"Are you going to force me to go with you?"

Exasperated, he shook his head. "Of all the stubborn, pig-headed females I ever saw, you take the cake! I don't know why I told Jacobs I'd help you find that friend of yours!"

Briefly gratitude gleamed in her eyes. Then it faded as quickly as it came.

"I don't need your help."

"Maybe you don't," he told her angrily. "But you're goin' to get it anyway. Now, what do you think of that?"

She smiled regally at him and swept by. She was still smiling when she reached the general store and went inside. She bought a length of yard goods as a gift for Mrs. Corrigan and opened her purse to pay for it.

"Are you the young lady whose fiancé was murdered the other night?" the storekeeper asked.

Her body stiffened. "What do you mean, 'fiancé'?"

"The man you were going to marry. The missus and I were talkin' about it again this morning. It was a real nice thing you done, prayin' over his grave that-a-way. I don't care *what* Ferguson says!"

Melinda's lips were thin as the blade on an Arkansas toothpick, and there was no color in her face.

"Ferguson? You mean the undertaker?"

He nodded. "I ain't surprised you'd not remember his name, bein' so upset and all."

Her eyes blazed.

"What did this—this Mr. Ferguson say about me?" she demanded.

The storekeeper looked up and for the first time saw her anger. He swallowed against his Adam's apple, and it bobbed convulsively.

"What did he say?" she repeated, her voice rising.

"I—I forget."

She glared angrily at him, spun on her heel, and stormed out.

"Know somethin'?" a clerk said as Melinda disappeared from view. "You almost put your foot in it."

The balding storekeeper mopped the sweat from his forehead with a soiled handkerchief.

"The next time a woman comes in here, remind me to keep my mouth shut," he said.

Melinda Grainger's shoes beat a fierce tattoo on the boardwalk; her features were stormy. She should have known something like that would happen with a mouthy man like Mr. Ferguson. She knew at the time she should have gone over to him and set him straight, but even that might not have helped. It might only have given him more to talk about.

She had planned to go to a number of places where Cassie might have been seen and try to find someone who remembered her. But she couldn't do that now. How could she talk to people she didn't know when she was so upset she could scarcely remember what they told her?

At the next corner she stopped, paused for a moment, and turned back, walking as rapidly as before. The storekeeper must have seen her coming and supposed she was going to stop and talk to him again. Hastily he put out a CLOSED sign and shut the door, though the afternoon sun was scorching and every other business along the street had their doors and windows open.

Melinda didn't slow her pace until she reached the marshall's office. Hank Corrigan was sitting at the desk, poring over a stack of posters. He looked up to see her in the doorway.

"Come in, Melinda."

"I've got to talk to you," she exclaimed.

"Come in and sit down." When she did so, a smile cracked the serious set to his features. "What have I done to put you in such a black mood?"

"It's not you."

"I'm thankful for that."

"It's that Mr. Ferguson."

"The undertaker? What's he done?"

"He's been talking about me. That's what he's done. Telling all sorts of things that aren't true."

He leaned forward and folded his gnarled hands in front of him. "About you and Hunter bein' lovers?"

She nodded. "And I don't know what else." Her voice broke, and he thought she was close to tears.

"It's nothing worth crying about."

"I'm not about to cry!" she exploded. "I'd like to get my hands on him, just for one minute! That's all I'd need."

"You shouldn't be so upset," he reasoned. "People who know you will know the stories he's been tellin' ain't the truth. And as for those who don't know you, it doesn't matter."

Her gaze met his. "That's why I stopped here," she said. "You'll tell me the truth. Just what *is* he saying about me?"

Hank traced a triangle with his finger in the dust on his desk. "You can't pay attention to him, Melinda. That tongue of his is clatterin' all the time."

"What's he saying?"

"He's worse than a gossipy old woman."

"What's he saying?" she demanded again.

It was a moment or two before he looked up. "Like I said, he's been tellin' that you and Hunter were—were goin' to get married. That was why you came to the funeral and said a prayer over his grave."

"That's not all. I know that."

"I—I guess you're right. That's only part of it. You see, he saw you and Breck together somewhere and got the idea you was after him."

"John Breck? Breck and me? He's got to be out of his mind!"

"That's what I've been tellin' people."

Her features darkened. "Just as I thought—the stories are all over town!" She took a deep breath. "What else has he said about me?"

Dismay edged Hank Corrigan's voice. "You don't want to hear this. It'll just make you more upset."

"If I didn't want to hear what he's tellin' everybody," she snapped, "I wouldn't be asking you."

"All right, but don't blame me. I'm just

repeatin' what I've heard. As for me, I don't believe a word of it."

"Go on."

"He's been sayin' Hunter's body didn't have time to get cold before you started throwin' yourself at John Breck."

Melinda slumped in the chair, her face ashen. It was two full minutes before she could speak. "I knew he was going to talk, but I didn't think it would be so terrible."

"I said you shouldn't feel bad."

She looked up slowly, anger flaming in her eyes. "Feel bad?" she echoed. "Who feels bad? I wish I was a man! I just wish I was a man!"

"Do you want me to talk to him?" Corrigan asked.

"No," she replied quickly. "I'll take care of it myself."

"What do you figure on doing?" he asked hesitantly.

"I don't know yet." She spoke slowly, each word deliberate. "But I'll think of something."

"Don't go gettin' yourself in a mess," the marshall cautioned.

She got to her feet without answering. At the doorway she stopped and looked back. "Thank you very much, Mr. Corrigan."

"You remember what I told you!"

She left the building and marched deliberately up the street in the direction of the general store. The proprietor wasn't expecting her to return and was surprised when she appeared at his door.

"I've already told you," he said, "I don't remember what Ferguson said, but it wasn't anything to get upset about. And that's a fact."

"I didn't come in here to talk about Mr. Ferguson. I want to buy a gun."

His eyes widened. "Sorry, but I don't carry no derringers or little stuff. There ain't enough call for it. Course I can get it for you out of Denver if you ain't in too big a hurry."

"I am in a hurry," she said, "but I don't care for a little gun. I want something big enough to do a man's job."

"How about a Smith & Wesson .32?" he suggested. "It's lighter than the Colt and easier to handle, but it still packs a wallop."

He laid the gun on the counter hesitantly. She examined it for a moment, twirled the chamber, and tried the action.

"It's a nice gun," she murmured.

"You've used a six-gun before?" he asked.

"I can shoot," she told him.

"What're you aimin' to use it on?"

"Snakes!"

She bought the weapon and a box of cartridges, loaded the chamber, and put the gun in her purse.

"Here," she said, thrusting the package of yard goods and the box of cartridges into the shopkeeper's hands. "Keep these for me."

"Where are you goin'?" he demanded. "And what are you fixin' to do?"

"I'll be back." She strode purposefully out the door.

The storekeeper stared after her in alarm. As soon as she was gone, he called to his clerk. "Mike! Get yourself down to the marshall's quick as you can. Tell him that fool girl who's stayin' at his place has gone plumb out of her mind. She's bought herself a gun and is fixin' to kill Ferguson!"

Melinda paced grimly up the street toward Ferguson's establishment. She met Jacobs near the hotel and he spoke to her, but she did not reply. He doubted that she had even seen him, she was so intense. He stopped and turned to watch her curiously as she crossed the wide thoroughfare and went into Ferguson's.

The undertaker came out of the back room, rubbing his slender hands together and flashing his best smile.

"Good afternoon, madam. You must forgive me, but I seem to have forgotten your name."

Her eyes slitted angrily. "I haven't forgotten yours. You've been telling lies about me, Mr. Ferguson."

"My dear young lady," he said, "I don't understand."

"Neither do I. You don't know one thing about me, but you have started stories all over town. First about me and the late Mr. Asa Hunter, then about me and John Breck."

"I'm sure there's some mistake."

"The only mistake, " Melinda replied angrily as she opened her purse and the Smith & Wesson appeared in her hand, pointed straight at him, "was the one you made when you opened your mouth and started spreading lies."

Horror muddied his features. "Madam!" he cried. "That's a gun!"

"I'm well aware of that!" Her voice was like ice.

"And it's pointed right at me!"

"I'm aware of that too. Now come on!" She motioned toward the door with the weapon.

"B-but I can't leave. I'm expecting someone."

"You can see them when you get back—if you get back."

He stepped gingerly ahead of her, and she followed close behind.

"W-where are we going?" he managed to stammer.

"To the places where you talked about me. You're going to set them straight. You're going to tell them the truth."

"But I didn't—"

She shot near his feet, and he leaped into the air.

"Don't try to tell me what you didn't do!" Melinda cautioned grimly. "*I* know!"

"Madam, I'm sorry if you think I caused you any trouble. I—I'll make it up to you in any way I can."

"I know you will. Come on!"

At the Eagle's Nest Saloon she stopped him and ordered him inside.

"You ain't goin' to take me in there," he exclaimed. "That's no place for a lady."

"But it's a good place to talk about a lady, isn't it?" she said as she prodded him in the back, and he stepped through the swinging doors.

"That's far enough. I've still got five slugs, you know."

"I wasn't going any farther, I swear it," he pleaded.

She remained just outside the building, but called loudly to the men inside. "Gentlemen! Gentlemen!"

Nobody paid any attention to her. Pointing the gun skyward, she fired into the air. That stopped them. A hush settled over the noisy crowd, and every eye was fixed on Ferguson and the slim young woman behind him.

"Mr. Ferguson has something he wants to tell you."

Silence hung over the saloon. "I—," he began hesitantly. "I—" His voice died away.

"Go on!"

"I—I came to tell you I made a mistake about this young lady. She wasn't fixin' to marry that man Hunter we buried and—" He swallowed hard.

"Go on. You're doing fine."

"And she never threw herself at that John Breck fellow. They're just friends and was eatin' together when I seen 'em."

The men at the bar were grinning.

"There's more, Ferguson." She pushed the gun into his back.

He looked plaintively over his shoulder. "Do I have to?"

"You have to!"

"I—I'm sorry I done it! I ain't goin' to tell no more stories about this here lady or no other ladies in town."

"You've done well, Mr. Ferguson." Melinda directed her attention to the men in the saloon. "Thank you kindly."

She ordered Ferguson outside once more, and a roar of laughter went up as the door closed behind him.

"We're going to see everyone you talked to, Mr. Ferguson. When we've done that, you can go back to wherever you want, but not until then."

"But—"

"Step lively, Mr. Ferguson. We don't have all day."

The undertaker was just finishing at the second saloon when Hank Corrigan came striding up.

"What's goin' on here?" he demanded.

"Marshall Corrigan!" Ferguson said. "Am I glad to see you. This young woman is out of her mind."

"Melinda," he said sternly, "I told you not to get yourself in a mess."

"I'm not. I'm just setting the record straight."

"Let her alone, Marshall!" someone from inside the saloon exclaimed. "She's doin' old Ferguson a world of good!"

The marshall weighed the situation, summed up what was happening, then turned to Melinda.

"How'd it be if I went along just to see that there ain't no trouble?"

"It's fine with me," she told him. "As long as you make Mr. Ferguson do what he's supposed to."

"Oh, I thought I'd leave that with you," the marshall said, smiling. "You're doing a pretty good job of it."

13

Breck went into the Bon Ton at his usual time that night and pulled out the chair at his favorite table. Before he was seated Adolph came out, a broad grin creasing lines in his plain features.

"You should have seen her, Mr. Breck. You'd have been real proud of her, you would."

John looked up curiously, hard gray eyes fixed on the waiter. "Who are we talkin' about, Adolph?" he asked, mildly.

"That pretty little freckle-faced gal you had supper with the other night. Or did you hear about it?" Disappointment crept into Adolph's voice at the possibility that someone else had told Breck first.

"Haven't heard a thing." Whatever it was, it wouldn't surprise him. She was a firebrand; unpredictable and quick-tempered as a wild mustang.

Adolph chuckled. "She stuck that old hog leg into Ferguson's backbone and marched him all over town, makin' him take back what he said about her bein' sweet on that murdered guy and—" His voice trailed off as he suddenly realized where the rest of the story would take him.

"Go on."

He glanced helplessly at the kitchen, hoping

the cook would call him before he had to finish the story. A voice at his elbow spared him.

"Good evening, Adolph."

He turned gratefully to see Jacobs standing there.

"Good evening, Mr. Jacobs. I'm right glad to see you. Sit down."

The waiter took their orders and scurried away.

"Well, our little gal made quite a name for herself," the Pinkerton agent said.

"So I hear."

"She's the talk of Buffalo Gulch. They just might laugh that undertaker plumb out of town. It's mighty miserable for him right now."

"He'll probably think a long time before he has any stories to tell."

"Leastwise about Melinda."

Adolph was back with their coffee in time to hear what they were talking about.

"Don't that beat the cards!" He chuckled at the thought. "I can just see her takin' him up to the door of the Eagle's Nest—she wouldn't even go in, you know—but she made him tell those guys it was a lie about her and Hunter and about her throwin' herself at you, Mr. Breck."

John's eyes widened. "At me?" he echoed.

"Oops!" The waiter's hand flew to his mouth. "I didn't aim to tell you that." He set their cups on the table and fled to the safety of the kitchen.

Jacobs grinned, but didn't say anything.

"I can tell you this much," Breck replied. "If she's been throwin' herself at me, she's had a funny way of doin' it."

Adolph brought their ham and eggs, and Jacobs asked for more coffee.

"Did you tell her you're goin' to help find her friend?"

Breck nodded.

"Pleased her, didn't it?"

"Not so's you could notice." He started to eat. "But that makes no difference. I told her I was in on the case whether she liked it or not."

Jacobs started to explain to Breck how he should launch the investigation, but remembering Corrigan's warning about itching ears in the cafe, he stopped. Adolph meant well, but he was always moving around, hearing snatches of every conversation. And he talked continually. If he heard it, he told it—perhaps to the wrong people.

"We'll go back to my room and go over things," the Pinkerton agent said.

Clouds moved in during the night, shielding the early morning sun and cooling the wind that soughed around the buildings and across the bleak, treeless prairie. Relief from the oppressive heat and the promise of rain, however slight and transitory, brought joy to the hearts of everyone. Even the hostler, grumpy and disagreeable as a man with a stone in his boot, had a smile and a cheery greeting for Breck that morning.

John strapped his slicker to the back of the saddle and led the dun out of the livery barn. He was about to mount the wiry bronc when a footstep from behind stopped him.

"Going somewhere?" a familiar young voice asked.

"Oh, it's you. I was just headin' your direction."

"To tell me good-bye?" she asked.

"You know better than that," he grumbled.

Lowering his voice, he went on. "Jacobs and I went over things last night. If you'll just go back to the marshall's and wait, we'll get to you with news as soon as we can."

Her face was stormy as the sky. "John Breck," she exclaimed darkly, "do we have to go through that again? I'm grateful that you're helping me, truly I am. But I'm going with you. Cassie's my friend, and I'm going to do what I can to help find her."

He didn't argue with her. He knew that would be useless.

"All right. Get your horse so I can get him saddled. We ain't got all day."

"He's already saddled," she informed him coldly. "I was on my way to the hotel when I saw you and came back."

They mounted and rode slowly to the far end of the main street while Breck repeated what Jacobs had told him about beginning the investigation. The plan the Pinkerton man had developed was simple enough. So simple Breck wondered how he managed to get and keep his job. If Cassie and her Uncle Edwin were somewhere around Buffalo Gulch, they would have to have supplies. That meant one or the other would be forced to risk showing up in town once in a while.

"It could be either one, I suppose," John said. "But I wonder if Knox would let his niece run the risk of being recognized coming into Buffalo Gulch."

Melinda agreed.

"Her Uncle Edwin was real protective of her."

"We'll ask about him first."

A few drops of rain fell as the wind came up.

He tried once more to get her to go back to the marshall's place.

"There's no need of you getting wet," he said. "Soon as I check things out along the street, I'll come over and tell you everything I found out."

"I've been wet before. But I have my slicker along, so it won't be too bad."

He hadn't expected Melinda to do as he asked, but had felt compelled to try once more to get her to be sensible. It wouldn't be his fault if she caught pneumonia.

They got off their horses, put on their slickers, remounted, and rode on. By this time the storm was getting worse. Lightning split the heavy clouds, and thunder rumbled in from the plains. The rain pelted their faces and soaked the felt of Breck's battered hat. He glanced reproachfully at Melinda, but her jaw was firm. It would take more than a summer storm to turn her back, now that she had begun to search for her friend.

They stopped at the blacksmith shop and dismounted. The smithy was at the forge, but when he saw them he laid aside his hammer and met them at the open door.

"Come in out of the wet. It ain't much of a day to be ridin' anywhere, that's for sure." He eyed Breck approvingly. "You're the one who stopped that train robbery, ain't you."

"Just one of them."

"That ain't the way I heard. I'd like to shake your hand, Breck. I'm right proud to meet a man like you."

John told him what they wanted.

"Nope," he said in answer to the question, "I ain't seen any one by that description around here."

He wiped beads of sweat from his forehead with the sleeve of his tattered shirt. He appeared to be as wet as his visitors, and they had been out in the rain.

"You're sure of that?" Melinda asked, disappointment edging her voice.

"I'm mighty sure, young lady." He paused and a smile crept into his eyes. "And that's the plain truth. Don't you get no ideas about marchin' me around town with that six-shooter of yours makin' me tell people I lied to you."

Her cheeks colored delicately, and for an instant John wondered what she might do, but she remained silent. He thanked the smithy, and they turned to leave.

"You'd better wait 'til that storm lets up a mite," he told them, still chuckling to himself. "There's no need of gettin' wetter than you are already." But they shook their heads and left, bending into the storm.

They rode up the street a short distance and separated. Breck tied the dun to the hitching rail in front of the barber shop while Melinda crossed the muddy street to the Bon Ton Cafe. She was going to start there, then check the feed store, the land office, and the general store on that side of the thoroughfare. He talked to the barber and began to check the saloons.

The saloons were the best places to ask; they were usually more than just places to drink. Even those who seldom, if ever, touched liquor often found themselves frequenting them. The saloons were meeting places where business could be discussed and transacted.

Breck soon understood Corrigan's concern about the gunfighters who were flocking to Buffalo

Gulch. He hadn't noticed them before, but now the saloons were sprinkled with them. They were drifting in from wherever they holed up when they weren't working. Lean, hard-drinking, hard-gambling strangers in fancy, handmade boots and expensive clothes. They were at the bars wherever Breck went—and at the gaming tables.

The conversation was hushed, save for those whose tongues had been loosed by whiskey. In general they were a quiet, deadly breed, given to action but not a lot of careless talk.

Breck attracted their attention wherever he went. They saw the way he wore his gun with the tip of the holster tied in place, and the way his gaze missed nothing in the room. Few were able to place him, but they all knew he was one of them. There was no camaraderie and few friendships among them. It was best not to have friends, they reasoned. One never knew who he would be called on to take out. No one in the first three saloons Breck visited even spoke to him, except the bartenders he approached.

Like the blacksmith, they also professed not to have seen Edwin Knox in town or even to have heard anything about him. They acted strangely secretive though, as if something was going on that they wanted no part of.

It was not until Breck reached the Eagle's Nest, the largest and most expensive saloon in town, that any of the patrons spoke to him. The instant he entered, before he had opportunity to seek out the bartender, one of a trio at the far table got to his feet.

"Breckenridge!" he exclaimed loudly. He had been drinking heavily and had to grasp the table to support his wobbling legs. "What are you doin' down here?"

Breck recognized the speaker and his companions—Billy Brooks, Tighman, and Skunk Curley. He sauntered over to their table.

"We figured you'd still be up north on that ranch of yours!" Curley said. "Sit down. Sit down. It's been a long time since we seen you, John."

"That's a fact!" Tighman added. "Have yourself a shot to cut the dust." He filled his glass, spilling whiskey on the table. He wiped it dry with his sleeve and set the bottle in front of Breck. " 'Tain't good stuff by a long shot, but it's the best they've got in this two-bit town."

John pushed the bottle away. "You guys know me well enough to know I don't use it."

"Don't you remember?" Billy Brooks said. "He don't drink nothin' stronger than coffee. Always has been funny that way."

Breck studied their faces individually. "What are you doin' here?" he asked. "This ain't exactly your stompin' grounds."

"We've got us a job," Curley answered, grinning widely. "Best job we've ever had. Hardly no work to it. Nothin' much at all. And the pay's the best we've seen for a coon's age." Slowly his expression changed as he thought about Breckenridge. "What're *you* doin' in these parts, John? Pickin' up a little extra change on the side?"

"Not the way you're thinking. I've got a few loose ends to tie up. Then I'll be goin' into the hills lookin' for color."

Tighman laughed. "You'd better join up with us. The way I hear it they're hirin' most anybody. And it's a heap better than chasin' over them hills where you run the risk of losin' your scalp."

"I'll take my chances."

He shrugged. "It's your hair."

Breck was about to leave the men he used to ride with and go talk to the bartender about Edwin Knox when a stocky, well-dressed stranger approached their table. Tighman and his companions spoke to the newcomer warmly. It was obvious that they considered him someone very important.

"Know how to use that thing?" the stranger asked casually, pointing at the Colt Peacemaker Breck was wearing.

"Well enough to get by," he said.

"Well enough to get by?" Brooks echoed, the whiskey adding volume to his voice. "Know something, Mr. Clevenger? This here's John Breckenridge. Ain't a gunfighter in all Colorado Territory can stand up to him." He glanced at the men who rode with him. "Now ain't that a fact?"

They nodded in agreement.

Clevenger was interested in Breck immediately. He thrust out his hand. "I'm right glad to meet you, Breckenridge. I haven't heard about you since I've been out here. You must not have been active recently."

John made no reply.

"You sound like you're exactly the kind of man we are interested in recruiting."

John's gaze came up, cold and expressionless. "Sorry, I've already got all the job I want."

"You'll do well for yourself to hear me out," Clevenger said. "The pay's the best and like your friends'll tell you, the work isn't all that hard. Actually you'll only be keeping the peace. You probably won't even have to use your gun. You'll not get another chance like this in a long time."

"We've already told him that," Curley explained, the words slurring over his thick tongue. "But it wasn't no use. He just ain't interested."

The easterner ignored the others. "Come over to my table, Breckenridge," he said, "and we'll talk about it. I don't know what your objections are, but I'm certain we can work out something that will be agreeable."

"It's like Curley said," Breck answered, "I'm just not interested."

"Is that *final?*"

"It's final."

Anger gleamed in Clevenger's eyes. "If you won't even talk to me, that means you're workin' for the other side."

"I'm workin' for my own side." Breck got to his feet and glanced down at Skunk Curley. "You'd better lay off that rot-gut. It'll be the death of you."

Tears leaked from the outlaw's eyes, and he began to slobber. "That's what Ma used to tell me," he said drunkenly. "But I never paid her no mind. I'm no good, John. I'm just plain no good."

"Shut up!" Tighman exploded. "It's gettin' so you can't drink no more but you start goin' on about your ma and what she told you. We're tired of it."

Curley was still mumbling incoherently, but no one paid any attention to him. He wiped his eyes with a red bandana and continued to sniffle.

"I've got to be on my way," Breck said. "I've got things to do."

Clevenger's stocky frame came erect, suspicion darkening his small, round eyes. "If you're workin' for the other side, I might have to send your friends against you. I'd hate to do that."

John moved closer. His good hand grasped the easterner by the coat lapel and lifted him onto his toes. "You do whatever you've a mind to,

Clevenger. But let me set you straight. You try that and I'll be comin' after you. Not them—*you*. Understand?"

Clevenger's features paled, and he was trembling slightly. But when he spoke, his voice was clear and firm.

"If that's the way it has to be—" He left the rest of the sentence unsaid.

"That's the way it has to be!" With that, John strode to the front of the saloon where he spoke to the bartender in low tones.

As he left, Billy Brooks lowered his voice to a hoarse whisper. "You ain't sending *me* out to gun down Breckenridge, boss. Let's get that straight. I'll quit first."

His companions nodded soberly.

"You're hired to do what I tell you."

"We know that, and we appreciate what you're doin' for us. But we want to live to enjoy all that money we're gettin'—so count us out," Brooks went on.

"A rancher up north of Denver sent us to get John once," Tighman explained. "Only thing that saved us, we backed off when we found out this poor excuse of a man had killed John's wife."

Skunk Curley nodded in agreement. "He got both that fellow and his pa at the same time, and they were real good with a six-gun. Right then we decided *nobody* was goin' to have us facin' John Breckenridge again."

Clevenger turned and stalked away.

"There's others," he muttered over his shoulder.

"Not as can put John away, there aren't," Billy said quietly.

Breck talked with the bartender about Edwin Knox, but he had seen nothing of him, or so he said. He detected a certain uneasiness in the bartender's manner, a reluctance to talk once he heard the name of the man John was looking for.

"You've heard about Knox?" John persisted.

"Me?" Nervously the barkeep picked up a dish towel and began to dry glasses. "Now, how would I hear about anybody like that? I'm kept busy with my job. Never do have time to go anywhere so I could learn anything about anybody."

Breck wasn't sure he was telling the truth, but he could not accuse him of lying. "Keep your eyes open. I'll be stopping back in a few days to see if he's been in."

"That I'll do," the bartender said quickly, a bit too quickly to be convincing to John Breck. "You want I should tell him you're lookin' for him, or do you want me to keep quiet? 'Til you come in, I mean."

"Don't tell him anything, but remember when he was in and who was with him." He was about to add that he really wasn't looking for Edwin Knox. He wanted to find the man's niece. But he didn't. There was no need in giving out any information he didn't have to.

14

The rain had almost stopped falling by the time John went through the swinging doors and out onto the boardwalk. The clouds were racing eastward, shoved along by a harsh, cool wind. To the west a little patch of blue shone through. "Dutchman's britches" his step-pa, Waddy Ross, used to call it.

Breck approached the hitching rail where he had tied the line-back dun. Melinda was there waiting for him. She had finished talking with her people some time before and rode her horse across the street where she sat motionless in the sidesaddle, her back hunched against the wind.

"So you finally decided to come out," she said distantly.

"Met some men I used to know." That was no explanation, but it was all she was going to get.

"It's a wonder you're in shape to talk to anyone."

"For your information I don't drink."

"If you hang around those places, you will!"

He loosed his mount, brushed the water from the saddle with his hand, and swung aboard. "I was in there for you, remember?" he said coldly. "Trying to find someone who's seen Edwin Knox so we can get a line on where to look for your friend Cassie."

Her belligerence seemed to abate. "Did you learn anything?"

"Nobody will admit to having seen him. He either hasn't been in town in recent months or everyone's afraid to talk."

"I feel the same way," she admitted. "I couldn't understand it. They acted like they were afraid of me."

"I can understand that. It's because of Ferguson. They're scared you'll draw on 'em!"

Her eyes flashed. "He got what he deserved!"

"I won't argue with that."

They rode for half a block without speaking.

"I saw something a little while ago," she continued at last. "I'm not sure, but it may be helpful. I saw it while I was waiting for you. I waited a long time, you know."

He faced her.

"Well, what was it?"

"The rig that took the Nesters out on the prairies was back in town. I saw it go by a little while ago and stop in front of the general store."

Breck turned in the saddle and glanced up the street. "I don't see it."

"Of course not. It isn't there now. It drove in and stopped. They loaded up some things, and the driver went off like he was in a big hurry."

"Did you happen to see him?"

She nodded. "It was Charles Snyder."

Breck's features hardened. There was no knowing what that meant, if anything, but it could be significant. "This might be what we've been waiting for. We'll go over to the Bon Ton and get a quick bite to eat. Then I want you to check with the women in their homes. See if they might have seen your friend. They won't talk to me, but they might to you."

"Just how would they know anything about Cassie?"

"They wouldn't unless she comes in for supplies. If that happens, some of them would see her in the stores, and if they did they would remember her. Women pay attention to other women—especially young, pretty ones."

Melinda wasn't quite ready to accept his reasoning.

"I don't know that I believe that." She changed the subject abruptly. "What will you be doing while I'm talking to them?" she asked suspiciously.

"I'm goin' to track that rig and find out where it's heading."

"We aren't looking for the Nesters," she informed him coldly. "It's Cassie Knox I'm after."

He was exasperated and showed it.

"Sometimes I wonder why I ever let myself get into this mess."

"You can get out any time you want to," she retorted.

He frowned and dug his fingers into the dun's shaggy mane. "I'm goin' to track Nester's rig," he explained tautly, "because I've got a hunch they might help us find your friend Cassie."

"Do you think they know where she is?"

"We won't know that until we find them, will we?" He answered her in terse tones, spurring his horse back to the hotel.

Adolph hovered over Melinda and Breck while they were eating. He was constantly at the girl's elbow wanting to know if she had enough coffee, if she would like more bread or butter or potatoes.

"We aren't supposed to bring seconds," he whispered, "but with you it's OK. The cook and me both like what you did to that big-headed Mr. Ferguson. Him treatin' us like dirt and all. We look on it as you helpin' us get even with him."

They finished eating and went outside.

"I'll be back as soon as I can," he told her.

"I'd feel better if I were going with you," she said reluctantly.

He scowled his disapproval. "We need to find out whether anyone in town has seen your friend."

"They wouldn't admit to having seen Mr. Knox," she countered. "Why would the women tell us if they'd seen Cassie?"

"The women would be more free to talk than their husbands. And besides, talking about a girl to a girl is going to seem harmless enough. You might not get anything from them, but you might strike paydirt the first time you put your spade in the ground."

Reluctantly she watched him ride off. He did not look back.

Breck knew that Jacobs would have wanted him to stop at the hotel long enough to tell him what was going on, but he couldn't take time for that. He had ridded himself of Melinda, at least momentarily. He didn't intend to give her the opportunity to change her mind.

Once out of town, he waited until the storm was over and supposed Snyder would have done the same. A seasoned hand might have left in the rain, especially if he had a reason to get back in a hurry, but the driver of the rig was a tenderfoot. He wasn't likely to brave bad weather.

The storm stopped as suddenly as it began. The wind died away, and the sky began to clear.

It wasn't long before the ominous black clouds were gone, save for a rim along the eastern horizon that still was split occasionally by sudden slashing swords of fire. They appeared briefly, speeding fingers of light plunging toward the ground, quivering like slender, fine steel blades slammed point-first into the pines.

The heat had been overwhelmed by the brief cooling of wind and rain, but now was in control again, spreading its oppressive blanket over everything. It soon brought out the sweat on Breck's face and neck and on the withers of the big dun.

Still, he was in no hurry to leave Buffalo Gulch. He wanted to give Snyder time to get far enough ahead so he would not realize he was being followed. Finally, he headed out on a western road, keeping an eye out for the wagon's wheel tracks in the mud. He was not too disappointed when he didn't find them. Since Snyder wouldn't know his way around the back country, he would have to stay on the main road, at least until he reached the turnoff to the place where they were staying. There would be time enough to be concerned about finding the tracks after they were out of town a few miles.

Breck soon realized that the driver of the rig must have left town earlier than he thought— probably during the storm. He should have been able to catch a glimpse of him in the distance ahead by now, or at least to find a track made since the rain. But the prairie before him was empty, and there were still no tracks unwashed by the storm.

He didn't know exactly what could come from finding out where Nester and his party were. But it might add one small piece to the larger puzzle. He hadn't even thought about them after seeing them leave town the morning after Hunter had been murdered. Now he was nagged by unanswered questions.

Where were they? What were they doing? Why would they leave town so quietly? If he found out, he might discover a clue as to what had happened to Edwin Knox and his niece, although at that point he didn't know how the two could be tied together.

Come to think of it, there was another piece to the puzzle that made it even more confusing; a wild card that threw everything out of kilter. Where was *Fannie* Knox? She had come sweeping into Buffalo Gulch like a reigning dowager-queen demanding homage from her subjects. Everyone in town knew who she was. She saw to that. Then, as suddenly as she appeared, she was gone again. He hadn't seen her since the night Melinda confronted her quite by accident in the cafe.

What had happened to her? Had she too gone with the Nesters, wherever they were? And why had she come? It was obvious that she was not the sort to deliberately choose such a place as Buffalo Gulch to live. She had to have a reason—a good reason—for coming. Was it because of her husband? She didn't appear to think enough of him to be concerned about his disappearance. Then why was she there? Was she involved in his disappearance? Maybe Pinkerton's informants were wrong and she actually wanted him found. But what part did Sam Richards play in all of that?

Breck rode slowly, trying to sort out the tracks of the spring wagon in the sloppy road. At first there was so much water on the rutted trail he could not make out anything with certainty. Once or twice he thought he saw the fuzzy slash of the narrow wheels in the mud, but he couldn't be sure.

Then, at a slight rise in elevation, some tracks had emptied themselves of water, and he could read them more clearly. He followed the trail for several miles, across a creek and up a gentle incline on the other side. The main road continued north, but the rig he was following turned to the west. It hadn't rained so much there, and the ground was hard, resisting the marks of the wheels. He could still make them out, faint though they were.

He traveled up a long rise that must surely have slowed the team. He skirted a long limestone outcropping that seemed strangely out of place among the soap weed and sagebrush and ended at the base of a steep, fluted butte. Juniper, scraggly and twisted from constant battles with wind and heat and drought, crowded on the lower reaches of the hill's base and were scattered less frequently up the sides.

Shading his eyes, Breck looked up at the deepening shadows that surrounded the small mesa. Though the hour was still early, it was already difficult to make out details in the sharp, time-scarred crevices and fissures that ringed the butte.

The road went on, but the tracks of the spring wagon ended abruptly on a stretch of rocky ground as surely as though some giant hand had plucked it off the earth. Breck looked about cautiously with the vigilance that came from years on the frontier where carelessness, even for a moment, could cost a man his life. Satisfied that no one was close by, he got down and bent over the road. At first he could see no sign that the rig had passed that way. It was an old wagon trail and the ruts were still evident, but the hard-packed soil showed no trace of anyone using the road recently.

Leading his horse, Breck moved forward, studying the narrow, little-used route meticulously. He noted the soap weed fronds broken off by turning wheels and sagebrush that had been crushed in the same way. There was evidence enough that the road had been traveled, but there was no indication it had been used recently.

Then, a hundred yards from where he dismounted, he found the white line left by an iron tire slipping off a small piece of limestone. There was another and another, signs so slight that a less skilled tracker would have missed them completely. But he had traveled with the best and read them easily. A spring wagon had gone by within the last day and probably within the last few hours.

The sun was moving lower on the horizon and night would soon come, but he continued to track the rig. It had skirted the small mesa and then headed off across the prairie in the direction of a distant hill. Breck stopped and stood in the stirrups. In half an hour the sun would be down. In an hour it would be too dark to continue his search.

He could now see a home some distance ahead and a mile or so off the trail. The log house, built with uncertain hands of whatever trees the settler-turned-carpenter could find, furnished a shelter against the harsh winters. The barn, smaller and even more poorly constructed, gave the livestock a measure of protection against the cold, wind, and snow.

From a distance John could make out a well midway between the house and the barn, a small corral that kept four scrawny horses from roaming, and a cornfield that had been planted so hopefully in the spring and now was such a sorry affair, the plants stunted and withered by heat and the lack of rain.

He turned the dun in that direction and touched him lightly with the spurs. The stallion responded quickly, leaping forward in an easy distance-eating gallop that soon took his rider close to the buildings. Breck pulled him back to a brisk walk, eyeing the house and barn warily.

There was no one outside, which seemed strange to him. Most settlers had a number of kids working or playing about the yard. He was thirty yards from the house when a whiskered farmer in a pair of patched overalls came out quickly, a Colt repeating shotgun at his shoulder.

"Hold it, mister!" he rasped, fear etching his voice. "Stop right where you are. Don't come any closer."

"I don't mean any harm," Breck told him. "I'm not goin' to hurt anybody."

"I know you ain't. I got this shotgun on you. One funny move and I'll let you have it right in the belly!"

"Pa!" a woman's voice cried from just inside the door. "He's the one I was tellin' you about. The one who saved the train from bein' robbed."

The settler hesitated, and for a moment the gun wavered.

"I'm beholdin' to you for keepin' my wife from bein' robbed when she was on that train," he said. "But that don't cut no ice now. You can go back and tell that boss of yours that he's goin' to have to kill me before he can run us out. I'm prepared for the likes of you."

"I'm not workin' for ranchers tryin' to run you out," Breck said. "I just stopped to say howdy and see if you'd seen a rig go by on the road in the last few hours."

The settler was perplexed. He wanted to believe Breck but wasn't certain that he could.

"How do I know you ain't lyin' to me?"

"You don't. You'll have to take my word for it."

"And I ain't about to do that." His voice grew louder. "Now turn that stud horse around and get outta here before I lose my temper."

Breck backed the dun slightly to indicate he was leaving.

"What about the rig?" he asked. "Did you see it?"

"I wouldn't tell you nothin' one way or the other."

"Pa! That ain't no way to treat a man who's done for us what he's done."

"Get back in the house, woman, and shut your trap."

The man kept the gun trained on Breck's belly, so he slowly reined the dun around and headed back the way he'd come. Somethin' was goin' on here, that much he knew for sure. But he'd have to wait for a better time to find out just what. For now, there was no use making more trouble between himself and the dirt farmer. From the looks of things, the settler had enough problems already with his heat-shriveled stand of corn and the shrill tongue of his wife. Breck could hear her still jawing at the man as he rode on.

15

Once back on the trail, Breck headed the dun toward town. He would need daylight to pick up the trail once more. When he looked up to check the sky he noticed that a new line of clouds was beginning to march out of the west. In the dim light there was little chance for him to read them, to see how threatening they actually were. But lightning indicated another storm was probable. It forked from the sky in sharp, savage thrusts and flickered from cloud to cloud like so many distant campfires leaping to life and burning fiercely for a few brief moments, only to disappear, leaving the night blacker than before.

He glanced apprehensively at the clouds. If it rained again before morning, he would have little hope of picking up the trail and no chance at all of finding where Nester and his party had gone. He urged the line-back dun to a brisk trot.

The incident at the farmer's still bothered him. He was not concerned about the man's hostility. Fear could cause otherwise sensible men to do strange things, and the settler was afraid—desperately so. But that did not jar Breck. It was something else. Something more subtle, a strange knawing sensation that something around the little farm was out of place, something didn't belong. It was there, grating on him, but he could not quite identify it.

He reined in for a moment, frowning thoughtfully into the darkness. Had there been someone in the dilapidated shack the settler called a house who didn't belong there? Someone who ordered him to get Breck out of there? That would account for the shotgun and his being ordered away.

But the wife's nagging wouldn't fit. She, too, would have been frightened. So frightened she would have said nothing. Or perhaps she was more frightened of their being alone with the visitor.

Even that didn't quite make sense to him. There had to be another explanation for his vague uneasiness. One not so obvious as those that came quickly to mind.

He rode back to town, unsaddled his mount, rubbed him down, fed and watered him and went back to the hotel. Lights were still on at the marshall's and for an instant he hesitated, wondering if he should go over and tell Melinda what had happened.

But what could he tell her? That he had lost the trail in the darkness and, if it didn't rain, he might be able to locate it again in the morning? There was small comfort for her in that.

Jacobs was sitting in the lobby when he entered the hotel, a week-old paper stuck in front of his face and an unlighted cigar clamped firmly in his teeth. He looked up as the door opened and went back to his reading, without acknowledging that he knew his associate.

Breck paused on the bottom step and glanced over at the corpulent Pinkerton agent. The paper moved slightly, and Jacobs whispered to him with his eyes. John knew he would be having a visitor soon, almost before he reached his room.

A few moments later there was a guarded knock at his door and he opened it, allowing Jacobs to enter. He closed it behind his guest and locked it.

"Anything new?"

"Not exactly. Lost the trail when it got dark, so I came back to town. I'll have another go at it tomorrow."

"If it don't storm." Jacobs dropped heavily into a chair and crossed his thick legs.

"If it don't storm—which it looks like it's going to do."

Breck sat on the bed and pulled off his boots, realizing for the first time since getting up that morning that he was exhausted. He wanted nothing more than to throw himself on the bed and go to sleep, but that was not possible—at least for a time. Jacobs was there, and obviously he wanted to talk.

"Your friend's back," the Pinkerton agent told him.

"My friend?"

"Yeah. The one and only Fannie Knox. Came in on the afternoon train from Denver."

"I've been wonderin' what happened to her."

"I saw her coming out of the cafe and Adolph told me—you know Adolph over at the Bon Ton?"

Breck nodded. "Everybody knows Adolph."

"Well, Adolph said that she explained all about her husband when she was in tonight. She said she had come out here from New York to look for him. He left home on business and was supposed to have come home months ago, but he didn't. Then even his letters stopped coming. Finally she could stand it no longer, so she took the train out here to Buffalo Gulch to see if she could locate him."

163

"Interesting, ain't it?"

"It is, for a fact. But that ain't all." Jacobs chewed on his cigar. "She did everything around here that she could to find him, and all she learned was that he had gone up to Denver. So she took a train there, and she thinks she found out where he is. She located an old friend who claimed to know exactly where he had gone—back in the hills someplace west of Denver. She doesn't know what he's been doing there or why he didn't write. But she sent someone to find him and get him to come here to be with her—at least for a little while." He breathed deeply. "Adolph was so touched he almost bawled."

"Me too."

Breck went over to the dresser, poured a basin of water, and began to wash up. "I'd give a heap to know why she came out here in the first place," he said, drying his face and hands. "And why she went up to Denver—if that's where she was."

"She was there, all right. I checked it out."

"You can be sure it wasn't because she missed her husband so much."

"That's for certain. She's into whatever is goin' on up to her little pointed ears."

The next morning Melinda was waiting in the lobby for Breck when he came down for breakfast. "I didn't expect to see you so early this morning," he said.

"I'm sure you didn't," she retorted. "You probably planned to sneak out before I could get to you."

"The thought had crossed my mind," he admitted cheerfully.

"You should have known it wouldn't work. I was waiting up for you last night, but you didn't come. And you said you were going to let me know how things went."

"I didn't say when."

"No, but you sure let me think you'd stop last night."

He grinned down at her. "Let's go over to the Bon Ton. We can argue over breakfast as well as we can here."

"I've already *had* breakfast!"

"Then sit with me while I eat."

They went out of the hotel together.

The sky above was clear, but clouds blanketed the northwest and the wind was strong and menacing. The butte, usually visible from town, was shrouded by rain.

"Did you find where the Nesters are staying?" she asked curiously.

He frowned and shook his head. "Nope. I lost Snyder when it got dark. From the looks of things over that way now, the rain's goin' to beat me out of a chance of findin' 'em this time. We'll have to wait 'til they run out of supplies and come back in again."

Disappointment crept into Melinda's voice. "You don't sound upset about it," she told him. "Don't you care whether we find Cassie or not?"

Breck didn't answer her.

They went into the cafe and headed for a table near the rear, a place where Breck would have his back to the wall and could command a view of the entire room. They hadn't moved ten feet when he spied Fannie Knox at the table she had appropriated as her own. She saw him about the same time, and smiled and waved at him. The instant they were seated she got to her feet and bounded over to them.

"I'm so glad to see you, my dear," she said to Melinda as though they were close friends. "I've had such exciting news. You were Cassie's best friend, so I know you'll be thrilled about it too. Dear, sweet little Cassie. I think it is so wonderful that you would come all this way just to find her. It shows how devoted you are to her and how brave. You must love her very much."

The girl's expression did not change. "Is that what you wanted to tell me?"

"Oh, no." She managed a thin laugh. "I'm so excited I—I'm afraid I'm somewhat flustered. But I wanted you to know that my trip to Denver was a great success! I've found Edwin!"

Melinda's eyes widened, and fear crept into her features. She had been so positive Cassie and her uncle were together. Now she didn't know. "Are you sure?"

Fannie scooted her chair closer to the table and leaned forward as though Breck and Melinda were the only ones worthy of hearing what she was about to say.

"I got word that he had been in the Denver area a few weeks ago," she said, the words bubbling out. "As soon as I heard that, I got my things packed and went to Denver on the next train." She paused dramatically, and her voice was almost a whisper. "But when I got there I was too late. You'll never know how crushed I was. After all these months of waiting, I wasn't going to be able to see him. He had left just a month before to go back into the hills. There was something about a mining claim or some other mining property he owned that he had to find out about. I don't know for sure what it was." She shrugged helplessly. "I don't understand about such things. Anyway, he felt that he *had* to go into the hills to see about it."

"I was very fortunate to find someone who knew my husband—an old prospecting friend and associate of Edwin's. And would you believe it? He knew exactly where that man of mine had gone. I hired him to go out where Edwin was and tell him I'm here in Buffalo Gulch. I'm sure he's as anxious to see me as I am to see him. I expect him here any time now." Her voice raised until everyone in the building could hear her plainly. "Isn't it wonderful?"

Adolph came out just then with her breakfast. He had been completely captivated. "You want me to serve you here, Mrs. Knox?" he asked.

"Oh no, Adolph. I'll go back to my own table. I—I don't want to impose." She stood. "I hope and pray that you are as fortunate in your search for Cassie, my dear, as I've been in looking for Edwin. All of my family and friends thought it the most ridiculous thing that I would come so far alone to try to find him, but I would rather have died than to lose him forever." With that, she went back to where she had been sitting, eyeing the other patrons as regally as though she had been clapped back onto stage at the close of a performance.

"Ain't it wonderful about her findin' her husband?" Adolph paused long enough to whisper to Breck and Melinda. "Just like a storybook!"

Melinda's features were pale, almost lifeless, and her lips trembled. "Do—do you think that's true?" she asked Breck quietly. "About finding Mr. Knox up near Denver?"

"Why?"

"If it is," she said, her voice weak with emotion, "Cassie isn't with him. Something must have happened to her!"

"We have no call to believe that," he told her. "When Edwin Knox shows up here—if he does—we can go to him and see if he knows anything about where Cassie is. He might surprise you by bein' able to tell you right where she is."

Melinda dabbed at her eyes with her handkerchief.

"It seems as though I've been looking for her for *so* long. And nothing happens. We're no closer to finding her than we were before I came west."

Breck knew how she felt, but there was nothing he could do about it. Every lead had turned out to be false.

They ate in comparative silence and went back out into the brilliant summer sun. By this time Buffalo Gulch was beginning to come alive. Two riders were on their way north, and a dray wagon was making its rounds with freight from the depot. The Wells Fargo door was wide open, as was that of the general store on the other side of the street. The smithy's forge was blazing, and a plume of black smoke drifted skyward above it. The saloons that never closed were beginning to pick up a few early morning customers— cowhands, prospectors, and drifters in town for a binge or to satisfy an uncommon urge to beat the gamblers at their own game, or simply because they had nothing better to do. They wouldn't be satisfied until their pockets were empty, their stomachs queasy, and their heads throbbing from bad whiskey and lack of sleep.

"What are you going to do today?" Melinda finally asked.

Breck shrugged his indifference. "I figured on ridin' west to see if I can pick up Snyder's trail again."

"I've got my horse saddled," she informed him, belligerence honing her voice. "I'm riding with you."

"You can't do that."

"I'm going with you, and we're *not* going to argue about it."

Breck fell silent. There had to be some way of keeping her at the marshall's where she would be safe, but he didn't know how.

They were almost in front of the general store when the settler who had held the shotgun on him the night before came out and climbed into the seat of a new spring wagon.

"Good-bye, Armenius," the storekeeper called after him. "And thank you kindly."

"Thank you, Mr. Fosberg. I'll be seein' you. I'll have to have another load of supplies one of these days."

"Come in any time."

The settler spoke sharply to the bony team and slapped the more alert animal on the rump with the reins. He stepped out briskly, and his companion followed suit.

Breck had stopped on the boardwalk until the settler had driven away. He stared after the rig, his lips parted slightly.

"That's it," he murmured.

"That's what?"

"I know now what was botherin' me at the settler's place last night. It was that rig. It didn't belong there."

Melinda had no idea what he was talking about.

"Everyone has a spring wagon," she said. "Why wouldn't Mr. Armenius have one too?"

"Everybody's got a spring wagon, true enough. But that one of his is a brand, spankin' new one. And the revolvin' shotgun he held on me was new too. But everything else around the place was old as the hills. And I mean *old!* The barn looks like a good kick on one corner would bring it down. The house didn't have a window or a door that was square, and the corral fence wouldn't hardly hold them scrawny flea-bit nags he calls horses. And you should see that corn of his. It's all dried up. He ain't goin' to get two dozen ears off the whole patch or I'll miss my guess."

"What do those things have to d with the wagon and shotgun?" she asked.

"Don't you see? He hasn't had money enough to do any real good building since he's lived there. Not even enough to fix things the way they should be. But all of a sudden he buys a new spring wagon and a new shotgun. Where did the money come from?"

"Maybe Mr. Fosberg let him have them on time."

"It doesn't sound likely, but we can find out. Come on." He went up the steps with Melinda at his side.

The storekeeper came from the counter and greeted them.

"What can I do for you?" he asked. He was talking to Breck but was staring at Melinda.

John went over to the counter and studied the gun on the wall behind it.

"Lookin' for a gun?"

"Not exactly."

170

"I've got a couple of top quality Colts and a new Winchester rifle."

He laid a rifle on the counter, and Breck picked it up.

"It's got a good feel."

"She's brand new! Maybe you've seen her?"

"The '73?"

"Right. She's a lever action with center-fire ammunition. A big improvement over the '66. Mark my words, she'll take over out here."

Breck worked the mechanism and sighted along the barrel.

"That man who just left," he said casually. "Been around long?"

Fosberg's eyes narrowed. "Long enough."

"He didn't seem like any ordinary settler."

"He's a cash-payin' customer, which is more than you've been up to now."

"I'd like a box of cartridges."

Fosberg glanced at his gun. "Forty-four's?" He nodded.

"This Armenius," Breck began as the storekeeper got the shells for him, "has he always paid cash?"

Fosberg dropped the box of ammunition on the counter with a resounding thud. "Just exactly what's that to you?" he asked coldly.

"Nothing. Nothing at all. I was out by his place yesterday. It's pretty rundown for him to be having a new spring wagon and harness. Sort of set me to wondering, that's all."

"So that was *you* nosin' around out there."

Breck nodded.

"You was lucky you didn't get yourself shot. He was fixin' to put you away, accordin' to him, when that old woman of his started givin' him argument." He shoved the shells across the counter, and the tall cowhand paid for them. "If I was you, I'd stay away from his place. Next time you might not get by so easy."

"I'll think on it."

"And I wouldn't ask so many questions if I was you. I don't think he likes that."

16

Breck and Melinda left the store and continued their journey to the livery barn.

"Still figurin' on going with me?" he asked.

The muscles around her mouth tightened. "You know I am."

"Somebody ought to be here to watch Fannie Knox."

"What for? She'll be here when we get back."

He saddled his horse and led him out into the brilliant morning sunlight.

"Confound it, Melinda, you shouldn't be traipsin' over the country with me. People are goin' to talk and you're too nice a girl for that."

Her blue eyes flashed. "I don't think they'll be sayin' much."

"You don't *know* they won't!"

"Leastwise Ferguson won't," she said. "And that's a fact."

Breck just shook his head as they mounted up and headed out of town together. Though the morning was young, the sun was already burning a horizon-wide furrow across the prairie. The hot wind had sucked the moisture from the top few inches of soil, and the grass showed signs of withering again. There was no evidence that it had rained recently except for the thin stream of water moving languidly to the east in a creek that was usually dry at that time of year.

"We didn't find out much about Mr. Armenius," Melinda said thoughtfully.

"Enough to know that there's something unusual about him."

"Like what?" Scorn edged her voice.

"He's payin' cash for the things he buys. That's a sight different than most dirt farmers I ever knew about. They're usually scroungin' to find enough money to keep the store from shuttin' 'em off."

"Maybe he brought money with him from back east."

Breck looked up from studying the trail. "I've been thinkin' on that. If he did, why didn't he build a better house than that barn? What he's got ain't hardly warm enough to get his family and his livestock through the winter." He reined in and faced her. "If he could have built better, he would have. That makes me believe he's got some way of gettin' money now that he didn't have when he put down roots on that piece of hard scrabble."

She fell silent for a time.

"Maybe he found gold."

"Out here? 'Tain't likely."

"Then how could he be getting it?"

"That's somethin' we don't know, but I aim to find out."

They covered another mile before either spoke again.

"Do you suppose he could be doing something for Mr. Nester?" she asked.

Breck thought about that. It was entirely possible. Nester struck him as being the sort who would use anyone he could to accomplish his goals.

But what could a man like Armenius do for the wealthy financier? He professed to own the land he farmed but undoubtedly was a squatter, appropriating the little chunk of prairie for his own use in the same way most of the cattle ranches got their grazing land. It was obvious that he had no money, and the farm was so demanding he had little time for anything else. It wasn't likely that Armenius would be of value to the easterner.

"There's got to be some other reason," he told her.

"Why?"

Breck shrugged. He didn't know why. He just felt that way.

"I think maybe I'd better pay our friend Armenius a visit," he said.

Her eyes widened, and for an instant fear robbed her cheeks of color. "You can't be serious."

"Who else knows how he suddenly came into money?"

"You can't just barge in and ask him."

"What quicker way is there of finding out what we want to know?"

"He pulled a shotgun on you the last time you set foot on his place," she reminded him. "I don't want you killed."

He smiled bleakly. "That ain't goin' to happen."

"I don't want him killed either. There's been enough of that already."

"That ain't goin' to happen either. Armenius is goin' to be glad enough to talk to me."

She hesitated, weighing his words. "You're sure?"

They followed the main trail north for several miles and turned off in the direction of the butte and the settler's farm. For the next hour Melinda scarcely spoke to Breck. When she saw the ramshackle farm buildings in the distance, however, she reined in.

"John," she said sternly, "exactly how are you going to get close enough to Armenius to talk to him without having him start shooting?"

"That's somethin' I ain't quite figured out yet," he answered, a smile teasing his lips.

Her temper blazed. "You act like it's some sort of a joke."

"I didn't say it was."

Melinda turned away, staring across the blistered prairie. Startled by their horses' hooves, a jackrabbit exploded from the shade of a clump of yucca and sped away. In the distance a coyote loped lazily into view and up the steep, fluted side of the butte. Finding Cassie had seemed so simple when Melinda considered the trip west. She would reach Buffalo Gulch, talk to people until she found someone who remembered her friend, and from there it would be easy.

The people in town that she remembered had been so warm and friendly, she had not anticipated any reluctance on the part of anyone to give her information. And they had been friendly enough when she returned. But she had been unable to locate anyone who could, or would, give her information about her friend. And some of them acted so strange she wondered if they knew where Cassie was or who had been with her and wouldn't say anything because they didn't want to get involved. The problem tore at her.

At the butte, which they reached half an hour later, Breck reined in.

"We're goin' to have to leave the trail here," he told her, "or Armenius will spot us for sure."

Her expression changed slightly, and she waited for him to continue.

"We'll go along the butte 'til we get to an arroyo that leads towards the squatter's place," he explained. "Then we'll work our way west until we get close enough or run out of cover."

"And if you don't find it or it plays out," she said, "what then?"

"We'll have to find some other way of gettin' closer without being seen."

"What if he sees us and we don't know it?"

"We'd be in bad trouble. But that ain't goin' to happen."

"You hope," she said doubtfully.

His eyes were smiling. "Don't you have any confidence in me at all?"

Not waiting for a reply he started off, leaving Melinda no choice but to follow. A short distance away they found a ravine that slanted from the butte in the direction of the Armenius farm, a deep fissure clogged with juniper and cottonwood and clumps of willow.

Melinda turned on him accusingly.

"You *knew* this arroyo was here, didn't you?"

He nodded, grinning. "I saw it when I was out this way yesterday."

"And it goes all the way to the Armenius place, doesn't it?"

"That I ain't sure about. It might and it might not. But I don't think it'll make all that much difference. There are some small hills over that way. They'll hide me until I can get close to the barn."

"And me!" she added firmly.

"You're stayin' with the horses."

"I am *not*."

His voice grew louder. "Don't you argue with me! You'll do as I say!"

"I told you I was coming along," she retorted defensively.

"You *are* along, as far along as you're going. I'll take you to the place where I leave my horse, but that's it. You ain't goin' another step farther."

Melinda fumed inwardly but did not reply. This time there was no arguing with him. His mind was set, and there was no changing it.

They went over the lip of the ravine and down to the bottom among the trees. Breck tensed as they left the trail and was alert to every movement, every whispering sound. He looked for changes in the behavior of the squirrels and birds and watched the ears of the big horse for a sign that the dun caught something he could not detect—the scent of a man or another horse. Melinda started to speak, but he turned in the saddle and put a finger to his lips in warning. The color fled from her cheeks, and her hands were trembling on the reins. She wondered what Breck suspected, and why he had changed so suddenly.

One thing Breck did not expect was for anyone to be lying in wait for them in the ravine. His was the natural caution of a man who had to be constantly on the alert for trouble. For him every clump of trees, every depression in the ground, every boulder large enough for a man to hide behind was a potential source of danger. The only way a man like Breck could be sure of safety was to anticipate trouble, to be keen-eyed and attentive to every danger spot.

They made their way down the arroyo without incident. It was fairly wide at the place where they entered, but as they traveled west it narrowed perceptibly and grew more shallow. The trees were thinner and scraggly, providing less protection from prying eyes.

"Do—do you think he'll *see* us?" Melinda managed.

Breck had been wondering the same thing. It would certainly have been easy enough for Armenius to spot them if he had had a mind to be suspicious. If that happened he would shoot first—John was certain of that. Fear robbed a man of reason, and Armenius was desperately afraid. But the lanky cowhand was counting on the settler's lack of experience and his confidence in believing he had run Breck off the place and that he would not dare come back.

The stand of trees thinned more and more the closer Breck and Melinda got to the nondescript little farm. The buildings were just ahead when Breck motioned to his companion and they left the trees on the opposite side of the ravine, using them as a screen. He rode as silently as possible across the narrow stream and to the far side of the steep hill.

"Now what do we do?" Melinda Grainger asked.

"I'll take you as far as I go by horseback. You'll wait there with both horses while I go up to talk to Armenius."

"You can't do that! He'll kill you!"

"Trust me, Melinda," he said under his breath. "I know what I'm doing."

She eyed him uneasily and in that instant realized that he mattered a great deal to her—

and not only as someone who was helping to find her friend.

Breck dismounted, placed the reins of the line-back dun in her firm young hand, and made his way around the hill while she watched tensely. He moved cautiously on cat feet, making no noise save the muted crunch of parched grass beneath his boots. He stopped now and then, listening intently for some sound that was out of tune with the prairie around him.

Beyond the hill he saw a thin shaft of smoke struggling skyward. A baby was crying plaintively, and a dog barked. Breck scowled. A dog was something he hadn't counted on. It could give him away.

But he couldn't stop now; he had to go on.

The horses in the corral caught wind of him. Their heads came up, and their ears twitched expectantly. Breck froze. For an instant he remained motionless. If Armenius was alert, he was undone. The settler would be coming around the corner of the barn with his shotgun at the ready. But he might not know about the instincts of his horses, especially western-bred horses with a strong strain of wild blood. He might miss the tell-tale signs that betrayed the presence of strangers. Only time would give the answer.

Two minutes passed and then three. There was no evidence that the settler had noticed the uneasiness of his horses. Relaxing slightly, John moved forward. He ducked through the corral fence and approached the dilapidated barn from the rear. Opening the back door of the old building he went inside, ducking to avoid hitting his head on the rafters that held up the loft. Armenius was a short man and, like so many necessity-born builders, had allowed only enough room for himself and his horses to stand comfortably inside. Tall men either stayed out of the barn or hunched uncomfortably.

The barn had not been cleaned in months. Manure and hay were ankle deep, and a stench squeezed Breck's nostrils until he fought for air. He went up to the manger where the floor was a bit cleaner and moved to the front door, where he waited. Armenius was working around the yard. It wouldn't be long until he came to the barn for something. Breck knew his kind. So he waited. After a few minutes the farmer, talking to himself, sauntered in that direction, measuring a length of board with a piece of rope. As he opened the door and came inside, John Breck stepped forward suddenly.

"Hold it, Armenius."

The farmer blinked at the gun in Breck's big fist.

"I knowed it! I should have pulled the trigger when I had you dead to rights."

"I want some straight answers, that's all. I ain't goin' to hurt you."

"I suppose all you want is for me to pack up my stuff and move off K Bar T range."

He moved closer and motioned the farmer farther into the barn, far enough so they wouldn't be seen from the house. Breck didn't want that woman sneaking up behind him with the shotgun. She had stuck up for him the day before, but that didn't mean a thing if she thought her man was in danger. He didn't doubt for a moment that she could draw down on him and squeeze the trigger. There was a streak of toughness in that one—a wildness that was capable of anything if she, her man, or her young ones were threatened.

"Who's the K Bar T?"

"You ought to know! They're payin' you and the guys you work with good wages!"

"I don't work for the K Bar T."

The settler's lips curled bitterly. "Don't expect me to believe that."

"I don't much care what you believe, but go on—what's this about the ranch and the guys I'm supposed to be workin' with?"

Breck had to give Armenius credit. He was frightened, but he was no coward. He didn't back off an inch. John had the uneasy feeling that the wiry little man might jump him any minute.

"You know the story as well as I do," the settler said evenly. "The wealthy eastern ranch owner hires a passel of gunmen to burn out the farmers and chase 'em out of the country so he can have the land. But it ain't workin' with us. Emily and me talked it over. We're sticking. You'll have to shoot us first."

Breck changed the subject.

"You've been payin' cash to Fosberg for supplies lately."

"How'd you know that?" Armenius asked, coloring slightly.

"It's the truth, ain't it?"

"I ain't tellin' you or anyone else whether it's true or not."

"Where are you gettin' the money?"

Armenius squared his shoulders and planted his feet some distance apart. "Ain't none of your business."

"You workin' for the K Bar T too?"

"Them's fightin' words, mister!"

"Are you?" Breck repeated the question.

"I'm goin' to pretend you never said that."

Breck prodded him in the ribs with the snout of the big Colt. "Who's the easterner that owns the K Bar T?"

The settler spit contemptuously at Breck's feet. "If you don't know, I ain't goin' to tell you."

"You're mighty hard to get along with."

He took a deep breath. "I don't know who you are, mister, or why you're nosin' around my farm. It don't make no real difference. I am goin' to tell you this much. I've been payin' cash at the store lately. Before that, Emily and me and the kids had a rough go puttin' food on the table. More than once we'd have gone hungry if it hadn't been for Mr. Fosberg. But it ain't that way now. We ain't got all the money we need, but we're careful an' we're gettin' there!"

"I figured as much."

"There's somethin' else I want you to know, mister. Whatever we've got, we've got honest. We're God-fearin' people. We never stole nothin' and we never lied to nobody. But that's *all* I'm tellin' you."

Breck's gaze met his.

"You're a good man, Armenius. A man to travel the river with."

His expression did not change. "I'd just as soon you don't come back. Emily and me don't want any truck with your kind."

"You told me the truth," John said, ignoring the barb in the settler's voice. "Now I'm goin' to tell you the truth—again. I ain't workin' for the K Bar T or anyone else that might want to come against you. And I ain't goin' to be."

Armenius stood for a moment measuring Breck's words and watching his face. Then he thrust out his hand impulsively, and Breck took it. "Sorry to have drawn down on you," the farmer said, "and I'm sorry for what I said just now. You come by any time. You're mighty welcome."

Breck nodded, relieved that the settler finally believed him. "Thanks for that. Can't say I blame you for gettin' riled—alone like this and thinkin' somebody's out to get your place."

Melinda was waiting for him when he returned a few moments later. "You're safe," she breathed prayerfully.

He nodded.

"And what did you find out?"

Breck shrugged. "I'll have to let you know later. Maybe something—maybe nothing. We'll know more when I check it out."

They mounted and rode back along the arroyo.

"He's gettin' money from somewhere," John continued. "That's for sure. But he ain't gettin' it dishonest. I'd stake my life on that. That fella would plumb starve himself to death before he'd take somethin' that wasn't his."

"Any idea how he comes by it? The money, I mean."

Breck glanced at her. "Like I said, when I find out for sure, I'll let you know."

17

Jacobs squirmed uncomfortably in the saddle and glanced toward his companion, anguish marring his bulbous features.

"I knew we should have rented a rig," he complained aloud. "If this horse is as sore as I am, he won't be walking tomorrow."

"You'll get used to it," Breck remarked, chuckling.

He groaned again. "If it don't kill me first. How much farther?"

"Just beyond the butte—I think."

"Think?" he exploded. "Don't you know?"

"I know there's a trail to it and that it's over there somewhere. What's an extra mile or two?"

"I ain't exactly built for this kind of traveling. Remind me to fire you when we get back."

It was growing late in the afternoon when they approached the butte from the south. It looked smaller to Breck now than it had the day before—lower and narrower. But that could have been because of the way the sun gleamed on it. The golden ball of fire was far down on the horizon. It silhouetted a rocky peak in the nearest range and cast long shadows across the prairie from every tree and sage and clump of soap weed.

"What did she tell you when you said she couldn't go along?"

"The usual." Breck shrugged. "Said she was goin' with us the next time, no matter what."

"Know something?" His jowls quivered with amusement. "You've got yourself a hard-headed little filly."

"She ain't mine."

Jacobs chuckled again. "You tried to tell *her* that?"

John fell silent.

Breck wasn't certain why Jacobs was so anxious to get out to the K Bar T. He hadn't seemed interested until he heard what Armenius said about an eastern owner. Then his eyes came alive, and he got to his feet immediately.

"That's right fascinating," he had said. "I think maybe we'd better have us a look-see."

"Tomorrow?"

Jacobs squinted up at the blazing sun. "We've got time enough today if we get a move on." He hesitated. "Suit you OK?"

They were on their way out of town when John asked the question that had been nagging at him. "Mr. Devin ain't interested in ranching, is he?"

"Nope." There was a long silence. "But that eastern rancher who's supposed to own the K Bar T just might be interested in railroads."

Breck had been wondering about Nester and his party. When they were talking to him and Hunter in Devin's private car, they talked as though they were going to stay there until the railroad president was ready to go back home. They talked about buffalo hunting and Indians, and he figured them to be ordinary tourists who had come to see the sights. But they hadn't stayed around town long once they got there. They'd found a rig and left. As far as he knew, no one in Buffalo Gulch had any idea where they had gone. When young Snyder came in for supplies the day before, he left town in the direction of the K Bar T. They could be staying out there.

He couldn't figure out why they were so secretive. Perhaps Jacobs was wondering too. That could be the reason he was so anxious to check out the ranch.

The two men traveled along the main road and turned west on the trail that served both Armenius and the K Bar T. At the arroyo Breck had used the day before he took Jacobs into the trees and told him to wait until he got back.

"What're you fixin' to do?" the Pinkerton agent asked curiously.

"I'm aimin' to do a bit of back-trackin' to see if we're bein' followed. I ain't too keen on bein' surprised by someone comin' up behind us. And that's the pure truth."

"I could go with you," Jacobs suggested.

"I reckon you could," John said grinning, "but I figured maybe you'd like to give your saddle a rest."

"You've got something there."

Breck touched the dun lightly with his spurs and the broad-chested stallion stepped out effortlessly, making his way through the trees to the lip of the arroyo. Coming out of the ravine, the rider reined in. At first he listened intently for any sounds that were foreign to the breathless hush of the prairie. Then, standing in the stirrups, he studied the parched landscape. The Armenius farmstead reared stark and bleak against the deepening shadows and a buzzard wheeled high above, searching the desolate prairie for a meal. A prairie dog, sitting erect just outside his hole, was also studying the grassland around him.

John was satisfied that everything was in order and was about to urge his mount forward when the dun's powerful body stiffened. His ears came up, and his distended nostrils began to quiver. Listening, Breck could distinguish nothing save the soft soughing of the wind and the rustle of leaves. Yet, there was something amiss. He couldn't quite put his finger on it, but something was there that didn't belong. He had been on the trail long enough to know that he could trust the senses of his mount better than his own.

Quickly he backed his horse into the ravine where he would be screened from view by the trees. The line-backed dun obeyed immediately, but he was not in time. A rider came out of a narrow, treeless slash in the prairie two hundred yards ahead. Behind him rode four others, their hands on their weapons.

Breck wasn't positive, but he thought in that quick moment that he had seen the leader before. Yet things happened so swiftly he could not be sure. The leader shouted in warning and jerked his rifle from its boot, firing across the saddle horn.

Breck read the sudden movement accurately and threw himself to the ground. That lightning-quick reaction saved his life. A bullet screamed past his ear as he fell. His own gun was in his hand as he hit the ground, and he fired twice in rapid succession.

Bullets slammed into the leader, and he rocked uncertainly in the saddle. His mount plunged to one side frantically and the man dropped his Winchester, clutching his shoulder. Someone behind the injured man shouted a warning.

But it was too late. He pitched forward, his lithe frame jerking. As he fell a third slug struck him in the neck.

A shot sounded to Breck's right. Without looking, he knew what was taking place. Jacobs had heard the shooting and was on his way to help, wriggling hurriedly through the brush and trees. The Pinkerton agent's gun barked again. Another rider fell and his horse stumbled, falling to his knees. That broke the will of the three men who were left. They fled with a flurry of shots that showered harmlessly into the trees above Breck and Jacobs.

For several minutes John and his companion remained under cover, listening intently for some sign of the attackers coming back. The leader had not moved since he fell. He had been dead shortly after he hit the ground. There was no question about that.

The other gunman lay motionless for a time, but stirred and tried to struggle to his feet. Somehow he managed to get up on one knee and fought to raise his gun, but couldn't. His body buckled and he sprawled on the hard ground, blood staining the parched vegetation.

Breck glanced at Jacobs. "I'm obliged to you. I don't reckon I could have held 'em off alone."

"If I'd thought about this ride you're taking me on, I think I'd have let them feed you to the buzzards," the Pinkerton man said grumpily.

They went over to where the dead men were lying facedown. Breck turned the leader over on his back. He *had* seen him before—in the Eagle's Nest the day he met Curley and Tighman and Billy Brooks. The fellow had been at the bar nursing two fingers of whiskey and a grouch against the world.

Jacobs went through the dead man's pockets, but there was nothing there to indicate who he was or where he was from. He had a small sack of gold pieces tied with a string of rawhide around his waist. There were cigarette makings in his shirt pocket along with the picture of a beautiful young woman and a boy six months or a year old.

Breck straightened and stared into the distance. The picture was undoubtedly of his wife. She was probably waiting hopefully for him to return to their Missouri or Iowa or Indiana farm— she and the boy. They would be waiting and praying for him to return safely and soon.

Remorse swept over Breck. He had been the one to destroy their dreams.

Jacobs must have guessed what he was thinking. He finished examining the other body and went over to Breck.

"It wasn't your fault, John," he said softly. "All five were after you. It was either you or them. You didn't have a choice."

He took the gold coins, the cigarette papers and tobacco, and the picture and put them in his saddlebag along with the dead man's Colt Frontier. He would put the dead man's rifle in his scabbard and carry his own. After what had happened, it would only be good judgment to have a gun at the ready.

Both men were strangers to him. It didn't seem reasonable that men he had never met would try to kill him. Yet, even as he asked the question he knew the answer. They were hired killers, outlaws whose guns were available for a price to enforce the will of ruthless men on those around them. Somebody in Buffalo Gulch considered him a threat and apparently was determined to have him removed.

"It has to be because of that Knox girl I'm lookin' for," he said thoughtfully.

"Somebody sure don't want her found," Jacobs added.

"Or her uncle."

Breck looked down at the bodies on the ground. "We don't have a shovel," he said. "What are we goin' to do with 'em? It don't seem right to leave 'em for the coyotes to tear to pieces."

"What do you figure on doing?" Jacobs asked.

"We could catch their horses and take them into town. Maybe Corrigan or someone else will know them."

The horses the two had been riding had not gone far. They were on the edge of the arroyo where the grass was thick, grazing peacefully as though nothing had happened.

Breck shook out a loop and urged his horse slowly in the direction of the others. But the rope was unnecessary. They were able to approach the horses, dismount, and take them by the reins.

"Notice the brands?" Jacobs asked.

John Breck nodded. He had seen them before, when the horses were running from the scene of the gunfight.

"The K Bar T," Jacobs said aloud. "They must be involved."

"Could be." But Breck was thinking something else. If the ranch or its owner was implicated in whatever was going on, why would they use their own horses for the guns they had brought in? Why let everyone know the hired guns were working for them?

He led the horses over to the place where the bodies were lying and threw them across their saddles, tying their hands and feet together so they would not slip off. Then they started back to Buffalo Gulch, leading the horses with their grisly cargo.

It was dark, and Hank Corrigan was home when Breck and his companion stopped to see him. He came out into the yard.

"What've you got here?" he asked.

"We were headin' out toward the K Bar T," Breck said. "I had an uneasy feelin' and backtracked to see if anyone was on our trail. Five riders jumped us. These two didn't leave like the others did."

Corrigan struck a match and bent down to look at the faces of the dead men.

"I've seen 'em both," he said. "Hired guns who came in town a week ago. I got concerned and ordered the whole bunch to clear out."

"They didn't go far."

"Not far enough," the marshall retorted.

"You might be interested in knowin' that they were both ridin' K Bar T stock."

The marshall straightened slowly. "That's a strange thing," he said. "I just had a visitor from the K Bar T reportin' two horses stolen. One black and the other a roan."

Breck looked from one horse to the other.

"Like these," he said.

"Like these."

Jacobs asked, "Who reported the thefts?"

"Let's see. . . ." Corrigan frowned thoughtfully. "He was a young guy by the name of Snyder. Charles Snyder."

Breck jerked erect. Snyder! He had caught a glimpse of one of those bushwhackers. Now he realized that he looked a lot like the young man from the East.

18

Hank Corrigan asked Breck and Jacobs to wait until he got back.

"The boy and I will take these two down to Ferguson," he said. "Go in and ask the missus to fix you a cup of coffee. I'll have to get a report from you when we get back."

"I'll go with you," Jacobs said. "It'll give me a chance to put some of the starch back in my legs."

They were about to leave when a thin, musical voice spoke from behind them. "W-w-who are *they?*" She pointed to the bodies.

For the first time Breck saw Melinda. He didn't know when she came out of the house or how long she had been standing there listening, her eyes wide with horror.

"You'd better go back inside," Corrigan said gently. "This is nothing for you to see."

She was stunned, as though her ears were stopped and she had not heard him. "Who are they?" she repeated.

Breck shrugged. "Never saw either of 'em before I came out here on the train."

"What happened?"

"They acted like they knew me," he said. "They started shootin' soon as they saw who I was."

Jacobs and Corrigan led the horses away. Melinda remained motionless, her gaze fixed on Breck. He shifted uncomfortably from one foot to the other.

"Got somethin' on your mind?" he asked.

"I—I want you to stop looking for Cassie."

He stared down at her.

"When did you decide that?"

She spoke hesitantly. "What difference does that make?"

"Don't you want to find her?"

"Two men have already died because I've been looking for her. I—I don't want you to be the third."

"I ain't goin' to be. I promise you that!"

"Just stop right now," she blurted. "Get your supplies or whatever it is you need and go prospecting like you wanted to."

"And what're you goin' to be doin'?"

"What difference does that make?"

"Listen, Melinda." He grasped her shoulders gently. "I didn't want to get into this mess. You know that as well as I do. I fought it, but I'm in now and I'm goin' to stay in 'til we find your friend and set things straight. Understand?"

Her gaze met his, tears quivering under her long lashes.

"I don't need your help!"

"You're gettin' it anyway, so just stop badgerin' me."

A tear escaped and trickled down her cheek. She wiped it away with the back of her hand. "I wish you wouldn't," she said softly.

"Sorry." For a moment they eyed each other. "I know why you want me to stop," he said huskily, "and I'm obliged to you for thinkin' about me, but I can't quit now. I just ain't made that way."

She turned abruptly and marched into the house. He followed a step behind her. They sat down in the parlor across from each other. Melinda's cheeks were still fiery, but the tears were gone, wiped away hurriedly when her back was turned to him. He squirmed uncomfortably. He wished he had had sense enough to have gone with the marshall. He wouldn't be sitting here feeling like something the dog wiped his feet on.

"I don't suppose you found out anything this afternoon," she began at last.

"Not a thing." His coarse fingers fumbled with the rim of his battered hat. "Of course we didn't get any farther than you and I did this morning. I went back to have a look-see to find out if anyone was followin' us. These five guys must have been on our tail. They came chargin' up the hill, their guns barking."

Dora Corrigan joined them at that moment, learned that Breck and Jacobs hadn't had anything to eat that evening, and insisted on fixing a meal for them.

"Nobody ever leaves my house hungry."

"I'll help you," Melinda said, getting quickly to her feet.

"You can come out in the kitchen with us, John," Dora said to Breck, "if you've a mind to."

"I think I'll stay here. I'd only be in the way."

Melinda Grainger paused at the kitchen door as though she was about to speak, then decided against it and followed Mrs. Corrigan into the other room.

Breck remained in the parlor, staring at the flickering kerosene lamp until Corrigan and the Pinkerton agent returned. By that time Dora and Melinda had supper ready and herded the men to the kitchen table.

"I ain't hungry myself," Hank said, "but I reckon I can stand another cup of coffee."

"You can always stand another cup of coffee," his wife replied pleasantly.

The kitchen had started to cool off after the evening meal. Now it was hot again. Dora's cheeks were florid, and sweat moistened her graying hairline. Melinda got a cup from the shelf and poured Hank a steaming cup of coffee. He dumped a little into his saucer to cool and turned to his guests.

"I've been thinkin' about the K Bar T and what happened to you two over that way this afternoon. Then that Snyder fellow comin' in to tell me about a couple of K Bar T brand horses that were stolen. It doesn't add up. I reckon I ought to go out and pay 'em a little visit in the morning."

"If I was you, Corrigan," Jacobs put in, "I believe I'd be doin' the same thing. There's somethin' goin' on that ain't what it should be, the way I see it."

Breck listened quietly. Going out to the ranch was a good idea, but if it was up to him he wouldn't be waiting until morning. He'd leave that night and be wherever he wanted to be come daylight. Early morning would be a better time of dropping in on the gunmen he was sure were there.

"What do you think about that Nester fella?" the marshall asked. "He made quite a splash comin' into town in that private car with the president of the railroad and everything. But he left and ain't been seen since the day after your man, Hunter, was murdered."

"I don't know what to tell you," Jacobs continued. "I've talked to Devin about him. He trusts him all the way. But me—I ain't so sure. I'd bet my bottom dollar that he's out at the ranch too. And I've got a hunch that he's in on whatever's goin' on, just like the others."

Breck wasn't so sure. "Nester's capable of it," he said. "He's a hard man. It's in his eyes. But he's got those daughters of his to think about. I've seen the way he is with them girls. He ain't goin' to hurt 'em if he can help it. I don't reckon he'd have them within a hundred miles of that ranch if he was into anything crooked."

Jacobs took a cigar from his shirt pocket, bit off the end, and was about to light it when he caught Dora Corrigan's disapproving frown. Reluctantly he returned the cigar to where it came from.

"I don't know about that," he said. "Havin' those girls with him makes a mighty good way to hide what he's up to."

"The girls aren't there now," Melinda announced firmly.

Heads turned quickly to stare at her. "You don't know that," Breck exclaimed.

"You're not the only one who can find out things! I happen to know that they rode into town in the spring wagon with Charles Snyder yesterday and were mad as could be at him because they got caught in the rain."

"Are you sure of that?"

"Of course I'm sure. Snyder didn't come in for supplies like we thought. He bought a few things, all right—some ammunition and flour and coffee. But he really came in so they could go to Denver on last night's train."

Corrigan strummed the oil cloth with his fingers without speaking. Finally he looked up. "I suppose you've got a good reason for sayin' that?"

"The depot agent told me," she said triumphantly. "He said they were bored silly sitting around the ranch. They got so tired of being cooped up out there that they finally coaxed their pa into letting them go to Denver to do some shopping and have a little fun."

"I'll bet they had to talk awful hard to get to make the trip," the marshall said, sarcasm edging his voice. "Sounds to me like he got 'em out of the way before the trouble starts. Just what I'd have done if I was in his boots." He breathed deeply. "I reckon I'd better go up there the first thing in the morning. Wanta go along, Jacobs?"

The Pinkerton man hesitated. "On a horse?" he asked.

"How else?"

"I'm about to come apart at the seams from that ride today. And that was on a horse. I don't reckon on getting aboard another ugly critter for love or money." He squinted at the marshall. "Even when I was in the field all the time and had to use one of those miserable creatures to get around, I hated them. And now that I've been in the office for a few years it's even worse. I'm plumb out of practice, and I sure ain't got the shape for it." He patted his bulging stomach with a pudgy hand.

"Suit yourself. But I don't want to hear you complainin' about getting beat out of all the fun, that's all."

"If bouncin' around on the back of a horse is fun," Jacobs exclaimed, "I've got another name for it." He turned to Breck. "You get along good on a horse. How about takin' my place?"

The muscles at the corners of John's mouth hardened. "I was already figuring on it, whether you asked me or not."

Melinda heard that and spoke quickly. "So was I," she said. "What time are you leaving?"

"It shouldn't matter to you," Hank told her mildly. "You ain't going."

"Give me one good reason why," she flared.

"It's official business—that's one. And I never take anyone along on official business who don't belong."

"What about him?" She indicated Breck with a small gesture.

"I'll deputize him before we leave."

"You can deputize me too."

"I ain't deputizin' no woman," he said bluntly.

"And why not?"

"It ain't legal."

"There's no law against deputizing a woman that I know of."

Color crept into his cheeks. "Then you don't know nothin' about the law here in Buffalo Gulch," he retorted defensively. "We've got us a law against women deputies!"

"Since when?"

"Since I said so."

"That doesn't make it the law."

"It does here. And even if I was of a mind to deputize a woman—which I ain't—I wouldn't be takin' her along when we might be facin' a bunch of gunmen. So relax and forget about it. You ain't goin' nowhere with me tomorrow."

"You men—you're all alike!"

Breck and the Pinkerton man left the Corrigan house presently. "Keep your eyes open out there, John. We've got to find out how that ranch figures into what's going on."

"You could go along."

"I know." He nodded in agreement. "But I

thought I ought to spend a little time checkin' out Fannie Knox. That woman's up to something, but I don't know what."

"Then it wasn't ridin' a horse that's keepin' you in town?"

"Not exactly." He chuckled to himself. "I can't say riding is my favorite sport, especially now that I've sort of gone to belly, but I thought I needed a little time to devote to Mrs. Knox. At this point I didn't much want the others to find out what I was doing. Besides, you can do as well going with Corrigan as I could. Maybe better." He glanced significantly down at Breck's Peacemaker. "If push comes to shove, that hog leg of yours will come in mighty handy."

"How do you look at the K Bar T?" Breck asked.

"What do you mean?"

"Think it could have something to do with Cassie and her uncle disappearing?"

"It might. It just might."

19

Melinda knew Breck and Corrigan were leaving early for the K Bar T. She awakened as the first gray slivers of light streaked the eastern horizon, robbing the night of its Stygian blackness. She could hear the sounds of a fire being built in the kitchen stove and water being dipped from the reservoir on the side. Moments later the heavy iron skillet clanged as it was placed on the stove. As usual, Dora had gotten up to fix breakfast for her man before he left.

Melinda stared at the flowered walls and the grimy ceiling in the little bedroom. Those men had intended to kill Breck when they jumped him the day before. And if they tried once, they would try again. It was all because she was so determined to find her friend. Why couldn't he have listened when she insisted on dropping the search? Why was he so stubborn?

She should have stopped it long ago, when the first Pinkerton agent was killed. If she had, John would be looking for gold or silver now. He wouldn't be in the danger he was in.

She sat up, pulling her nightgown close about her neck, and stared at the window. She remained in that position until she heard Breck's saddle creak as he dismounted to open the gate. It was him! She got out of bed as quietly as possible and went to the window in time to see him approach the house.

"Come in and have a bite," the marshall said.

"Don't mind if I do. We've got quite a ride ahead of us, and Dora puts out a mighty good spread."

Melinda listened to the voices from the kitchen. At times she could hear everything that was said. Moments later they were speaking so quietly she only caught snatches of the conversation. She wanted to dress and join them, but that wouldn't do. Breck and the Corrigans would think her forward.

It didn't take long for Dora to fix breakfast, and even less time for the two men to eat. In a few minutes she heard the kitchen door open noisily, and they went outside together. Melinda stayed at the window, watching, until they mounted and rode out of sight.

When they were gone, she dressed and went into the kitchen where Dora was sitting motionless at the table, staring blankly at the door. She looked up as Melinda joined her.

"You're up early this morning."

"I couldn't sleep."

"That's what I tell Hank. When he goes off this way I might just as well get up to stay. I couldn't sleep any more."

Melinda poured herself a cup of coffee and sat down across from her older friend. "Is it hard to have Mr. Corrigan go off like this?" she asked.

The older woman smiled and reached across the table to pat her new friend on the arm. "It's hard, Melinda. I try to keep from thinkin' about it, but that don't work so good. I know what can happen and what might happen."

She sipped her coffee. "Did you ever ask him to quit—to go into ranching or get a store?"

"I used to. Lots of times. But that's his life. He'd be miserable doing anything else. And I couldn't be happy if he wasn't."

Melinda nodded. She could understand that.

"Hank always says somebody's got to bring the law to the West so it's safe for decent people to make their homes here. He believes we ain't goin' to have families and schools and churches unless the men who live by the gun are rooted out and brought under control. And that's his job."

"He's right, of course."

Dora was silent for a full minute. "I know he is, but I keep wonderin' what kind of a price I'm goin' to have to pay. One of these days Hank might go out like this and not come back." She sighed deeply. "I don't talk to him about it any more, but I keep thinkin' on it."

"Would you go through it again?" Melinda asked. "If you could do it over, I mean?"

Dora set the cup on the table and looked up. "Are you thinkin' what I think you are?" she asked quietly.

The girl stared at her and turned away without answering. How could she? Her mind was in such a tumult she didn't know what she was thinking.

They cleared the table presently, and Melinda did the dishes while Dora Corrigan brought in wood for the stove and swept the floors. Neither talked any more than was necessary.

They were just finishing the morning's work when there was a knock at the door. Melinda went to answer it. Fannie Knox was on the porch, folding her pink parasol carefully. Her face lighted when she saw the girl.

"Oh, there you are, my dear. I was hoping I would find you home."

"Won't you come in?" Melinda asked cooly.

"Only for a moment." She stepped inside, adjusting her hat with a practiced hand.

"I presume you have something you wish to talk with me about," Melinda said.

"I was going to stop by last night, but Edwin wouldn't hear of it. The poor darling has been so lonely he'll hardly let me out of his sight, now that we're together again."

"Mr. Knox is in town?" Melinda asked, startled. She ushered Fannie across the parlor to the most comfortable chair in the room, a massive, high-backed rocker. She took a chair across from Mrs. Knox.

Fannie smiled warmly. "My dear, Edwin wants to see you. He has some news that should make you very happy."

The girl's heart leaped. "About Cassie?"

"I really shouldn't have told you that. But I have been almost as excited as he is because he is so happy to be able to talk to you. Edwin has always had a warm spot in his heart for you. Cassie means so much to him, especially since his only brother died. Any friend of his niece is very important to him."

"Please tell me—does he know where she is? Is she all right?"

Fannie's smile was reassuring. "I'm sorry Melinda, but he made me promise that I wouldn't say anything to you that would ruin his surprise. I'm afraid I've said too much as it is. But I can assure you that you will be very happy when you hear what he has to say."

"Where is he?" she asked excitedly. "Can we go see him now?"

"I'm afraid not, Melinda. He didn't know whether it would be possible to see you this morning, and he's very busy." She paused momentarily. "So he thought it best that I make an appointment with you so he would waste a minimum of time."

"I can see him whenever he wants to," she assured her guest. "Any time he wants to."

Mrs. Knox leaned forward, touching the side of her nose with an index finger.

"Edwin and I have an appointment with Mr. Richards—Mr. Sam Richards. We're going to have some legal papers drawn up. I think that's such a bore. I don't understand those things at all. Edwin says 'sign,' and I sign. I really don't know what I'm signing." She glanced at the clock on the wall and stood quickly. "Oh, dear, I've got to dash. We're due at Mr. Richards' office in twenty minutes. You will meet with us for dinner at noon today, won't you?"

"At the Bon Ton?"

"Why don't we pick you up at the hotel, if you could come down there to meet us."

"I'll be there."

Melinda stared after her guest momentarily, then as soon as the door closed behind Fannie, she hurried to the kitchen.

"Oh, Dora," she cried, "God has answered my prayers. I've finally found somebody who knows something about Cassie."

The older woman turned to her thoughtfully. "Are you sure?"

"As sure as I can be about anything right now."

A smile broke the worry lines in Mrs. Corrigan's face. "It must mean a great deal for you to find your friend. I'm very happy for you."

Melinda hurried to her room, changed clothes quickly, and combed her hair. She was ready to leave the house at 11:00, though she wasn't to meet Edwin and Fannie Knox until noon.

She sat down in the big rocking chair and tried to imagine what Edwin's news could be. Perhaps he had received a letter from Cassie saying she was well and happy and would be out to see him soon. Perhaps someone else had seen her—someone who knew her well and assured him that she was alive and content to be where she was. She might even have fallen in love and married. That would be a good reason why she hadn't written.

A few minutes before noon she left the house and went to the hotel. The morning had started with blistering heat that indicated it would be the hottest day of the summer so far. But by the time she went down the path that led past the jailhouse to Main Street, a few heavy clouds had moved in, shutting off the relentless rays of the sun. A cooling wind made the day comfortable.

A cumbersome wagon covered with canvas rattled noisily up the road. It passed Melinda and the Richards Law Office and moved toward the corner of the Bon Ton Cafe, pulled by a ponderous team of oxen. A milk cow, bony hips and ribs showing, was tied to the tailgate, forced to plod wearily wherever the wagon went. From somewhere beneath the canvas cover a baby cried and a mother's off-key crooning tried to lull it back to sleep.

As Melinda reached the hotel she saw that the wagon was traveling eastward, heading for a little used trail that led toward the river and, more than likely, to a little piece of ground where a young couple would try desperately to build a home and eke out a living. It would be a hard life, but even that would be better than what Dora Corrigan had—never knowing from one day to the next whether her man would come home or not.

Melinda went into the lobby and looked around. Her heart sank. Fannie Knox and her husband weren't there. Maybe they weren't coming! Then she saw Jacobs, sitting in his favorite chair, his cigar and his newspaper firmly in place. Seeing her he crunched the cigar in the ashtray, laid the paper aside, and got to his feet.

"Looking for someone?" he asked.

She nodded.

"They went up to their room a few minutes ago."

She stared at him. "How do you know who I'm looking for?" she asked.

"It's my business to know things." He smiled broadly. "When I saw Fannie Knox go out this morning all dolled up like a Christmas tree, I figured you'd be showing up sooner or later."

She moved closer. "Is *he* with her?"

"You mean her husband?"

"Who else would I be interested in seeing?"

He started to speak, but paused and gestured toward the stairs. "Look for yourself."

She turned to see the smiling couple on the stairs. The thin, cadaverous features of the man clinging to Fannie's arm lighted, and he waved at her.

"Mr. Knox!" she cried, rushing toward him.

"Melinda, my dear."

They met at the foot of the stairs. For an instant he acted as though he would take her in his arms. He stepped away from Fannie and held out both hands. She took them with trembling fingers.

"It's so *good* to see you, Melinda."

She tried to speak, but could not.

"What brings you out here?" he asked tenderly.

She stepped back. "Don't you know?"

"Of course." His smile came back. "I just wanted to hear it from you."

Fannie touched his arm. "Don't you think we should go to the cafe?" she asked, glancing at Jacobs who appeared not to be paying any attention to the scene that was taking place, but was obviously hearing all that was said.

The lights in his eyes faded, and he motioned toward the door. "Shall we, Melinda?" he asked. "We can talk there."

Reluctantly she went out the door with them and up the boardwalk in the direction of the Bon Ton. There was something about Edwin Knox that disturbed her. She didn't doubt his identity, but he was older than she remembered. There was more gray in his hair, and the lines in his face were deeper. His voice had a different quality, as though he was coming down with a cold, and his cheeks were pale, which seemed strange for one who had been out in the hills.

She asked about it.

"You're still the same intelligent, observant young lady I used to know," he told her. "My mine holdings west of Denver are quite extensively developed. I've either been in the office or down in the shaft supervising some new exploration, so I couldn't get any sun to speak of."

Her face flushed in embarrassment, and for an instant she didn't know what to say.

"Tell me," he continued, changing the subject, "do you still play the piano?"

Her eyes widened. "Do you remember that?"

"Why wouldn't I?" he laughed. "Cassie and you used to play the most beautiful duets. Can't remember the name of them right off. Never could. But I loved them. And you girls knew how to work me.

"If I forbade her to go over to your place or do something else you wanted to, you'd go to the piano and start playing. You'd melt me every time. The first thing I knew, the two of you would be dashing out the door with my blessing."

"That was such a long time ago." Melinda giggled as she thought about it.

"I hope to be able to do that again some time," he said, "even at the risk of giving in to you young vixens."

"Now, Edwin," Fannie said indulgently, "you'll only spoil them again."

"A little spoiling never hurt anyone."

The last slim doubts Melinda had about Edwin Knox had vanished.

They approached the cafe, and he held the door open for the ladies.

"Let's see," he continued, following them to a table, "you went to Cranbrook School for Girls. Right?"

She nodded. "Cassie and I were roommates."

"I know, I know. The head mistress used to write your papa and me often enough. I can still remember the letters I used to get from your not-so-patient Miss Elsie Darrington.

" '. . . I dislike bothering you again, Mr. Knox, but something is going to have to be done about your niece and her roommate, Melinda Grainger. They were caught putting oatmeal in another girl's bed and sneaking down to the kitchen where they ate most of Miss Webber's birthday cake. The poor soul thought we had forgotten her again and locked herself in her room for an entire day. . .' "

"I remember that. We had to apologize to Miss Webber and bake her a cake ourselves. Only that didn't work out either. We forgot to put soda in it, and it fell."

They were seated, and Adolph took their order.

"You must be Mr. Knox," he said to Edwin.

"That's right."

"You should have seen your wife. When she came in here at first, she was so upset she ate like a bird. I'm right glad she found you."

Fannie Knox colored. "That's enough, Adolph. You embarrass me."

He glanced at her wistfully. "I wish I had a pretty lady like you worryin' about me."

He left for the kitchen abruptly, as though he had said too much. Edwin turned to Melinda who by this time was squirming uneasily. She waited for him to start talking about Cassie.

"I'm afraid I've been unnecessarily cruel, my dear," he began, covering her fingers with his own. "I don't mean to be, but I so wanted to have the right setting to tell you the good news."

Melinda gasped. "You've found Cassie?"

"I've found Cassie, though I should say that she found me."

"I don't care *how* it happened. Where is she?"

"I'm coming to that." He paused and looked over at his wife. "I guess it's no secret that Cassie's Aunt Fannie and I have had our differences in the past."

Melinda nodded.

"We're both thankful that all of our troubles are in the past—aren't we, darling?"

"I was *so* miserable." She laughed happily. "But now we're as happy as two lovebirds. Aren't we, Edwin?"

"Melinda doesn't care to hear about us. She wants to know about Cassie."

Adolph came back with the coffee, and conversation ceased until he left.

"After coming out here, I got so involved with various business ventures that I neglected to write home. That upset Cassie. She thought something terrible had happened to me and came out to find me."

"Yes?" Melinda said, leaning closer to him.

"It took her a spell because I had gone on to San Francisco. Had some things out there to tend to. Anyway, when I came back she learned I was here and looked for me until I heard about it and hunted her up."

"Where is she?" Melinda broke in. "Is she all right?"

"That's the good news I have. She's fine. As well as I've ever seen her. I told her a few days ago that Colorado Territory must agree with her."

She closed her eyes momentarily. "Thank God!"

"Yes," Fannie said, "isn't that wonderful? I knew you'd be thrilled to hear Edwin's news. I could hardly sleep myself, I was so excited."

Melinda eyed the other woman critically. From what Cassie always told her, Fannie Knox had no use for her. It didn't seem possible that she could have changed so quickly. Cassie's pa used to preach about such a transformation when a person confessed his sin and put his trust in Christ, but there was no evidence in Fannie's life to indicate that had happened to her. Her eyes were cold and hard, and the lines in her face were harsh.

The girl turned away from Fannie toward Mr. Knox. "Where *is* Cassie, Mr. Knox?" she asked.

"Right now she's on the train with a lady companion headed for Omaha and Philadelphia and later New York. I'm probably old-fashioned, but I didn't like the thought of her traveling all that way alone. So I did some inquiring and learned of a more mature woman who is making the trip. She agreed to take her. She will be stopping with friends in Omaha and relatives in Philadelphia, but I thought that was better for Cassie than making the trip by herself."

"She'll be home in a couple of weeks," Fannie put in. "So we thought it would be wise if you were to notify Pinkerton's that Cassie is found. We're sure your papa would appreciate your not spending any more money looking for our niece."

Melinda stared at her.

"How did you know about that?" she demanded.

Fannie swallowed hard. "I—I—after all, Buffalo Gulch is a small town. Everybody knows everything about everyone else."

"And," Edwin added, his voice reassuring, "it isn't wise to have them continue to look for Cassie when she has been found, is it?"

20

It was a long, hot, dusty ride, and half the morning was gone by the time Breck and the marshall reined in at the crest of a little hill and looked down on the buildings that glistened white in the sun.

"First time I've ever been over this way," the marshall murmured. "It's quite a spread."

"There's money down there," Breck observed quietly. "And he never made it runnin' cows. Not to get a layout like that in this part of the country. In Texas, maybe, but not here."

The house, a two-story structure bigger than anything in Buffalo Gulch except the hotel, dominated the ranch. The front porch was decorated with fluted round pillars that supported the roof along the outer edge. A bay window as big as any Breck had ever seen stretched a third of the distance between the front door and the corner of the building. Stained glass sparkled from the upper quarter of the other windows in the big house, and a broad stone chimney revealed the presence of a large fireplace in the parlor.

The barn was smaller but just as substantially built. It was a hip-roofed structure white and shining like the house, with a hayloft over the horse stalls.

There was a bunkhouse some distance from the main dwelling, a long, single-storied building with a door at one end and a row of windows along the side. While they watched, two men came out and walked briskly toward the house.

"They ain't regular cowhands," Corrigan observed. "I can tell that from here."

Breck's lips parted, but he didn't have an opportunity to speak. The dun's ears came up, quivering, and he looked about, nostrils testing the breeze. Someone was approaching from behind the bushes to their right.

Hank Corrigan caught the warning signals at about the same time and pulled his Winchester from its boot. With his six-gun in his hand, Breck whirled his mount and dove to the ground in the same instant. He came to his feet with the big Colt trained on the clump of brush.

"All right," Corrigan ordered loudly, "throw out your gun and come out with your hands in the air."

There was no sound from whoever had been sneaking up on them. Cautiously, Breck moved away from the marshall, his feet inching over the hard ground as quietly as a wolf stalking his prey.

Corrigan repeated his command, but there was still nothing more than the uneasiness of their mounts to indicate anyone was there. Then a horse snorted, and the dun whinnied in reply. John skirted the brush and waited tensely, straining to catch a glimpse of their would-be assailant. A moment later he saw him, a patch of dirty shirt through the leaves.

"Hold it!" he ordered coldly. "Hold it right there!"

Movement stopped.

"Throw your gun out here!" Corrigan said sternly.

"Suppose you come and get it," a gravelly voice snarled.

In answer Breck pulled the trigger and the bullet slammed into a branch just ahead of the stranger. "If that ain't enough," he said coldly, "we'll send another one in to fetch you."

Immediately a gun was tossed in the marshall's direction, and a pair of bronzed hands came into view.

"I'm coming," the strange voice retorted.

Breck snatched his rifle from its scabbard and plunged into the brush at a position where he could look down on the ranch building. He knew the sound of his six-gun would bring riders pounding up the hill to see what was wrong. Sure enough, half a dozen hard-bitten men were riding recklessly toward them, rifles out and ready.

Corrigan slapped the handcuffs on the prisoner and raised the Winchester to his shoulder. When the others were two hundred yards away, he fired over their heads. They slid to a halt and were about to leap from their mounts and start shooting when the leader recognized Corrigan.

"It's the marshall from Buffalo Gulch," he cried. "Hold everything."

"That's right," Hank rasped. "Put your guns down—I want to talk to you."

They did as they were told.

"I'm Colonel Morgan," the leader said. "I met you once when I came down from Denver to see about buying some cattle for the army."

Hank nodded curtly. "You're sort of far from your post, ain't you?"

Morgan laughed.

"I'm out of the army now. Workin' for the K Bar T. The hours are good, and the pay is a sight better."

"I'm sure it is." Corrigan surveyed the men behind him. One was a former Pinkerton man who had lost his job when he got careless about how and when he used the guns he carried; two were former sheriffs from east of Buffalo Gulch. The other was obviously a gunman, a ruthless, cold-blooded individual who asked no questions about using his weapon if the pay was right. The marshall turned to the former law officers he recognized. "What're you men doin' here?"

The older of the two, a grizzled, weather-beaten character who had gone by the name of Silas Tarry when Corrigan first knew him as a Kansas marshall, spoke up.

"Like Morgan said, the hours are good and the pay's better than wearin' a badge."

"What's goin' on here, Tarry?" the marshall demanded.

The former sheriff's cheeks tinged with color. "Ain't nobody here by that name. You've got me mixed up with somebody else. My name's Cy— Cy Turner."

Corrigan's expression did not change, nor did it bother him that the man he had known by one name now called himself by another. What a man did was the main thing. It didn't matter who he was.

"What about it, Turner? What's goin' on here?"

"You'll have to talk to Morgan," he said with a jerk of his head.

Morgan spoke up quickly. "Really you should see the boss."

"Suits me. Get your man on his horse and let's go." He motioned to his prisoner.

Breck came out of the brush, caught up the dun, and mounted.

"Who's he?" Morgan asked.

"A new deputy of mine. He came along to help keep you honest."

The leader stared at Breck.

"I've seen you somewhere," he said evenly.

"I've been around."

"You weren't taking chances, were you, Hank?" the former sheriff asked him.

"You ought to know by this time that you don't grow old takin' chances in this business."

They rode into the yard, where Morgan led them up the steps and into the parlor of the mansion. Nester and young Snyder were there, along with another man about Nester's age.

"Breck," Nester said, coming forward and taking his hand, "I didn't expect to see you way out here."

"Apparently not. Your men did everything they could to take care of me yesterday."

"Just what do you mean by that?"

"Ask your man Morgan. His crew tried to kill me."

Nester faced the colonel. "What is this man talking about?"

"I think I know," young Snyder broke in quickly. "You remember my telling you somebody stole a couple of K Bar T horses a few days ago and you had me go in and report it to the marshall? The only thing I can think of is that Breck tangled with the horse thieves and thought they were our men."

The older man nodded. "Then it wasn't our crew who shot at Breck?"

"It wasn't our crew," Snyder repeated.

Breck didn't believe them, but said nothing.

"Charles," Nester said, "don't you think you should introduce the marshall and his deputy to your father?"

"I reckon so," he muttered, "but I don't like the idea of being accused of taking the law into our own hands. Pa, this is Marshall Corrigan and John Breck. Breck is the one who saved the train from being robbed. Gentlemen, this is my pa, Ian Snyder."

They shook hands, and Nester invited them to sit down.

The questioning didn't go as well as Corrigan had hoped. He asked what he wanted to know, and they seemed willing enough to answer him; but when he finished, he realized that he actually had learned little, except that Ian Snyder was also on the railroad board of directors. A very minor stockholder, Nester assured Corrigan. When the interview finally ended and the marshall and Breck were on their way out, Morgan whispered something to the ranch owner.

"By the way, Mr. Corrigan," Nester said, "Colonel Morgan reminds me that you have one of our men in custody. I'm sure his putting a gun on you was an innocent mistake."

Hank turned to face him. "And I suppose you would like to have me release him?"

"We would be very grateful. I will assure you that it won't happen again."

Corrigan shrugged. "I was figurin' on turning him loose when we leave."

Colonel Morgan went out to their horses with them.

"What are you men doin' here?" the marshall asked suddenly.

"Mr. Nester told you. Working cattle."

"Don't give me that. There's not a cowhand in the lot. You've got a collection of gunmen, and I want to know why."

Morgan's eyes narrowed. "I don't cotton to bein' called a liar."

"And I don't cotton to bein' taken for a fool. I've lived here all my life. I know a workin' cowboy when I see him."

Morgan and Corrigan faced each other a few paces apart, hands poised above their guns. One word, one wrong move and the situation would explode. Men behind them moved cautiously to one side or the other.

Claude Nester saw from the porch that trouble was coming and strode forward quickly.

"We're glad you came by, marshall," he said, stepping between the two men and edging Hank toward his mount. "Come back any time."

"I'll be back," he said tersely as he stepped up into the saddle. He looked down at Morgan and Nester. "And when I come I'm goin' to expect some straight answers about these gunfighters and why you've gathered them."

"What gunfighters?" Nester asked blandly.

For an instant Corrigan glared at him, then turned and rode off. Breck followed him.

"I thought we were headed for a showdown," John said when they were on the trail back to Buffalo Gulch.

"Not against that bunch. Too many of 'em would be glad to cut us both down, just to show Nester they're earnin' their money."

Breck nodded. The men on the K Bar T were a hard bunch. Like Corrigan, he hadn't seen a cow-puncher in the lot.

"I don't know what that outfit's doing," Hank went on, "but we've got to find out. That many gunmen can only mean one thing. Trouble . . . *big* trouble."

21

When Corrigan and Breck rode back into town that afternoon and went to the Bon Ton for a late dinner, Adolph joined them, his lean face beaming.

"That pretty freckle-faced gal of yours don't have to hunt for her friend Cassie no more, Mr. Breck," he said.

"Is that a fact?"

"Yes, sirree. I heard it my own self. Mrs. Knox—she's that nice lady who was lookin' for her husband and found him—the two of them—Mr. and Mrs. Knox—came here with your girl this noon, and they was tellin' her all about it. He found his niece right in Buffalo Gulch. Would you believe it? Cassie Knox was here in town, only nobody knew it 'til he found her. Now she's on her way back to New York, and they was talkin' to Melinda Grainger about goin' back there too. Said there weren't no need for her to be here."

"That's very interesting," Breck said skeptically.

"Ain't it, though?" Adolph thought he read doubt in the lanky cowman's eyes. "And if you don't believe me, you can ask that fat Mr. Jacobs. He heard it all, same as I did. He'll tell you."

"Was he in the cafe here when they were?"

Corrigan asked. "Did they know he was listening?"

Adolph shook his head. "Nope. They didn't have no idea he was there, and I know enough to keep my mouth shut." He read their concern and pulled out a chair to sit down between them. "They hadn't hardly got sat down at the table near the kitchen door—the one Mrs. Knox always uses—when this Jacobs came into the kitchen. He give me and the cook fifty cents each to let him come in and set for a spell. And as soon as they left, he did."

When he finished, he turned to the marshall for approval.

"I figured you'd want to know them things, Hank—I mean Mr. Corrigan."

The marshall smiled. "I'm 'Hank' to all my friends, Adolph," he said, "and you did the right thing by tellin' us. I need to know what's goin' on in this town."

"You know what else people's sayin'?" Adolph asked, getting to his feet. "Sounds like there's goin' to be real trouble. There was some shootin' over on the Great Western tracks where they're headin' for the pass through the hills to Leadville. Some of them hired guns the Missouri Pacific has on their payroll jumped the crew layin' rails. Never heard whether nobody was hurt or not, but you can take it from me, the Great Western ain't goin' to let that happen without a fight."

"I'll have to look into that, Adolph. Thanks." He turned to Breck. "I'm near starved. How about a pair of T-bones?"

"I'll see you get a couple of extra-special big ones, Mr. Corrigan—I mean Hank. And heavy on the spuds and coffee, right?"

"Right."

He looked at the marshall's companion. "I know what just about everybody in this town eats," he said. "My regulars, I mean. I see 'em comin' and I go tell the cook what to fix."

They said nothing until they finished eating, paid for their meals, and went outside, away from Adolph's prying ears.

"What do you make of it?" Corrigan asked.

"I ain't buyin' it—about Cassie being found. Why would Knox rush his niece out of the country so fast? That makes no sense to me. And why would he try to get Melinda to leave too?" He breathed deeply. "Appears to me they're in an all-fired rush mainly to get Melinda out of here. Do you suppose they're afraid she's getting close to findin' out somethin' they're anxious to keep her from knowing?"

Hank kicked the boardwalk with the toe of his boot. "If it was Fannie Knox, I'd believe you. I don't trust her half as far as I can see her. But I can't see why her husband would be so anxious to be rid of Melinda. From what I hear, he's a nice sort who was so crazy about that niece of his that anyone who was her friend stood high with him."

"I've got to agree with you. But that only bothers me more. There are things goin' on here I don't understand and don't much like the looks of. Like all them gunfighters out at the K Bar T."

"I've been tryin' to figure that one out ever since we left there. Like we said, them guys ain't cowhands and Nester or whoever owns that spread ain't payin' 'em the kind of wages they're getting just to herd cattle."

"I've got a hunch, Hank," Breck said, stopping to face his companion. "But I can't do nothin' about it without your help."

"All right. Tell me what it is."

"You'll help?"

"I trust you. What is it?"

"Take me into Fosberg's store and ask some questions for me."

"You know him. Can't you do it yourself?"

"I already tried. He wouldn't tell me anything. I couldn't get the time of day out of him."

The marshall's eyes slitted. "Breck. . . . " He was suddenly suspicious. "You know somethin' I don't?"

"I don't know anything for sure. I just got me a fist full of questions I'm hankerin' to get the answers to."

"You'll let me in on it when you find out?"

"I'll let you in on it just as soon as I know for sure."

They walked up the street in the direction of the general store. As they did so, Breck outlined the questions he wanted Hank to ask.

Fosberg was alone when they went in. He got up quickly and joined them. "Good afternoon, marshall," he said, ignoring Breck as though he wasn't there. "More cartridges?"

"Ain't got rid of the last batch yet. We just want to ask you a few questions. This is John Breck, my new deputy."

Fosberg's eyes iced. "We already met. He was askin' questions that time too."

"This is different. It's official business."

The storekeeper hesitated. "Do I have to answer 'em?"

"I wish you would," Hank said. "We're gettin' ourselves a man-sized pack of trouble headin' our way like one of them new Baldwin locomotives. You know about them gunfighters that have been comin' into town?"

"I reckon everybody in Buffalo Gulch knows about 'em."

"Well, there's another batch holed up at the K Bar T, and nobody knows why. I'm lookin' for real honest-to-goodness fightin' to break out any day now. I want to do everything I can to head it off."

Fosberg's expression softened slightly. "And you think answerin' these questions of yours might make a difference?"

"Could be."

He wiped his hands on a greasy rag. "You wouldn't be askin' questions about that settler over K Bar T way, now would you?"

"I reckon I would."

"I don't know why you're botherin' Armenius, marshall. I tell you he's a fine man. Ain't a harder worker on the prairie 'twixt here and Denver. Minds his own business a sight better than this character." He indicated Breck with a jerk of his thumb. "And he stays out of trouble. There ain't nothin' he's doin' that's the concern of the law."

"Most everything you say's true," Hank agreed. "Far as I know he ain't in no trouble and ain't goin' to be. We just need to know where he's gettin' the cash money he's usin' all of a sudden."

Fosberg flinched. "Who said he's usin' cash money?" he hedged.

"He is, ain't he?"

Reluctantly the storekeeper admitted it. "But he's comin' by it honest. I can vouch for that."

"How does he get it?"

The storekeeper took a stubby pencil from the counter and studied it intently.

"He ain't told me."

"You've got an idea."

"Yeah," he admitted, "I have an idea. Mind you I don't know for sure, but I know there ain't no crooked stuff goin' on. I'd trust that boy far as I would my own son."

"Go on."

"Well, Armenius buys his supplies in here and he's been havin' a hard time. A real hard time. Two or three times I've been tellin' myself I *had* to cut him off, but I just couldn't do it. Not with that wife of his out there tryin' to take care of their kids and hardly buyin' enough to keep so many pigeons alive."

Hank knew how hard it was for the settlers, especially the new ones who hadn't had a few crops to give them a start. He knew exactly what Fosberg was talking about. He had felt that way himself just seeing the ragged dirt farmers trying to make both ends meet.

"Anyway, about five or six weeks ago he come in and paid some on his bill. Said he was workin' now. Not all the time, but enough to start whittlin' on what he owed me. And whittle he did. He started buyin' lots more stuff and payin' cash for it, plus he paid on the bill he owed here—more than I figured he dared."

"Orderin' anything different?" Hank wanted to know. "Anything he didn't buy before?"

Fosberg scratched an ear with a stubby finger.

"Cartridges is about the only thing. Before, he only bought a box or two. Somethin' to have on hand for the coyotes or cougars that stray down from the hills, or a deer for some fresh meat."

Hank had a few more questions which the storekeeper answered.

"Will you tell me when he comes in and buys supplies again?"

Fosberg's cheeks heated. "Hank," he said, "that's a terrible thing to ask a man to do. I ain't never carried tales on a body in my life—leastwise a friend. I want to live up to the law, but don't tell me I've got to do that."

"How about me furnishin' you with a clerk for a few days. OK?"

"Clerk? What would I do with a clerk?"

"This place could do with a good cleaning."

"I can't afford no clerk. I just let one go."

"This wouldn't cost you nothing. She'd tidy this place up so's you'd hardly know it."

"And move stuff around so's I couldn't find nothing. I ain't about to go for that."

"She could wait on your customers and give you the chance to do the cleanin' or work on your books."

Fosberg thought about that. "Just what would *you* get out of a deal like that?"

"Well, if she happened to be in here when Armenius came in, you wouldn't have to tell her about it. It wouldn't be your fault that she found out."

Fosberg turned around and hitched himself up on the counter. Hank went over to stand in front of him. "And who might this clerk be?" he asked.

"That little gal who's stayin' with us right now."

"She'd be good. There's no doubt about that."

"Then I can send her over?"

"But if it don't work out I can send her home. Agreed?"

"Agreed."

227

Fosberg chuckled. "It might be nice havin' a fiesty little filly like her around here—as long as she don't start shootin' up the payin' customers."

Breck and the marshall left the store.

"Well, what do you think? Did you get the answers you thought you'd get?" Corrigan asked.

"I found out I'd guessed right on what the dirt farmer's doin' to get money."

"Buyin' supplies for someone who's scared to come into town?"

"Right."

"And who might that be?"

"I've got me an idea about that too, but I ain't ready to go into it yet."

"Remember, you're goin' to tell me soon as you find out."

"I'll give you my word."

Corrigan stopped by the house and told Melinda what he had arranged. She would do it, she said, but only because he asked her to.

"There is really no use in looking any further. I've found Cassie."

"Breck seems to have some questions he'd like to have answered."

"Breck!" she exploded. "When I *wanted* him to help look for Cassie, he wasn't going to do it. Now that I've found her, he's got questions. He's the most obstinate man I ever knew."

"But you will go down to Fosberg's? And when Armenius comes in for supplies, you'll come over to my office and tell me, soon as he leaves?"

"I'll be there first thing in the morning," she replied. "And I'll come over and tell you as soon as Armenius comes in."

"Don't let him know what you're doing."

She nodded. "I don't like it, but because you're asking me, Mr. Corrigan, I'll do it."

Shortly after seven the next morning, she went to the store to work. Fosberg had opened a short time before and was sweeping the front steps when she arrived.

"I don't know what's behind this," he grumbled, "but come on in and I'll show you where to start."

Fosberg has just received a shipment of yard goods and was hoping to attract the attention of the women in Buffalo Gulch to buy material for new fall and winter dresses. He had it strewn about the store wherever he could find space for it. Melinda cleaned out one corner, arranged the material attractively, and put a bolt in the window with a sign in front: "NEW FALL COLORS ON DISPLAY INSIDE." She hadn't finished when Fannie Knox went by, saw her there, and came in.

"Good morning, Melinda," she said, hostility edging her voice.

"Good morning. Is there something I can do for you?"

"I thought you were leaving for home."

"Right now I'm helping Mr. Fosberg," she said.

"Edwin is going to be very disappointed."

Melinda drew herself up to her full five feet and two inches. "What does he have to do with whether or not I go back to New York right away?"

"I thought you wanted to see Cassie as soon as possible."

"Mrs. Knox," Melinda said, "when I get ready to go home I'll go, and not before!"

She was trembling when her friend's aunt flounced out of the store.

"That ain't no way to treat a customer," Mr. Fosberg said. "A lady like that might be good for two, maybe three pieces of yard goods. Now you've run her off."

"She wasn't a customer!" Melinda blurted. "And she sure isn't a lady!"

22

Three days later Breck was sitting in the cafe when Melinda rushed in.

"Oh, there you are. I'm so glad I found you. I've got—"

He stopped her with a glance. "I'm just leaving."

"I need you right away, Breck," she protested. "I—"

He tossed a nickle on the table for his coffee and got languidly to his feet. "I'll walk with you as far as the marshall's office. We can talk on the way."

Her cheeks were livid as he marched her outside, beyond Adolph's hearing.

"Now," he said, "what was that all about?"

"I've decided to talk to Mr. Corrigan," she informed him primly. "He'll listen to me!"

"So will Adolph," he retorted. "That's why I got you out of there before you shot off at the mouth."

She walked half a block without speaking. "I was *not* shooting off at the mouth, as you call it. I had some important information for you."

"Fine. Tell me."

"I don't think I'm going to."

He stopped. "I'd just as well go back and finish my coffee, then."

"Oh, you!" she exploded. "I came over to tell you that Armenius was in the store just now."

"He was?" Breck's lithe figure tensed, revealing his emotion. "What did he buy? What did he say?"

"He bought a lot of things. He and Mr. Fosberg talked about the weather and the corn he's afraid won't make it this year and his sick horse. He's afraid it'll die. Then he'll have to buy another one, and they're expensive."

He grasped her by the arm. "All right, I admit I deserve that. Now tell anything *important* that he said."

"The only thing that seemed significant to me was that he said he was in a hurry this time. He had to get right back."

"Did he say why?"

She shook her head. "And Mr. Fosberg didn't ask."

Lights gleamed in Breck's gray eyes. "This may be the break we've been waitin' for."

Edwin and Fannie Knox went up the stairs to their hotel room.

"I don't like this, Fannie," he said. "You told me there would be no complications. Now you say that girl isn't leaving. She's staying in town."

She faced him, eyes blazing.

"The least you could do," she whispered, "is to wait until we're in our rooms before you start an argument."

Fannie unlocked the door, and they went inside. Once she locked it again, she turned back to him.

"Now, what were you saying?" she asked, keeping her voice low.

"I'm through, Fannie. I've done everything you asked me to. I've made up like Edwin Knox and fooled the girl into believing I am your husband. I've appeared with you here in town enough to establish myself as Edwin Knox. I've even signed the power of attorney in Richards' office to give you the right to vote with your husband's stock at the coming board meeting. That's all you asked me to do and all I agreed to do. Now give me my $500 and my ticket back to Denver. I'm pulling out."

"Now, Paul," she said, flashing a winsome smile. "There's no need to be frightened. That stupid girl thinks you're Edwin. She doesn't suspect a thing. All we need is two more days. Then the telegram from Denver will come, calling you back to the city immediately, and no one will know you're not who you say you are. In two days everything will be perfect."

"That's what you've told me all along. Everything is going to be perfect. Nobody will know what we're doing. But that's *not* the way it's been. You were in the cafe just now when Adolph came over babbling about Melinda coming in all excited to see this Breck fella but he didn't know why. I tell you, they're onto something. I want out now!"

She hesitated, measuring a corner of the bedspread with her hand.

"My brother was supposed to bring me the money to pay you. I—I won't be able to get it now."

"What do you mean?" he demanded angrily.

"I'll have to get word to him and have him send it in. It'll take a little while."

He hesitated. "How long?"

"Tomorrow afternoon."

"You're sure you'll have it for me by then?"

"Positive."

"If you don't, I'll go to the marshall with the whole story."

Her face turned ashen and her lips quivered. "You wouldn't dare!"

"Wouldn't I? Just try me, Fannie Knox!"

"It's against the law to impersonate someone else. You'll go to prison if you tell anyone what you've done."

He paused, but only for an instant.

"I'll go to Devin. He'll be so glad for the information, he'll not only get me off, he'll give me the $500 besides."

She leaned forward and hissed, "You wouldn't *dare,* you miserable, little, double-crossing worm!"

"Call me what you wish," he said, a mocking grin lifting one corner of his mouth. "I'll wait no longer than tomorrow. Then I'm going to get my ticket and my pay for the job or I'm going over to the other side. Is that clear?"

"Perfectly." Her smile switched on as though she had suddenly touched a match to the wick. "You'll get your money and your ticket in time for the late evening train."

He picked up his hat and put it on.

"Now what are you going to do?"

"I'm going over to the Eagle's Nest for a drink," he informed her. "Then I'm going to find a place where it's safe to spend the night."

"You should stay here, you know. People expect it."

"My dear, I wouldn't trust you with a two-cent piece. I sure wouldn't spend another night here. You might use a knife on me or that little derringer you carry in your purse."

"I feel like it," she snarled, her smiling fa-
cade slipping.

"Don't worry about it. You're not going to
get the chance. I will see you tomorrow." With
that, he lifted his hat to her and strode off.

She muttered a curse and closed the door
behind him. That was the trouble with men. They
weren't cunning, and they didn't have enough
nerve to see a project through. All he had to do
was to sit tight. That stupid Melinda had been
completely taken in. She hadn't suspected a thing.
She was probably staying in Buffalo Gulch because she had a crush on that Breck fellow.

Fannie locked the door once more and went
over to the window where she watched her pseudo-
husband as he crossed the street in the direction
of the saloon. He must have known she would be
at the window. He turned, doffed his hat once
more, and bowed to her. Then he whirled and
marched quickly through the double doors of the
saloon.

Fannie sat down in the rickety straight-backed
chair. Now she would have to get in touch with
her "brother" and tell him about Paul and his cold
feet. He wouldn't like that. He didn't enjoy being
involved in any of the details. He had told her
explicitly that he didn't want to hear from her
until the job was completed.

But this was different. There was Paul to
think about, and Adolph at the cafe, who talked
all the time and said far more than he thought,
and Melinda staying in town. Not only that, there
was the important matter Melinda had come rushing into the Bon Ton to talk to Breck about. Why
couldn't Breck have let Adolph hear what Melinda
had to tell him? If only he had, they could have

gotten the story out of the waiter. Then they would know exactly how serious the situation was.

Breck was in no hurry to leave town. Armenius was a suspicious character. If Breck followed the rig too closely, there was a good chance he would be seen, and that would spoil their chances of learning anything. It was better to let the farmer get an hour or so ahead before he followed.

He left Melinda on the boardwalk and made his way to the hotel, where he talked for a time with Jacobs.

"You want me to go along?" the Pinkerton agent asked.

"Suit yourself."

"If you need me, fine. But I've got my report to Devin to finish. He's a bear for reports."

"I don't see any trouble comin' up I can't handle."

Jacobs rolled the cigar between his teeth. "Don't take any wooden nickels."

John got his horse at the livery stable and stopped at the marshall's office on his way out of town.

"I'd like to go with you, Breck," Corrigan said, "but I've got me a powder keg in that railroad fight that's about to go off any time. I don't dare leave."

"I'll get along."

"Be careful, Breck. You hear? If this thing's part of the railroad trouble, anything can happen. The stakes are big, and there ain't much law either side will pay attention to. They're goin' to do what they can to win."

John stepped into the saddle, and the big lineback dun fiddle-footed in his haste to be away. He was one of those animals that was born to run. But Breck tightened his grip on the reins and held him in. They might have a lot of miles ahead of them before the day and night were over. It would be unwise to waste the stallion's strength when it wasn't needed. More than once Breck had saved his neck by conserving his mount's stamina for the time he would need it desperately.

John went west to a little used side road that led north to the edge of Buffalo Gulch, avoiding the street that went by the Corrigan house. He wasn't taking Melinda along, no matter what, but there was no use in arguing about it if he didn't have to.

The wind was picking up as he trotted his mount to the main road and headed north. The clouds overhead were gone, swept toward the horizon by a sudden summer gale, hot as a campfire's breath. Dust devils curtsied and spun in an erratic two-step across the prairie, only to run out of breath and collapse in formless heaps. Moments later they were replaced by other spiraling cones, lifting up from the flat plains, hesitating as they gathered strength. Then, with the abandon of moths around a flame, they danced wildly across the buffalo grass, sage, and soap weed.

Breck left the main road and turned up the trail toward the settler's place and the K Bar T. Armenius had kept traveling. John could read the marks of the rig's iron tires. Another rider was following on a smaller horse from the looks of the tracks it left—a small, well-shod animal with a powerful stride.

A certain uneasiness crept over Breck. There was only one person he knew who rode a horse like that, but she was back in Buffalo Gulch. She wouldn't have had time to saddle up and ride out ahead of him so quickly that she was nowhere in sight. Or could she? He stood in the stirrups and, shading his eyes with his hand, peered into the distance. He could see faint wisps of dust ahead, but that could be the farmer's wagon. It would be traveling more slowly than a rider, especially with the bony, ill-fed team Armenius owned.

Breck held the dun to an even slower pace, and the dust ahead disappeared. The sun was a fiery ball above the distant scraggly peaks when he reached the ravine he had followed to Armenius's place several days before. Now, however, he was in no hurry. He would wait for darkness before going closer. He was determined not to give that dog any more time to alert the farmer than he had to.

He rode over the lip of the long gulley and dismounted among the trees. Loosening the cinch on the saddle, he put the reins on the ground to keep the dun from wandering off, and sat down against a rough-barked cottonwood. He had scarcely closed his eyes when he heard footsteps in the dry grass.

"There you are," an all-too-familiar voice said, approaching him. "I thought you'd never get here."

He knew her without looking. "You're supposed to be workin' in Fosberg's store."

She stared down at him. "Aren't you surprised?"

"The itch always comes back."

She made a face at him, but his eyes were still closed and he didn't see it. After a moment or two he opened them and squinted at her.

"You'd just as well get on that nag of yours

and get back to town," he said. "This is the end of the line. It's as far as you're going."

"You can't tell me what to do."

His frown deepened. Come to think of it, that was the truth. He wanted to turn her over his knee and spank her, but he couldn't do that either. There was only one thing he could do, and he didn't know if that would work.

"It's either you or me," he said sternly.

"What do you mean?"

"Either you go back to town or I do. And that's final."

"Breck!" She came over and sat across from him. "Listen to me. I've thought this all out. There's only one reason why Fannie Knox and her so-called husband want me to go back to New York."

"Oh? Maybe you're as big a nuisance to them as you've been to me."

She stuck her tongue out at him. "They want to get me out of here because they're lying about finding Cassie. I don't think they even know where she is, and I don't think they want her found. That's why they're trying so hard to get me to go home. They're afraid that I—that we'll find her."

He pushed his hat back on his head and nodded. "You might have something at that."

"If it wasn't for all the things he knew about Cassie and me," she continued, "I'd say that man wasn't her uncle at all, that the *real* Edwin Knox hasn't been found yet."

"Did you ever think he'd have some real good help in Fannie Knox if he wanted to pretend to be Cassie's uncle? She knows a lot about you and your friend."

"But he looked like him, too. That's another

thing that's bothered me. How could he look so much like her uncle?"

"Fannie's an actress," he said, "and she went up to Denver for a spell before she came back and said she'd found her husband."

Melinda's eyes brightened. "That's it! It all fits. She hired an actor to make up like her husband and taught him the things he'd need to know to fool me into thinking he was really Edwin Knox."

"I think you're right, but we don't know why— yet." He got to his feet and, pulling the rifle from the boot on his saddle, glanced about.

"See someone?"

"It just pays to be a bit careful." Satisfied that no one was near, he turned back to the girl.

"What are we going to do now?" she asked.

"*You* are goin' back to Buffalo Gulch."

"And if I don't?"

"I do."

Dismay clouded her features, and she sighed in resignation. "I don't know *why* I ever got you to help me in the first place."

He got to his feet and squinted at the dying embers of the sun. "Well, it's time to go. Which is it? You or me?"

Melinda started for her horse.

"And you be careful!" Breck called after her. "This whole stretch is bein' combed by K Bar T hired guns. I don't think any one of 'em would hurt a woman, but you never can tell."

She paused and turned back. "How do I know which trail to follow?"

"Keep your eyes on the iron tire tracks of the Armenius rig," he said. "He came straight out here. You'll have no trouble followin' it back."

She glanced up slyly. "And how do I do that

when it gets dark?" she asked. "It'll be dark before I get back to the Corrigans', you know."

Concern gleamed in Breck's grim features. He was beaten and he knew it. "I can't have you wanderin' around half the night tryin' to find Buffalo Gulch. But I'm warnin' you, Melinda Grainger. Next time you pull a stunt like this, I'll paddle you!"

"You wouldn't dare."

"For two cents I'd do it right now."

She smiled triumphantly, but not so he could see her.

"Are we going to leave?" she asked quietly.

"Yes, we're goin' to leave!" he snorted. "Get on that horse of yours. And don't talk. Just mount up and ride."

They made their way along the brakes. Breck was in the lead with Melinda close behind. They followed the tree-choked ravine down to the farm and around the buildings. The cowhand reined in and dismounted.

"Here's where we wait," he said, keeping his voice in a hoarse whisper.

She nodded and climbed out of the saddle without his help. "How long?"

" 'Til whoever is comin' gets here." He turned and found another big cottonwood to lean against. "You take first watch. If you hear anyone come up to the house or barn, wake me. But be quiet about it. If they know we're here, we'll never find out who Armenius is workin' for."

She made a face at him and sat down to wait. Darkness stole in silently, merging shadows and blotting out large areas of the grove around them. Night lay its feathery hand upon them, hushing the wind and hiding the home of the owl that called mournfully for his mate. After a time the moon came up, climbing into the sky, its silvery light easing some of the darkness, revealing the lip of the ravine and the yucca-cluttered prairie around the farmer's garden and field of corn.

Finally Breck stirred, opened his eyes, and allowed them to get used to the night.

"It's your turn now," he said at last quietly.

"Are you sure it's all right if I sleep?" she asked, sarcasm dripping from the words.

"It's up to you."

"Are you positive you don't want to take another nap?"

He laughed shortly. "That was for out-foxin' me on bringin' you along."

Her laughter was like music and so loud he warned her with a finger to his lips to be quiet.

She had scarcely gone to sleep when he heard the creaking of saddle leather and the sudden barking of Armenius' dog.

"What's that?" she demanded, raising on one elbow and staring into the night.

He got quietly to his feet. "You stay where you are," he ordered. "And I mean it! One false move, one sound that gets up to that dog or the settler and you'll ruin everything."

"What do you want me to do?" The tone of her voice indicated that this time he did not have to be concerned. She would follow orders.

"Stay with the horses and try to keep 'em quiet if you can."

He moved forward, inching one foot ahead of the other, noiselessly, the way his step-pa had taught him years before. At the edge of the gulch he dropped to his stomach and peered through the darkness at the buildings. There was a saddle bronc and a packhorse in sight, faintly discernible against the blackness of the house with its faint, yellowed lamp shining in one small window.

"I was afraid I wouldn't get back on time," he heard Armenius say loudly. "It took longer to load up than I thought it would. Fosberg had a new clerk, too, so he was able to help me carry the stuff out. But it seemed to take longer anyway."

The other voice was so muffled Breck was unable to make out the words being spoken.

"Well, even if you ain't in no hurry," the farmer continued, "I'm glad I was here when you got here." He paused for half a minute or more. "You weren't followed, were you?"

The lanky cowhand strained to hear the answer to that question, but could not make it out.

"The country's full of gunmen now. But I suppose you already know that, livin' where you do."

The other voice spoke again, and Armenius fell silent. Breck could see at least one shadowy form moving from the spring wagon to the packhorse and back again. Presently the farmer spoke again.

"Well, that's the end of it. Let me know when you need anything else. I'm glad to accommodate you."

The dog barked as the horses started to move, and Armenius spoke sharply to him, ordering him back to the barn.

John stole back to the place where Melinda was waiting with their mounts. "You did a good job," he told her. "Not a sound out of 'em."

"What's going on?" she asked under her breath. "What happened?"

243

"We've struck paydirt! All we have to do is follow those horses and we'll know who Armenius and his wife are helping."

23

They waited until the rider leading the packhorse was some distance ahead. Then they led their horses up the steep slope to the west edge of the ravine.

"You got a jacket along?" he asked abruptly.

"What business is that of yours?"

"Do you or don't you?"

"Yes, I have. Is that all right?"

"Put it on."

"But it's too hot for a jacket."

"Put it on! We don't want whoever's up there to see that white blouse a mile away."

"Oh." She was contrite. "I'm sorry."

She put on the lightweight jacket and mounted her horse. Breck was already in the saddle, waiting impatiently. They rode off single-file.

"We're less apt to be seen this way," he told her.

"Who do you think it is?" Melinda asked.

"I've got a hunch, but we won't know for sure 'til we get there."

Breck thought about moving faster and overtaking the courier before they reached the place he was going to, but decided against it. It was better to follow the horses to their final destination. Then nothing could go wrong.

They followed the rider and packhorse for two hours—into the rough, wooded foothills, across a small stream, and along a butte that reared high in front of them. A few hundred yards ahead, the faint outline of a cabin with a kerosene lamp showing from a small window was discernible.

Breck hesitated. There was no way of knowing whether the cabin was their destination, but it was quite likely that their long search was over. The situation at the moment was quite dangerous for both himself and his companion. The cabin, sitting against the sheer butte wall and surrounded by trees, was in almost complete darkness, while they were bathed in the soft light of the moon. To anyone in the cabin they could be seen from some distance.

"I don't like this," he muttered under his breath. "We're sitting ducks for anybody who's got half an eye."

There was no need for caution now, however. Anybody on guard would already have seen them.

They rode toward the cabin, and were forty feet away when a hoarse voice rang out, "Stop right where you are. One more step and I'll shoot."

Melinda gasped. "I know that voice. It's Cassie's Uncle Edwin!" Before Breck had a chance to respond, she shouted, "Uncle Edwin, it's me—Melinda—Cassie's friend!"

"A likely story."

"But I am! If she's with you, ask her."

"Don't give me that. I'm not so stupid as to believe you. Turn those horses around and get out of here before I change my mind and pull the trigger!"

"I wouldn't do that if I was you," Breck

warned, his powerful voice reverberating through the still night air. "You would be shooting two people who mean you no harm, and you'll hang. Is that what you want?"

"Who are you?" he demanded.

"You don't know me, but I helped stop a holdup on one of your trains a few days ago. This girl came out in Devin's private car to find your niece. She'd hired Pinkerton's to do the job for her, but when two of their best agents were killed she asked me to help. I don't know why I was fool enough to say I would, but here I am."

"You don't expect me to believe that!"

"Don't you know my voice?" Melinda pleaded. "I knew yours."

That stopped him. A long minute of silence followed. Then he whistled two short, piercing blasts. Almost immediately the cabin door opened, allowing a wedge of yellow light to spill out on the ground, silhouetting the figure of a girl.

"You want me, Uncle Edwin?"

Before he could answer, Melinda cried out quickly, "Cassie, don't you know me?"

"Melinda!"

"You must be Melinda," he admitted reluctantly, "but don't try anything. I've still got my rifle on you."

She scarcely heard him. She cracked her mount on the rump with the end of the reins, and he sprang forward. An instant later she leaped off and flew into her friend's arms. They were both laughing and crying at the same time.

A gaunt, tired man came out of the blackness and approached Breck.

"I'm sorry about pulling a gun on you, but you don't know what we've been through the last few weeks."

"We have an idea."

"And what's worse, they're closing in on us. Every day the search gets nearer. I'm beginning to wonder if we're going to be able to last it out."

Breck nodded. "The marshall and I were at the K Bar T a few days ago. That place is filled with gunfighters, and they ain't up there for their health. They've got to be lookin' for you or someone else in these parts."

By this time Knox had regained his composure. His voice steadied, and he became the charming gentleman Melinda had known.

"Let's go in the cabin. Cassie can boil us some coffee if we can get her away from Melinda long enough. You and I need to talk."

"Sounds good to me."

Over steaming cups of coffee Breck told Knox about Fannie and the bogus husband she had produced.

The older man's eyes narrowed. "Sounds just like her," he gritted.

"We couldn't figure out why she'd pull a stunt like that. It didn't make any sense to us."

"It doesn't to me either," he said, "but I can tell you this. She's figured a scheme to get some money out of it, or she wouldn't bother."

The girls were sitting off to one side, their heads together, talking and giggling in the excitement and joy of being together again.

"What I'm wondering," Breck said, "is how long it'll be 'til some of that K Bar T crowd stumble onto this place. They've got some capable men up there—army officers and former sheriffs and marshalls. They know how to track as well as shoot. One of these days they're goin' to come across the tracks in here and it'll be all over."

"That's why I've been so jumpy. Whoever's heading up the search has been taking the range piece by piece and combing it thoroughly. It's laid out like a regular military operation."

"That figures." Breck sipped his coffee before continuing. "Appears to me you'd be smart to move while you've still got the chance."

"I've had the same idea, but where could we go? We can't go into town. They'd know about it before we'd been there an hour. And this is just about the only half-decent hiding place in the whole area. I worked out here with our surveyors for almost two years trying to find a way over the mountains to Leadville. I'm the one who located that pass that's causing all the trouble."

Breck thought for a moment. "I'm not sure," he said, "but I might know of a place where you could hide for a few days."

"It doesn't have to be long. After the stockholder's meeting there won't be any reason for them to try to get rid of us." He set his cup back in the saucer and leaned forward. "Where is this place?" he asked, "and how do you know it'll be safe?"

"The settler who's been bringin' in your supplies could hide you at his farm for a while if he has a mind to. I don't know him, but he appears to be an honorable man. A mite quick-tempered but honorable. He's got himself a good reputation in Buffalo Gulch."

"He was completely trustworthy helping us with supplies." Knox thought for a moment. "It wouldn't hurt to try, I suppose."

They decided to pack up what they could and go back to the Armenius place. If he and his wife wouldn't allow them to stay, they would have to go somewhere else.

In twenty minutes they were ready to leave. They rode to the farmer's place, woke them up, and explained the problem. They glanced at each other and nodded.

"You've been helpin' us with cash money when we needed it somethin' terrible," Armenius said. "And besides, we don't want to see no harm come to you. You and the girl are good people."

"Better keep their horses in the barn," Breck warned, "so the K Bar T men won't see 'em."

"You don't have to worry about that none," the settler retorted firmly. "I have my shotgun, and the woman's tolerable good with a Winchester. There ain't *no* gunfighter stupid enough to face the two of us if we see 'em comin' first and get the drop on 'em."

The actor who was playing the part of Edwin Knox entered the hotel lobby shortly after seven o'clock and started for the stairs.

"Good morning, Mr. Knox," the clerk said curiously. "I didn't see you go out."

"You were dozing a bit, lad," he said genially, "and Mrs. Knox was still asleep, so I went out for my morning constitutional."

That seemed to satisfy him, but he looked at the actor in concern. "You won't tell anybody, will you?" he asked.

"About what?"

"About my—" he swallowed hard, "—about how I closed my eyes for a minute when I wasn't busy. Mr. Anderson—he's the owner—don't like it when I do that. Said I'd lose my job if it happened again." By this time he was pleading. "You won't tell him, will you?"

"I won't say a word to anybody, not even the Missus. It'll be our little secret."

"Thank you, sir. Thank you. Any time I can do anything for you, just let me know."

Fannie was sitting at the window staring across the roof of the store building next to the hotel when footsteps stopped at her door. At the sound of the key turning in the lock, she got to her feet.

"Good morning, my dear," Paul said, smiling broadly. "I trust you slept well."

"What do you care?"

"I don't, really." He closed the door and locked it. "But we must think of our fans, you know. As you say, the show isn't over yet."

He went to the only chair in the room and sat down, ignoring the fact that she was still standing, her jowls quivering with anger.

"By the way, did you write that note to your brother?"

"I told you I would, didn't I?"

"Please?" He held out his hand.

"What's that for?"

"I want to read it, my pretty little apple blossom."

Her cheeks went hot. "You don't trust anybody, do you?"

"Some people maybe, but not you, sweetie-pie." He stepped closer. "The note, please. We're wasting time."

She reached into the bodice of her dress and withdrew an envelope.

"I've already sealed it."

"But we can take care of that little matter, can't we?" He stuck a finger into the corner of the envelope and ripped it open. "Now, let's see what you told your brother."

EDWIN MUST GO BACK TO DENVER IMMEDIATELY. HE WANTS HIS $500 AND TICKET BY TRAIN TIME TODAY. IT IS URGENT THAT HIS DEMANDS BE MET OR WE WILL HAVE SERIOUS PROBLEMS.

SINCERELY,
YOUR LOVING FANNIE

He read the note a second time and bowed slightly, a mocking smile on his lips. "I'm touched by your tenderness toward your sibling, madam."

"Was it all right?" she asked.

"Commendable, darling. Commendable." He started to hand the note back to her, but withdrew his hand before she could take it and stuffed it into his shirt pocket. "I believe it would be better if I were to place this missive in the care of our courier. But tell me, do you honestly think Adolph can be trusted with such a responsibility?"

"Absolutely. He'll do anything I ask him."

"That is no recommendation, but let us take ourselves over to the Bon Ton for breakfast and get our friend on his way. Shall we?"

She stepped back to allow him to go through the door, but he declined. "After you, my dear."

They went to the cafe and took Fannie's favorite table. Adolph was there by the time they were seated. He took their order and listened while Fannie explained about the letter.

"Now, you know where to go, don't you?" Paul asked, handing the waiter the envelope after Fannie gave him detailed directions to find her brother.

"Course I know where to go," the waiter exclaimed. "I've lived in these parts most all my life. Ain't nobody around Buffalo Gulch who knows this country better than I do."

"That's fine. I just wanted to make sure you don't get lost."

"I won't get lost." He put the envelope in his pocket and winked broadly at Fannie, but Paul was sitting where he couldn't see it. "I'll go right away—soon as the breakfast business is over."

"Can't you leave before?" Paul asked. "It's most important."

"It wouldn't be right to leave my job before the breakfast rush is over, but I'll get it done, Mr. Knox. You can count on me. I'll take care of it as good as I do servin' you."

"That's fine, Adolph." The actor lapsed into silence, but while the coffee was being poured he spoke again, as though the thought just came to him. "And, Adolph, there's one other thing."

He scowled at Fannie's companion. "Yeah?"

"Don't say anything to anyone about this little matter, OK?"

"How many times do I have to tell you? I'll take care of it. You can count on me. And nobody won't know nothin' about it, either."

When they finished eating, Paul remained motionless at the table until Fannie opened her purse and extracted two quarters to pay for their meals. Taking the coins, he gave them to Adolph and they went out into the still morning air.

"I'm sorry, Fannie, but I have some matters of importance to attend to. I must leave you now."

Uneasiness crept into her eyes. "What's that supposed to mean?"

"I'll see you later and learn where to meet your brother or his representative to be paid for my services. Until then, adieu."

"The least you can do is to spend your last day in Buffalo Gulch with me. We have appearances to keep up, you know."

"*You* have appearances to keep up. I have my wages to get and my good-byes to say."

"You can't leave me as though we've had a fight. People will talk."

"I'll make a deal with you. After I am paid off, I'll spend time with you. How does that sound?"

She started to reply hotly, but saw the wife of the hotel owner approaching on the way to Fosberg's general store. She smiled graciously and spoke. When the woman was past them, she turned back to the false Mr. Knox and continued in low tones.

"You may have to go with me whether you want to or not. My brother is a careful individual, especially when it comes to money. It is most likely that he won't pay you unless we are together. He's never met you, you know."

"We can take care of that, my lovely. Don't worry your pretty little head about it."

He left her as quickly as possible, went to the livery barn, and rented a horse and buggy. He should have had a saddle horse for what he was up to, but he was more comfortable with a rig. They didn't teach horseback riding on the stages of Chicago and New York.

He drove out of town as though his destination was south, turned east, and made his way to the edge of town before turning back to make his way west and north by a circuitous route. Behind a dilapidated vacant house and barn he waited. It wasn't long until Adolph rode by at a brisk gallop, arms flapping as he bounced in the saddle. The actor let him get some distance ahead, then followed him several miles, until he was certain he was obeying instructions. Then, a smile on his face, he turned and drove back to town. Shortly before noon he went back to the hotel and found Fannie Knox pacing impatiently in the small, plainly furnished room. Her makeup was streaked, and her hair was slightly askew.

"I was beginning to wonder if you had changed your mind and gone off without your blood money," she said acidly.

"That would have made you happy, wouldn't it?" He sat down and crossed his legs. "I'm afraid I can't accommodate you in that regard. What have you heard from your brother? Or do I go to Devin and his associates with the whole ugly little story?"

Her cheeks flushed. "For your information, Adolph was just here. The dear boy almost missed getting back to work for noon, and that could have cost him his job." She was about to go on, but stopped significantly. "I suppose you'll want to read the note."

"Tell me what it says. I'll tell you whether I want to see it or not."

"My brother said that you and I should hire a rig and go for a picnic in the willows down on the river. He'll be waiting for us there and pay you what you have coming."

Greed lighted his eyes. "You know, Fannie, darling, I've never had $500 at one time in my whole life. This makes me feel like a millionaire."

"Don't forget, you've still got your part of the bargain to finish."

"Like what?" he asked suspiciously.

"Like pretending to be my loving husband until train time."

"With $500 in my pocket, even *that* will be palatable."

She glared darkly at him, but he didn't notice. He pulled out the big gold watch he carried, a gift from a former lady admirer, and noted the time.

"We should get our lunch packed and the carriage rented. We don't want to keep your loving brother waiting."

She examined herself in the mirror. "My hair's a mess, and so is my makeup. Go get the rig and stop at the Bon Ton for our lunch. I'm sure Adolph will find a basket for it. By the time you get back here I'll be ready."

He set the black bowler on his head at a jaunty angle, strutted down the stairs and out the hotel door whistling a gay tune from a musical he had had a small part in a long time before. For a while it looked as though the entire affair had gone sour, but he had gotten it straightened out easily enough.

He paused on the boardwalk, debating whether he had time enough to stop at the Eagle's Nest for a drink or two, but decided against it. There was time enough for that after he got the money. He walked briskly toward the cafe. He probably had made a mistake in asking only for the $500 they had agreed on previously. As easily as Fannie and her brother accepted his demand, he could have gotten twice that.

He stopped and glanced at his watch. What was to prevent him from getting the $500 and demanding another $500 or $1,000? By this time he realized he was playing in a big-stakes game. There was no use in settling for pennies and nickels when there were dollars to be had for the taking. He didn't quite know how he would manage it, but he would, and soon.

He stopped at the Bon Ton where he told a surly, uncooperative Adolph what he wanted and that he would be back in a little while to pick it up. From there he went to the livery stable, rented a rig for the afternoon, and picked up the picnic lunch. Fannie was waiting for him in the lobby. She came out, holding her parasol in one hand and a purse in the other.

"Oh, darling," she gushed, "I'm so glad you suggested a picnic. It's such a lovely day." She stood beside the buggy until he came around to her side and helped her in. "Thank you, Edwin." She was talking to him, but her words were spoken loudly enough for the loafers in front of the saloon across the street to hear everything she said. "You *are* the gentleman."

"Don't push it, my dear," he gritted softly before turning to go back to his side of the rig.

"I only wish you didn't have to go back to Denver tonight."

"You know how it is. Business calls."

"I know, but it seems that we're just getting acquainted again." She noted with satisfaction that the eyes of the men along the street were upon her as she and her companion drove south toward the river.

They went down to the willows along the stream to the place where Fannie said they were to wait for her brother. Paul got out, tied a rein to the hitching weight, and took the picnic basket from behind the seat.

"Aren't you going to help me down?"

"You can get down on your own or stay there—it's all the same to me."

She gathered her skirts and got out of the buggy angrily.

The gelding in harness raised his head, ears twitching as he caught scent of another horse or man. From a dense willow thicket fifty yards away a horse neighed. Paul straightened, staring in that direction. He heard a twig snap.

"Somebody's over there."

Fannie's cheeks paled, and she opened her purse hurriedly.

"Somebody's over there!" he repeated. "You set me up, Fannie! You—"

She whipped the derringer from her purse and aimed it at him. "You think I don't know what's going on in that slimy little mind of yours? You wouldn't be satisfied with $500 or $1,000 or $2,000. You would keep bleeding us for as long as you could."

He suddenly realized that she was about to pull the trigger and lunged forward, hitting the derringer with his hand as she fired. As they struggled for the weapon, a rifle shot rang out. The bullet hit Fannie and she jerked violently, blood staining her dress. She staggered backwards, clutching at her wound, then she collapsed.

"Fannie!" Paul shouted, kneeling over her. "Fannie!"

Her lips parted. "Help me," she moaned, then fainted.

24

Trembling, Paul picked Fannie up, laid her in the buggy, and drove to town, whipping the horse to utmost speed. The bowler hat was whipped off the frantic driver's head and rolled across the prairie to lodge against a clump of sagebrush. Sweat soaked his face and shirt, and his heart hammered fiercely against his chest.

Fannie Knox was still alive, but she was bleeding profusely. She groaned weakly, and he felt her stir beside him. The blood soaked his shirt and trousers where she lay against him.

The gelding was hurtling the buggy over the rough terrain at top speed, but Paul did not stop flailing the hard-running animal. He kept whipping him until the rig careened into town and dashed up the street to the doctor's office. Everyone in town seemed to be outside, drawn by the noises of the buggy and the hard-pounding feet of the horse. Paul jerked the gelding to a halt in front of the doctor's office and scrambled to the ground.

"Get doc quick!" he shouted.

He gathered Fannie into his arms and started for the office. The dyspeptic old doctor met him at the door.

"What are you standin' out there for? Get her in here and put her on the table."

Paul did as he was told.

The doctor set to work hurriedly, cutting away her clothes to expose the ugly wound.

"What happened?" he asked as he worked.

Paul didn't answer him.

By this time a crowd had gathered in front of the doctor's office. They were milling about muttering darkly to each other when Marshall Corrigan strode up.

"What's goin' on here?" he demanded crisply.

"That Knox fellow," someone said, "he shot his wife."

"Are you sure about that?"

"What do you think? We seen him bring her in. He shot her, all right. You could see that in his face."

"We ought to string him up," somebody else put in. "We don't hold with treatin' decent women that way. They might get away with that back in New York, but not out here."

"I don't want to hear any talk like that," Corrigan said sternly. "Now you men move on. If you have business, get to taking care of it. If not, move on anyway. If Knox killed his wife, we'll arrest him and have a trial to decide if he hangs or not."

"A trial's too good for him."

Corrigan pushed through the crowd to the spokesman. "Joe Hodges, we've heard enough from you. Go home and stay there. I see you downtown again and I'm runnin' you in. Understand?"

Hodges glared at the marshall, but left the crowd and plodded down the boardwalk muttering to himself.

The marshall then directed his attention to

the others. "All right, you men, go about your business. I'm goin' in the doc's office. Anybody who's here when I come out is goin' to jail. And that's a promise!"

He went into the office.

"How is she?"

The doctor looked up. "It's goin' to be a long haul, marshall," he said. "She caught a bullet in the chest. A bad one."

For the first time Hank seemed to notice Paul sitting in stoney silence across the room, his features pasty and colorless.

"Want to tell me about it?"

"I didn't do it!" the actor muttered. "She had the gun and was goin' to pull the trigger. I tried to get it from her, but—" He shuddered violently.

"Suppose you start at the beginning and tell me exactly what happened."

"I don't know, marshall, and that's the truth!"

"Listen, mister." Hank reached down, grabbed him by the collar, and hoisted him to his feet. "There's a bunch of mighty angry men out there talkin' about hangin' you. And they mean it. If I don't get some straight answers out of you so I can cool 'em down some, they'll get you. It might take a little time, but they'll get you. Sooner or later they'll put a rope around your neck or a bullet in your belly. So if you've got anything to say that'll help me convince 'em you don't deserve killing, you'd better start talking."

"You've got to protect me, marshall! I didn't shoot her!" He shuddered. "I've never fired a gun in my whole life. This is what happened."

He told how she lured him to the river and drew the derringer on him. "I—I knew she was goin' to shoot me so I—I jumped for the gun and hit it as she fired. The next thing I knew she was lying on the ground with blood all over her."

"What made her want to kill you?" Corrigan persisted. "Most women aren't that anxious to get rid of their men."

"I—I don't know," he stammered, grasping the marshall by the arm. "I swear it. She was nice as you please to me in town, but when we got out to the river she was like a tiger. Changed completely. Pulled that little gun out of her purse and—" The words trailed away.

"That's goin' to be hard to sell, Knox. I don't think that bunch out there is goin' to believe you."

"Take me with you," he pleaded. "Put me in jail. Don't let them get me."

Hank frowned. "That might be best at that. I don't believe all of what you've told me just now, but I don't hold with hangin' either. Not unless it's done proper, with a judge and a fair trial."

He turned back to the doctor, but before he could speak Jacobs came in.

"Who invited you?" the doctor growled.

"Nobody. I came on my own."

"Then go out the same way. Can't you see I'm busy?"

"I think Jacobs is here to see me, doc," Hank broke in.

The Pinkerton man nodded. "It's gettin' ugly out there, Hank."

Jacobs glanced at the woman and the doctor who was working over her. "Is she goin' to make it?"

"I doubt it," he said bluntly. "That slug went through her lung and must have hit her heart. She's still bleeding and I can't get it stopped. She keeps this up, she'll bleed to death."

"No derringer did that," Jacobs said firmly.

"Right," the marshall agreed. "She was shot by a .44 unless I miss my guess."

"That can't be," the actor blurted. "The little gun was in her purse. It wasn't as big as my hand."

Hank motioned him to follow. "Come on. I'll take you to jail."

"Figure you'll need any help?" Jacobs asked.

"Right now I need all the help I can get. I'd be obliged if you'd come with me."

Jacobs paused long enough to bite the end off a cigar and light it. Then, pulling a .38 from his shoulder holster, he took his place on one side of Paul.

The men out front had dispersed, but there was a small crowd on the walk in front of the Eagle's Nest and several others were staring sullenly from Fosberg's General Store.

"Give him to us," a drunken cowhand shouted. "There ain't no need of wastin' good grub on no woman killer."

Corrigan acted as though he hadn't even heard. They took the actor along the boardwalk past the store, the Wells Fargo office, and Sam Richards' office. The lawyer saw them and ran out the door.

"Marshall! Marshall! I must talk to you."

Hank stopped and waited.

"What are you doing with my client?" he demanded, hurrying up to the trio on the walk.

"Is this guy one of yours?"

"He certainly is."

"Well, if I don't get him in jail and keep him there, you're goin' to lose one client before dark. His wife's in Doc's office dyin' of a gunshot wound, and the guys along the street are thirstin' for blood. *His* blood."

"Then by all means put him in jail. His life *must* be safeguarded." Richards touched the actor reassuringly on the arm. "Everything will be all right, my good man. I'll be along to see you in a few minutes. That will be agreeable with you, won't it, marshall?"

He nodded.

Corrigan put Paul in a cell alone and locked the door behind him.

"Thanks, Jacobs," he said to the Pinkerton man as he came back to look out the window at the still muttering men outside.

"Seen Breck the last hour or so?" Jacobs asked.

Hank frowned. "Nope, but if you run across him, tell him to come over here pronto. Maybe you'd better come back, too."

Jacobs removed the cigar from his mouth and spat, hitting the spittoon with a wad of tobacco chewed from the end of his cigar. "It's that bad?"

"It's that bad. Believe me."

The Pinkerton man waddled away from the jail, still chewing on his cigar. He hadn't been gone more than five minutes when Sam Richards showed up at the marshall's office and asked to see his client.

"Don't take no longer in there than you have to, Sam," Hank said. "This thing's gettin' serious. We don't know what's goin' to happen."

He opened the cell door and locked the lawyer in with his client.

"How did you get to be my lawyer?" Paul demanded. "The only time I saw you was when we signed those papers."

"You're in jail. That means you do need a lawyer, doesn't it?"

"I reckon I do, but I don't want to get out of here right now. I'm happy right where I am."

"But you do want to get out of this mess, don't you?"

"That's a stupid question."

"Sign another set of these proxy papers and I'll see that you go free."

Paul's dark eyes narrowed.

"Like I said, I ain't wantin' to be free 'til those crazy guys are off my back."

"When I say free, I mean free and *safe!*"

Paul turned that over in his mind. "How come you want to get another set of those papers? What's that to you?"

"Those you signed were made out to your wife and I understand that she's dying. So we need more."

"Why?"

"That's all you need to know."

"You'll give me your word that you'll get me out of here and back in Denver safe?"

"Right."

"Make them out. I'll sign them."

"I thought you would, so I took the liberty of writing them up." He took the papers from his coat pocket. "Just sign here."

"They aren't made out to anyone."

"I know. I'll fill them in later."

Paul wrote the name Edwin Knox quickly.

Richards got to his feet. "Fine. You just stay right here until I can work things out to get you safely out of this part of the territory."

Breck and Jacobs met in the hotel, talked briefly, and went down to the Bon Ton for a cup of coffee before making their way to the marshall's office and the jail. Adolph's gaunt features were sadder than they had ever seen him.

"You heard what happened, I reckon?" he asked, almost tearfully.

They both nodded.

"That Edwin Knox ought to be hung. Gettin' her killed that way when she came so far just to find him. Hangin's too good for him. They ought to put a rope around his feet and drag him until he's dead."

"Maybe he didn't do it, Adolph," Breck said quietly.

"Don't make no difference." He scrubbed at his eyes with the back of his hand. "It was his fault. 'Twouldn't have happened if it hadn't been for him. Killin's too good for him."

"How about some coffee?"

Adolph went to the kitchen and came back with two big cups to set before them.

"I got to tell you something," he said. "I've waited on lots of people in my day. Women and girls as well as men. And they treated me like scum. Leastwise the women did. But not that Mrs. Knox. She was a real lady. She treated me nice. She never made fun of me with her eyes. The others didn't think I knowed what they was doin' when they laughed at me, but I did. Knew it as well as I know what I'm sayin' to you right now. She was a *real* lady. It just about tears me up to think about what he done to her." With that Adolph turned and hurried back to the kitchen.

The two men finished their coffee and left the cafe.

"What's that gal of yours doin' today?" Jacobs asked Breck, smiling slightly.

"She ain't my gal," Breck reminded him. "And

I don't know *what* she's doing. I don't keep track of her."

"You ought to. She keeps track of you." He glanced to one side, significantly.

Breck followed Jacobs' glance and saw Melinda hurrying towards them.

"Is it true?" she demanded as she reached Breck.

"Is what true?"

"About Fannie Knox?"

"She's still alive, if that's what you're askin', but it don't look too good for her."

"Where's her—her *husband?*"

"They've got him in jail now," they told her.

"Do they think he did it?"

"A lot of men do. He wouldn't be safe five minutes if they turned him loose."

"I—I was wanting to ride out in the country and thought I—I'd better see if it would do any harm."

"I'm afraid it would," Breck said. "Somebody might suspect you know somethin' and follow you."

"Then I'll wait." She started away but turned back, her eyes starry. "I haven't thanked you for—for finding Cassie for me," she said.

"That's all right," he said, embarrassment coloring his cheeks. "Forget it."

"I can't do that. If it hadn't been for you I—I wouldn't have found her."

"Just forget it," he retorted. "It's over and done with."

Standing on her tiptoes she kissed him lightly on the lips and fled, hurrying toward the Corrigan house.

"Yes, sir," Jacobs said, eyeing him narrowly,

"you got her broke, John. She's gentle as a kitten."

"Shut up, you fat galoot."

Jacobs was still laughing when they reached the jail.

Corrigan quickly joined them in his office. "I'm glad you're here. I've been gettin' reports from around town. The talk's gettin' uglier. And Fannie Knox is gettin' weaker. Stay here for awhile and spell me. I'm goin' to make the rounds and see what's cooking."

When Hank was gone, the actor called Breck to his cell. "You aren't going to let them get me away from you. You'll protect me, won't you?"

"Should we?" he asked, contempt edging his voice.

"I didn't kill her! I swear it!"

"Then who did?"

"If I knew, I'd tell you!"

The lanky cowhand thought about that. He had to admit that Paul was right. He would have nothing to gain by keeping the name of Fannie's killer to himself.

Hank Corrigan was away longer than Breck and Jacobs thought he would be. The sun disappeared behind the mountains and darkness crept over the tense main street and still there was no sign of the marshall.

"I don't like it," Jacobs said, fingering the shotgun in his hands. "I don't like it at all."

It had grown quiet outside—too quiet for a rough and ready town like Buffalo Gulch.

Breck went out front and stared up the wide street. In the growing darkness he could see a crowd of men marching toward the jail. The leader had a rope with a noose tied in it. The others were carrying rifles, revolvers, or clubs.

"Oh, oh," Breck said softly, "here they come."

"Ready?" Jacobs whispered.

"As ready as I'll ever be."

In silence they waited until the mob was thirty feet from the building.

"That's close enough," Breck rasped. "Take another step and I'll blow you apart."

They stopped, confused by the unexpected opposition.

"Who are you?"

"The new deputy, John Breckenridge!"

"Breckenridge?" Several men fell back involuntarily at the mention of his name.

"Who's Breckenridge?" somebody sneered. "Get out of the way, and you won't get hurt. We've come for that prisoner of yours."

"I'll tell you who Breckenridge is," a grizzled old prospector broke in loudly. "He's just about the fastest gun in these parts—or anywhere. And he's got ice in his veins. You can be stupid enough to face him if you want to, but not me. I'm goin' home." He turned and separated himself from the mob. Several others did likewise.

"That's good advice for all of you," Jacobs said. "Go on back where you came from, and nobody will get hurt."

But some of the younger men who knew nothing of Breck's reputation were unpersuaded. "Move aside. We're takin' that wife killer."

"She was still alive the last we heard."

"Well, she ain't now. She's dead. And he killed her. Come on, men, let's get him."

"Go ahead," Breck said to the self-styled spokesman coldly. "Some might get through, but not you. You'll have a hole where your belly ought to be. Now get out of here before you do somethin' you'll be sorry for."

The man stepped back, then turned to talk to the men around him. For a moment Breck thought they'd won, but then the men in the front turned back to the jailhouse and they started forward.

"Get ready, Jacobs," Breck whispered grimly. "Looks like this trouble just isn't gonna die down quietly."

25

As the mob drew closer, Breck and Jacobs searched the faces of the front row of men, trying to pick out the leaders, those the others would look to for making the decision to launch the assault or back off.

Breck chose his target and brought his Winchester to bear on him. Jacobs did the same. It seemed certain that the mob would storm the jail. Most of those men had been in the saloons since the actor brought Fannie Knox into town, fortifying their courage and indignation with cheap whiskey.

At that instant Hank Corrigan rode up. He came from behind the building on his big bay gelding, a gun in his hand. He spoke softly to Breck and Jacobs so they would know he was at their sides and directed his attention to the mob.

"I told you men to go home," he said coldly. "And I meant it."

"We want Knox," the spokesman shouted. A dozen others echoed the cry.

Corrigan fired over their heads, and a breathless hush settled over the unruly mob.

"The next one won't be in the air," he promised. "I want you men to listen to me and listen good. I told you I'd check this out to see if Knox was tellin' the truth."

"We don't believe nothin' he says."

"I ain't askin' you to believe him. I'm askin' you to believe me. I went out to where the shootin' happened. I found Fannie Knox's purse and the derringer with a cartridge in one barrel and an empty casing in the other. The empty chamber smelled of smoke, so it had been fired recent-like, but there was no sign of a heavy rifle."

"What's that got to do with it?"

"Everything. Mrs. Knox wasn't shot by a derringer. If you don't believe me, ask doc. Neither one of us has ever lied to you that I know of. Here's the slug that doc got out of her." He tossed it to Joe Hodges, who caught it deftly. "Take a look for yourself."

"It's a forty-four, all right," he admitted reluctantly.

"That don't prove nothing," somebody else said. "He could have stashed the gun before he came into town."

"Now wait a minute! You saw him racin' in here like Satan himself was after him. He wasn't thinkin' about nothin' but gettin' her to the doc. And that's the pure truth."

Some were still unwilling to believe that the man in jail hadn't been the killer, and they grumbled to each other in low tones. But when the leaders had decided and backed off, the others did the same.

"Now go home," Corrigan shouted after them. "I don't want to have to lock you up."

When the crowd had dispersed, Paul was ready to be released.

"They know now that I'm not guilty," he said, "so there's no use in keeping me here."

"Maybe you're right," Corrigan told him, "and

272

maybe not. They're gone now, and I hope they don't try again, but when they get to talkin' over a bottle of rot-gut they can make themselves believe the sun comes up in the west. We might have real trouble before morning."

"I figure you just better stay here 'til the train from Denver comes in tomorrow night. Then I'll take you to the depot, buy you a ticket, and put you on it."

Breck and Jacobs agreed. They had both seen lynching mobs and knew how little it took to set them off.

"Want us to stay around in case there's trouble?" the cowhand asked when they were back in the office.

"I'd be obliged. Why don't you go with me to get somethin' to eat," Corrigan said. "Then we can watch things while Jacobs goes. I don't reckon there's goin' to be trouble for a while."

They took a quick look around the jail and started for the cafe.

"If you hear a commotion up this way," the Pinkerton agent said, "come running."

They found a table along the wall in the Bon Ton and sat down with their backs to it. They could look out and see a wide expanse of street in case there was trouble.

Adolph came over to them as quickly as usual, but his eyes were bloodshot and he reeked of whiskey.

"What do you want?" he demanded, his lips twisted into a surly scowl.

"I've never seen you drinking on the job before," the marshall told him quietly.

"Why shouldn't I?" he blurted. "The best friend I had in the whole wide world was killed this afternoon." He glared at Hank. "Why did you do it, Mr. Corrigan?"

"Do what?"

"Keep us from stringin' up Knox! He don't deserve to live."

"We don't know that. Fact is, the evidence we've got points the other way—that he ain't guilty."

"Evidence!" the waiter exploded.

"If he's guilty he'll be hanged. But he has a right to a fair trial."

"That wife of his didn't get a trial. He just shot her and she was dead. Like that!" Adolph's lips quivered. "What are you goin' to have?"

They ordered steaks, and he fled to the kitchen, tears trembling on his eyelids.

"Adolph's takin' it mighty hard," Breck observed.

"She treated him good," Corrigan remarked, "and that's more than you can say about most people in this town. Somebody's always makin' fun of Adolph or playin' mean practical jokes on him. I try to keep an eye on things and stop it when it gets too bad, but I can't be in here all the time."

Adolph brought their coffee and slammed it on the table before them.

"You should have let us hang him, marshall," he muttered. "To tell you the truth, even that's too good for him."

With that he stormed away, leaving them alone. Only then did Corrigan haul a couple of cartridges from his pocket and hand them to Breck.

"Ever see any shells like these?"

The tall cowhand shook his head. "Nope. Not with those long casings and blunt noses."

"These're the same cartridges as killed Hunter. They fit that Swiss Vetterli I found in the lumber pile. Tried 'em a little while ago and they fit perfect."

"Where did you get 'em?"

"Same place I got this." He thrust a torn scrap of paper across to his companion. Breck read it aloud.

"Asa Hunter. Five feet eight, medium build. Well-dressed—gray suit, black tie. Uses shoulder holsters. Top Pinkerton agent."

"Where did you get 'em?"

"From Fannie Knox's purse."

Breck's eyes narrowed. "You mean she's the one who murdered Hunter?"

"She's got to be. You won't find cartridges like these any place in the territory except in the magazine of that gun."

"Then this fake Edwin Knox must be tellin' the truth about her tryin' to kill him."

"It sure seems that way."

"But why?"

"The way I figure it," the marshall said, taking a drink of his coffee, "she was in this railroad mess up to her pretty little ears."

Outside the cafe Sam Richards lurked in the shadows. He planned to meet the man he was waiting for over a cup of coffee in the cafe—but not with the marshall and John Breck inside. When the slight, well-dressed rider came up the street, Richards went to meet him, whispered in his ear, and motioned across the street in the direction of his office. The stranger rode around the small building to the back, dismounted, and tied his horse to a scraggly cottonwood, then waited for Richards to come through the building and let him in the back door.

"Good to see you, Ian," the lawyer said, offering his hand. "I've been waiting."

"I couldn't get away until my son Charles got Nester out of the way. It took longer than we planned. I'm afraid he's suspicious."

"We've got problems," Richards blurted.

"Can't we have a little light?"

"It's best nobody knows we're here. Like I say, we've got problems. That actor's still alive."

Snyder swore. "Didn't Fannie get him?"

"The fool she got to do the killing missed him and killed her instead."

"I told her to be careful about who she hired. She should have done it herself. She did a good job with Hunter."

"She was your sister?" Richards asked, curious that Ian Snyder showed so little emotion at the death of a close relative.

"That's what she told people. Thought it looked better that way. Let's say we were friends with a common purpose."

"We've got to get rid of this guy Corrigan's holding in jail. And we've got to do it before he talks. He's beginning to get suspicious. He could bring our scheme down around our ears."

"That's not our only problem. We've got the real Edwin Knox to get rid of so you can vote his proxy at the stockholder's meeting."

Richards nodded. "But there's the difficulty of finding him and that niece of his! He must be clever, hiding the two of them that way."

"Oh, we know where he is now," Snyder said, allowing himself a bleak smile, though it was too dark for his companion to see it. "He's over at that settler's. The boys tracked him there and are on their way to take care of both of them."

Richards was concerned. "I hope they do a neat job of it."

"They will."

"And that they keep me out of it."

Snyder laughed. "If this town finds out about you, Richards, it won't be the fellow in jail who'll get strung up."

"When will you learn how it went?" Richards asked, ignoring Snyder's caustic remark.

"When I get back to the K Bar T. I'll send Charles to tell you. He's the only other one up there who knows what's going on for sure."

"Excellent. Now, don't let anyone see you going out of town."

"Don't worry. I think as much of my neck as you do of yours."

Richards let Snyder out the door and watched until he mounted and rode out of sight, picking his way along the dark path. Then he went outside himself and locked the door behind him.

As soon as the marshall and Breck got back to the jail, Jacobs went to eat. The night was quiet save for the sounds of player pianos echoing in the still air. The moon came up, stealing silently through the cloudless sky and washing the town with soft, shadowless light that revealed the buildings and trees and hitching posts with horses fixed to them in a long line.

Breck walked slowly about the jailhouse, his rifle cradled in his arms. All was quiet, and there was nothing out of the ordinary in sight.

"Look all right?" Corrigan asked.

He nodded.

"I don't know why, but I've got an uneasy feeling that the trouble ain't over yet."

Breck felt the same, but he did not voice his concern. They would soon know if the mob would try their hand at taking the prisoner again. Jacobs came back presently, chewing on his cigar. He selected a double-barreled shotgun from the rack in the marshall's office and went out to stand guard.

"I don't like it," he told his companions. "I don't like it at all."

Before either John or Hank could reply, they heard a rig rattling noisily down Main Street, accompanied by the hammering of hooves on the hard ground. It approached the jail and whirled into the lot behind the building. The driver jumped out. It was Armenius.

"Marshall," he cried, "you've got to help us!"

His wife leaped off the wagon and pulled back the heavy canvas that covered the box. Edwin Knox and Cassie climbed stiffly to the ground.

"What is it, Armenius?" Hank demanded. "What happened?"

"Two men came sneakin' around the place. They seen Edwin and Cassie. I tried to stop 'em. I tried hard." His voice was trembling so, he could not go on.

"Jake killed one of 'em," his wife said loyally, "and filled the other's backside full of buckshot, but he got away."

By this time Armenius had regained his composure. "He took off in the direction of that ranch— the K Bar T. So we figured we had to get out of there or they'd kill us all."

By this time Melinda reached them, dashing across the field from the Corrigan house, asking

Cassie what had happened to cause them to leave the farm buildings.

"What do we do now?" Armenius wanted to know.

"We'd better get you back to the house," Hank said. "It'll be safer for you there than it would be here."

Before they could move, Breck saw a horse and rider some distance away, edging closer to the jail. He saw other riders too, both to the left and the right, moving toward the jailhouse, their rifles out of the boots and across the saddle horns in front of them.

"We're havin' company, Hank," he whispered hoarsely.

"There ain't time to get you over to the house," the marshall said. "Get inside. Quick!"

They ran for the front door.

Edwin Knox got a rifle from the rack behind Corrigan's desk, and Armenius checked the shells in his shotgun. Hank got Breck and the others inside as well, distributing the men to the windows with orders to hold their fire until he gave the word. "We've got plenty of ammunition if we're careful and don't waste it."

Breck waited, a deadly calm settling over him. He rested his Winchester on the windowsill and sighted down the barrel. A certain melancholy gripped him, the feeling that always came when he was about to use his gun again. Would the time *ever* come when he could put it away and know he would never again have to pick it up?

The approaching gunmen made no attempt to be quiet. There was no need. They soon had the jail surrounded and no one could escape.

"All right, Corrigan," a rough voice called.

"Give us Knox, and we won't cause you and your deputies any trouble."

"Come after him, Morgan."

"You *know* he killed his wife."

Breck, who had been watching the rear, saw a dark figure glide stealthily between the barn and the neighbor's board fence not more than fifty yards from the jail. Whoever it was carried something in his hand. Instantly John discerned Morgan's plan: the talk was to attract their attention while someone crept close enough to douse the rear wall with kerosene and touch a match to it. That would panic those inside and drive them out the doors and windows. Morgan was counting on the fire to distract the defenders just enough to give his gunfighters the edge they wanted.

Breck aimed at the can the fellow was carrying and squeezed the trigger. There was a burst of flame and screams of terror as the fire ignited the clothes of the hapless individual. The fight was on.

Morgan threw himself off his mount and scrambled for cover; his men on horseback did the same. The hired gun at the leader's right jerked violently and collapsed, staining the ground a dirty brown as the blood gushed from his side. Jacobs crouched at the window and fired. An attacker cursed and grasped his shoulder.

Armenius found a target and opened fire. The first shot went wild, but the second found its mark, slamming a pattern of shot into one man's legs at forty yards. The man dropped his own weapon and writhed on the ground, hands grasping at the ugly wound below the knees.

Edwin Knox was at a window beside Breck, firing carefully. It was obvious that he knew what he was doing. He found a target, held the Winchester steady, and squeezed the trigger expertly.

By this time, the gunmen who were alive and unwounded had retreated behind nearby buildings. One crouched in back of an old buggy that belonged to one of the town's spinsters. Another lay behind the wooden watering trough.

But that didn't mean they were defeated. They were shrewd, cunning men, in spite of the fact that they much preferred to follow the course of least risk in carrying out their nefarious responsibilities. If the situation demanded it, they could be deadly in close quarters, especially when they were fighting for their lives.

They continued to fire, laying down a deadly barrage. The wife of Jake Armenius let out a faint cry as a bullet seared her arm, and the actor, crouching in his cell, caught a bullet in the leg. He cried out loudly for help.

Melinda got the key from Corrigan and went in to take care of him while Cassie cleansed the woman's wound and wrapped it with a piece torn from her own white petticoat.

Breck kept a sharp eye for a man with another can of kerosene. He doubted that Morgan would give up the plan just because it had failed the first time. He saw a shadowy figure dart from behind the fence and start for the barn a little farther from the jail. That didn't seem to make sense, but he shot and the man dropped. A big hat rolled a dozen feet toward the barn, and the fellow cried out in agony.

Two more gunfighters were dropped, and then Morgan took a bullet in the abdomen. Uncertainty gripped the remnant of gunmen. Their leader was gone, and men they had lived with for days and weeks were dead or wounded. Nobody seemed to know what to do or to have the stomach for doing it. The shooting stopped, at least momentarily, and silence reigned.

The group in the building waited tensely.

"What do you think, Breck?" Hank asked.

"They may feel they've had it. Men like these are practical. If the odds are against them, they'll quit so they can live to fight another day."

Five minutes passed, then ten. Melinda and Cassie were talking in low tones, and the false Edwin Knox began to look relieved.

"Think they've given up?" he asked the marshall.

"Something's happened." Corrigan turned to Jacobs and Armenius. "Cover me."

"You can count on us," Armenius murmured.

Hank went out the door and shouted, "All right, drop your weapons and put up your hands."

There was no movement or sound.

He repeated the order.

"I don't think there's anybody there," Armenius said between gritted teeth.

Corrigan moved stealthily forward, a step at a time. His backup men followed, their guns at the ready. At Morgan's body, the marshall stopped and looked down. The man was already dead.

Corrigan didn't need to look any further to know that any of the others who hadn't been badly wounded or killed were gone. The battle was over, for now.

26

Breck stood alone several feet from the building. He had expected the townspeople to flock in, eager to see what happened. But for a time no one came. They were probably waiting as cautiously as those in the jail had been, wanting to be certain the gunfight was over before exposing themselves. He moved forward tensely, his Colt in his hand, straining to see into the semidarkness of the moonlit night.

Someone was lying some distance behind the jail, sprawled grotesquely on the ground. Breck saw the remnants of the kerosene can lying twenty feet away. As he stared, the man moved and Breck heard a faint groan. Cautiously he moved forward, the hammer on his hog-iron cocked and ready to fire if the groaning proved to be a ruse to get him to lower his guard.

As he drew nearer, he saw that there was nothing to fear from the wounded man. He was burned along one side where the exploding can had thrown fire on him, and the bullet had left a crimson stain just below his ribs.

The wound was bleeding profusely.

Then he recognized the man who was lying there.

"Adolph!"

The wounded man opened his eyes and with difficulty focused them on Breck.

"I couldn't do nothin' right," he muttered, remorse clouding his pain-filled eyes. "She was the only friend I ever had, and I couldn't even help her when she needed me. I couldn't do nothin' to make things easier for her."

Breck knelt on one knee beside the dying man. "What do you mean?"

He paused as though refusing to speak, then shook his head and struggled to get out the words.

"It don't matter now," he said, the hurt in his heart rushing back. "I was the one who did it! I killed her! That husband of hers was treatin' her so bad she couldn't stand it. So I said I'd take care of him for her, but I didn't. I bungled that, same as I bungled everything else. They started fighting, and I aimed at him, but didn't hit him. I hit her and killed her!" He started to cry again. The sobbing choked off, he shuddered violently, and the life ebbed from his body.

Breck stared down at him, not even hearing the marshall approach.

"Adolph was in on it," Corrigan exclaimed. "I wouldn't have believed it."

"Neither would I."

"But why would he get involved? He didn't have a mean bone in his body."

Breck got to his feet slowly. "He wasn't with the rest of them. He was out to finish the job he tried to do this afternoon. He died because a woman who wasn't worth the tip of his little finger was nice to him and tried to use him."

Back in the jail, Edwin Knox approached Corrigan. "We want to thank you, marshall. You saved our lives."

"Thank Breck and Melinda. They learned where you were and got you out of that cabin—and just in time, the way I understand it."

"We owe a lot to all of you," Cassie broke in.

The color flared into Breck's cheeks.

By this time the townspeople had concluded that the gun battle was over and flocked to the jail, asking questions and talking among themselves. One of the group came to the door of the wooden building and called out to Corrigan.

"What's Sam Richards doin' gettin' ready to leave town?" he asked.

"Leave town? I didn't know nothin' about that."

"He's sure cleanin' out his desk at the law office. Was hard at it when I went by a little spell ago. Had the light on and he was goin' to it like he was killin' snakes."

Corrigan's jaw tightened. "Comin' along, Breck?" he asked. "I think we've got ourselves a live one."

"Don't mind if I do."

They reached the law office minutes too late. Richards had already gone.

"Now what?"

"The bank," Corrigan exclaimed. "He owns the bank too. He'll be over there cleanin' out the safe!"

They hurried to the bank four doors down the street and looked in. There was a lamp lighted in the window, though the shade was down. Breck went to the back door, and Corrigan hammered on the front. Moments later the rear door opened stealthily, and a dark figure stepped out.

"That's far enough, Richards," Breck said evenly. "Drop that satchel and put your hands in the air—away from that shoulder gun you're carrying."

"It's all right," Richards said, managing a thin smile. "It's just me, though I do appreciate your watchfulness. We can't be too careful, can we?"

Breck raised his voice. "We're back here, Hank. Our friend was on his way out of town."

"You make it sound as though I've done something illegal," the lawyer countered. "I resent the implication!"

A moment later the marshall came around the corner of the building. "What's up, Sam?" he asked blandly. "Takin' a little trip?"

"What if I am?" he demanded defensively. "There's no law against that."

"You're under arrest, Sam. We're takin' you over to the jail."

"You can't do that. I know my rights."

"You'll have plenty of time to think about your rights. Maybe twenty or thirty years if they don't hang you."

"If this is a joke, it's not funny."

"I quite agree. Let's go."

Richards lowered his hand, his fingers reaching for his holster.

"I wouldn't if I was you," Corrigan warned. "One of us would nail you before you cleared the holster."

"Why are you takin' me in, Hank? I've got a right to know."

"We want to ask you about your business with that actor who impersonated Ed Knox. There ought to be some interesting information comin' out of a talk like that. And I imagine some of the railroad attorneys will want to have words with you. Devin's attorneys, for example."

"I have done nothing I'm ashamed of," the attorney exclaimed, pulling himself erect indignantly.

"Then you don't have anything to worry about, do you?"

While Breck held a gun on the broad-shouldered lawyer, Corrigan searched him. He removed a Smith & Wesson .32 from a shoulder holster and a derringer from his sleeve.

"Take the bag, Breck," the marshall said. "I think we're ready to go back to the jail."

Corrigan put Richards in the cell with the actor.

"Why, Mr. Richards," Paul said. "Are you here because someone's after you too?"

"No, stupid," he blurted, turning his back on his cellmate.

"When I saw you, I thought you'd come to get me out. You said you were my lawyer."

Jacobs came to the cell which Hank had just locked.

"I think I'll go over to the car and ask Devin if he might want to send his men over for a spell."

"I'm not talking to anyone, lawyer or no."

"Don't tell me. Since I'm pretty sure Devin's lawyers will be here as soon as I can get word to Devin, you can tell them yourself."

Corrigan had put Richards' satchel on the desk and opened it in front of Armenius, his wife, Melinda, and Cassie.

"Looks like our friend was figurin' on some traveling," the marshall said, holding up a thick wad of bills. "I'd better go get the assistant bank manager and get him to put this back in the bank for safekeeping." He glanced toward the door to the cell. "Even if Richards hadn't done anything before, what happened tonight is plenty. We've got him for bank robbery."

The true Edwin Knox announced he would take his niece to the hotel and get rooms for them so they could rest.

"We've had a long, hard day," he said, "and I'm frightfully tired."

"I think I'll stay with Melinda," Cassie told him. "That is, if you don't mind."

"Suit yourself. I just think we both ought to get to bed."

"Why don't you wait 'til Jacobs gets back?" the marshall suggested. "He may have someone with him who will want to talk to you."

"Can't it wait until morning?"

"They'll be here soon."

Knox sighed and appropriated a chair for himself. The farmer, his wife, Cassie, and Melinda went back to Corrigan's house where Dora was waiting uneasily.

"It's all over?" she asked.

"It's all over."

"And everyone's all right?"

Melinda nodded.

Relief flooded her features. "Thank God!"

While Corrigan was gone, Devin and two well-dressed associates came into the jail building. The railroad president's eyes brightened when he saw Knox.

"Ed!" he exclaimed. "They found you! I was afraid something terrible had happened to you."

"It almost did."

They went into the other room and questioned Richards. At first he was adamant in his refusal to tell them anything, but when they revealed some of the information Jacobs had unearthed about his involvement in the plot to overthrow the management of the railroad and take control, his cheeks paled.

"Nobody's going to believe you," Richards said defensively.

"Shall we find out? Or maybe you'd like to hear a bit more of the evidence we have?" Devin glanced at Jacobs. "You have the file on Sam Richards, don't you?"

He opened the briefcase and handed it to Devin.

"Is—is all that about me?"

"And your associates."

He sighed deeply. "What is it you want to know?"

Once Richards started talking, the words spilled out. He outlined the part he played in the scheme: Fannie had contacted him, even before she came west, informing him that she and Ian Snyder and Snyder's son, Charles, were making the trip to see that Knox didn't surface at an inopportune time and ruin their plans. Nobody mentioned killing the stockholder when he was found, but Richards was certain that was the plan. If Fannie could not become a widow legally, she would find an actor to impersonate her husband, and after he had signed a proxy allowing her to vote with his stock, he would be disposed of. They hadn't spelled that out either, but Richards knew they wouldn't leave the actor alive so he could blackmail them.

"So it was Ian," Devin exclaimed. "I was beginning to think it was Nester, and that hurt. We were in the war together."

"It was Ian. He bought as many shares of

Great Western stock as he could in the names of people who were under his control. That was to be the base for the power play to get control of the railroad from Devin and his associates. When his son started going with one of the Nester girls, he used that as a way to get Charles out here without tipping off his hand to Devin. But at the same time he bought the K Bar T and invited Nester and his daughters to stay there. No one thought a thing about it."

"What about the gunfighters they gathered there?"

"That was my idea," Richards said proudly. "They had to try to find Cassie and Edwin Knox, and the Missouri Pacific had to have some gunmen in the area to fight off Devin and his associates if it came to that. I suggested using the K Bar T as a staging area. The gunmen were brought in to look for Knox and his niece and would be ready to put against the Great Western if they were needed."

The actor, who had been listening to what Richards said, broke in suddenly, "When do I get out of here?"

"I'm afraid the judge will have to decide that," one of Devin's legal representatives put in. "You've committed forgery, and more than a million dollars was involved. I'm afraid you're due to be here for a long time."

"What about the Snyders?" Richards asked. "They aren't going to be free, are they?"

"I've got a posse goin' after 'em right now. They ought to be there shortly after the K Bar T gets the word that things have blown up here," Hank said. "We'll have 'em locked up before morning."

"They're not going to like that," Devin said quietly.

"I don't imagine they will."

Knox turned to Devin. "What about the squabble about the pass?" he asked. "I haven't liked the looks of that. Hired guns coming in for both sides. It could be a bloody battle, Devin."

The railroad president's lips tightened. "If it were up to me," he said, "I'd have it out with that outfit. They throw their weight around like they own the world. I'd like to teach them some manners."

"It's probably better to compromise now than to fight," Knox said. "In the end, we'd have to sit down at the table and talk things out anyway."

"But that's not the way I like to do things." He smiled wryly. "I guess I enjoy a good scrap. Keeps the blood boiling."

Knox waited for him to continue.

"When this battle over control of the road came up, I sat down with two or three of the men in New York who were set on compromise. They'll stand by me in the takeover attempt if I'll agree to their terms. So we're working on an agreement for the other outfit to take the California route we were going to build. We'll get Leadville." He paused momentarily. "Now that we have your stock, Ed, we've whipped Snyder and his outfit. They may twist and squirm like a bucket of eels, but we've got them dead to rights!"

The next morning at breakfast, Breck was strangely quiet. When they finished eating, he called Melinda into the parlor so he could talk with her alone.

"What's the matter, John?" she asked.

"I've got to talk to you."

"What about?"

A lump rose in his throat, and he swallowed hard. "I—I—"

She reached out and laid a firm young hand on his arm.

"You're going on, aren't you?"

He nodded.

"I thought—" Her eyes grew misty.

"So did I. But it would never work." He patted the weapon on his hip. "This hog-iron has a way of runnin' my life."

"I talked with Dora Corrigan," she said truthfully. "It bothered me too, having you wear a gun and use it. But I know I can handle it. She does."

"But she ain't happy," he persisted. "You can read that in her eyes." He shifted nervously from one foot to the other. "We could never be happy as long as I'm wearin' this, and I can't quit. People won't let me."

"I'd never say anything about your wearing a gun."

"There is somethin' you don't know, Melinda," he said. "I ruined the life of a wonderful woman because of this gun. I can't take the chance of ruinin' another."

She looked up at him through her tears and saw that there was no use in pressuring him. His mind was made up. Standing on tiptoes, she brushed her lips lightly against his. "Good-bye, John," she whispered.

He ached to take her in his arms, but didn't.

"Good-bye," he said roughly, turning on his heel and striding out of the house in the direction of the livery barn where his line-backed dun and a pack mule were waiting.

A great loneliness enveloped him, but he knew what he had to do. Maybe someday things would be different. Right now, though, he only had one choice: to move on. He'd come out here to do some prospectin', and that's just what he was going to do. He would buy his supplies and head for the hills without looking back.

Other Living Books Bestsellers

THE BEST CHRISTMAS PAGEANT EVER by Barbara Robinson. A delightfully wild and funny story about what can happen to a Christmas program when the "horrible Herdman" family of brothers and sisters are miscast in the roles of the Christmas story characters from the Bible. 07–0137 $2.50.

ELIJAH by William H. Stephens. He was a rough-hewn farmer who strolled onto the stage of history to deliver warnings to Ahab the king and to defy Jezebel the queen. A powerful biblical novel you will never forget. 07–4023 $3.95.

THE TOTAL MAN by Dan Benson. A practical guide on how to gain confidence and fulfillment. Covering areas such as budgeting of time, money matters, and marital relationships. 07–7289 $3.50.

HOW TO HAVE ALL THE TIME YOU NEED EVERY DAY by Pat King. Drawing from her own and other women's experiences as well as from the Bible and the research of time experts, Pat has written a warm and personal book for every Christian woman. 07–1529 $3.50.

IT'S INCREDIBLE by Ann Kiemel. "It's incredible" is what some people say when a slim young woman says, "Hi, I'm Ann," and starts talking about love and good and beauty. As Ann tells about a Jesus who can make all the difference in their lives, some call that incredible, and turn away. Others become miracles themselves, agreeing with Ann that it's incredible. 07–1818 $2.50.

THE PEPPERMINT GANG AND THE EVERGEEN CASTLE by Laurie Clifford. A heartwarming story about the growing pains of five children whose hilarious adventures teach them unforgettable lessons about love and forgiveness, life and death. Delightful reading for all ages. 07–0779 $3.50.

JOHN, SON OF THUNDER by Ellen Gunderson Traylor. Travel with John down the desert paths, through the courts of the Holy City, and to the foot of the cross. Journey with him from his luxury as a privileged son of Israel to the bitter hardship of his exile on Patmos. This is a saga of adventure, romance, and discovery—of a man bigger than life—the disciple "whom Jesus loved." 07–1903 $3.95.

WHAT'S IN A NAME? compiled by Linda Francis, John Hartzel, and Al Palmquist. A fascinating name dictionary that features the literal meaning of people's first names, the character quality implied by the name, and an applicable Scripture verse for each name listed. Ideal for expectant parents! 07–7935 $2.95.

Other Living Books Bestsellers

THE MAN WHO COULD DO NO WRONG by Charles E. Blair with John and Elizabeth Sherrill. He built one of the largest churches in America . . . then he made a mistake. This is the incredible story of Pastor Charles E. Blair, accused of massive fraud. A book "for error-prone people in search of the Christian's secret for handling mistakes." 07-4002 $3.50.

GIVERS, TAKERS AND OTHER KINDS OF LOVERS by Josh Mc-Dowell. This book bypasses vague generalities about love and sex and gets right down to basic questions: Whatever happened to sexual freedom? What's true love like? What is your most important sex organ? Do men respond differently than women? If you're looking for straight answers about God's plan for love and sexuality then this book was written for you. 07-1031 $2.50.

MORE THAN A CARPENTER by Josh McDowell. This best selling author thought Christians must be "out of their minds." He put them down. He argued against their faith. But eventually he saw that his arguments wouldn't stand up. In this book, Josh focuses upon the person who changed his life—Jesus Christ. 07-4552 $2.50.

HIND'S FEET ON HIGH PLACES by Hannah Hurnard. A classic allegory which has sold more than a million copies! 07-1429 $3.50.

THE CATCH ME KILLER by Bob Erler with John Souter. Golden gloves, black bell, green beret, silver badge. Supercop Bob Erler had earned the colors of manhood. Now can he survive prison life? An incredible true story of forgiveness and hope. 07-0214 $3.50.

WHAT WIVES WISH THEIR HUSBANDS KNEW ABOUT WOMEN by Dr. James Dobson. By the best selling author of *DARE TO DISCIPLINE* and *THE STRONG-WILLED CHILD,* here's a vital book that speaks to the unique emotional needs and aspirations of today's woman. An immensely practical, interesting guide. 07-7896 $2.95.

PONTIUS PILATE by Dr. Paul Maier. This fascinating novel is about one of the most famous Romans in history—the man who declared Jesus innocent but who nevertheless sent him to the cross. This powerful biblical novel gives you a unique insight into the life and death of Jesus. 07-4852 $3.95.

LIFE IS TREMENDOUS by Charlie Jones. Believing that enthusiasm makes the difference, Jones shows how anyone can be happy, involved, relevant, productive, healthy, and secure in the midst of a high-pressure, commercialized, automated society. 07-2184 $2.50.

HOW TO BE HAPPY THOUGH MARRIED by Dr. Tim LaHaye. One of America's most successful marriage counselors gives practical, proven advice for marital happiness. 07-1499 $2.95.

Other Living Books Bestsellers

DAVID AND BATHSHEBA by Roberta Kells Dorr. Was Bathsheba an innocent country girl or a scheming adulteress? What was King David really like? Solomon—the wisest man in the world—was to be king, but could he survive his brothers' intrigues? Here is an epic love story which comes radiantly alive through the art of a fine storyteller. 07–0618 $4.50.

TOO MEAN TO DIE by Nick Pirovolos with William Proctor. In this action-packed story, Nick the Greek tells how he grew from a scrappy immigrant boy to a fearless underworld criminal. Finally caught, he was imprisoned. But something remarkable happened and he was set free—truly set free! 07–7283 $3.95.

FOR WOMEN ONLY. This bestseller gives a balanced, entertaining, diversified treatment of all aspects of womanhood. Edited by Evelyn and J. Allan Petersen, founder of Family Concern. 07–0897 $3.95.

FOR MEN ONLY. Edited by J. Allan Petersen, this book gives solid advice on how men can cope with the tremendous pressures they face every day as fathers, husbands, workers. 07–0892 $3.50.

ROCK. What is rock music really doing to you? Bob Larson presents a well-researched and penetrating look at today's rock music and rock performers. What are lyrics really saying? Who are the top performers and what are their life-styles? 07–5686 $2.95.

THE ALCOHOL TRAP by Fred Foster. A successful film executive was about to lose everything—his family's vacation home, his house in New Jersey, his reputation in the film industry, his wife. This is an emotion-packed story of hope and encouragement, offering valuable insights into the troubled world of high pressure living and alcoholism. 07–0078 $2.95.

LET ME BE A WOMAN. Best selling author Elisabeth Elliot (author of *THROUGH GATES OF SPLENDOR*) presents her profound and unique perspective on womanhood. This is a significant book on a continuing controversial subject. 07–2162 $3.50.

WE'RE IN THE ARMY NOW by Imeldia Morris Eller. Five children become their older brother's "army" as they work together to keep their family intact during a time of crisis for their mother. 07–7862 $2.95.

WILD CHILD by Mari Hanes. A heartrending story of a young boy who was abandoned and struggled alone for survival. You will be moved as you read how one woman's love tames this boy who was more animal than human. 07–8224 $2.95.

THE SURGEON'S FAMILY by David Hernandez with Carole Gift Page. This is an incredible three-generation story of a family that has faced danger and death—and has survived. Walking dead-end streets of violence and poverty, often seemingly without hope, the family of David Hernandez has struggled to find a new kind of life. 07–6684 $2.95.

The books listed are available at your bookstore. If unavailable, send check with order to cover retail price plus 10% for postage and handling to:

Tyndale House Publishers, Inc.
Box 80
Wheaton, Illinois 60189

Prices and availability subject to change without notice. Allow 4–6 weeks for delivery.